"Here it is, Babe,"

She watched the _____ as
crazy as hell, but _____ rk
that way, it probably wou_____ to
envision what the world of the meat-ma___ ___ta-
matrix? – would be like. God only knew much data
was stored in that world, taken out, manipulated, put
away. What would the great flesh machines, the massive
files of the giant conglomerates smell like? Taste? Feel?

And what would it be like to actually be there, in that
new place? For a moment she felt the one emotion that
truly moved her, the one she could not let anyone ever
see.

She shivered.

"...be it, then," he said. "Hairwire to a new world."

She watched the cable as she would a snake. Ozzie was crazy, he ... he was a genius. If he said it would work than ... it would work. For a moment she tried to remember the world of the consequences - the most immediate ... would be these? Do you know how much it was worth that well ... take her accumulated ... even. What would she ... that calculations, as she could she lies in the grill confront ... since 1142, no, no, No ...

And what would it be like to scramble to that on the ice... plane? Her frontier ... felt the one could to fon ... to find to her, like the ... world ... for its unknown ter...

# W.T. QUICK

# DREAMS

## OF

# FLESH

## AND

# SAND

Futura

An Orbit Book

Copyright © 1988 by William T. Quick

First published in 1988 by NAL Books in the USA

First published in Great Britain in 1989
by Futura Publications, a Division of
Macdonald & Co (Publishers) Ltd
London & Sydney

ISBN 0 7088 8287 0

Reproduced, printed and bound in Great Britain by
Hazell Watson & Viney Limited
Member of BPCC plc
Aylesbury, Bucks, England

Futura Publications
A Division of
Macdonald & Co (Publishers) Ltd
66–73 Shoe Lane
London EC4P 4AB
A member of Maxwell Pergamon Publishing Corporation plc

*This book is dedicated to my mother,*
*Della May Quick,*
*and my father,*
*Clifford W. Quick*

*and to*
*Theodore R. Cogswell.*
*Skoal, Brigadier!*

REPORTS SAID THEY got Collinsworth just after he stepped off the lunar shuttle. He picked up his suitcase from the luggage carousel and carried it out to the taxi stand, a matter of two or three minutes—long enough for the quarter-kilo of tailored petroleum derivative in the handle of the case to reach body temperature and go unstable. Somebody knew that machines do all the baggage handling. Half of him landed in the picturesque flower cart across the street, and the other half permanently ruined a nearly new San Francisco cab.

Aldocci was in a phone booth in Muncie, Indiana, when something crawled out of the face plate and bit him on the chin. It was a double bug, and the insect-vectored recombinant virus, an industrial job designed to do interesting things to calcium deposits in nuclear reactors, left a nasty puddle on the floor for the next customer of Midwest AmeriTech to find.

Tough little Marie, she of the legendary monomole switchblade, picked about the same time to go skydiving from the 237th floor of the State of Illinois building, carving a scalpel-thin wound in its skin on her way down.

None of this would have bothered Berg, but all three people had things in common. They were skilled in the arcane arts of camouflage and spookery. They were very hard to kill. They were pros.

And they were all coming to meet him.

\*     \*     \*

In some Chicago places, mostly the Old Labyrinth under what was once Michigan Avenue, you can still see high water marks from the time before they brought in Dutch engineers to dam up the rising lake. Ancient slime hangs petrified in black, ropy lines ten meters or so above the rotting basement bones of wrecked hotels. Down in the Lab, where abandoned roadways lie choked with rusted car hulks and loading docks gape like rotten mouths opened in the dark, new things lurk. Things that like the atmosphere of ruin and decay.

Berg caught a broken glimpse of his face in a shattered windshield. Pale, thin: he looked as if he belonged. His footsteps echoed sharply, like somebody pounding steel spikes with a hammer. The locals had strung surplus glowbulbs along the underside of the roadway in this section, marking off a meeting ground. They seemed to cast more shadow than light.

Everything smelled of damp, rust, decay. And a diseased sweetness, as if unseen, night-blooming plants waited somewhere, wafting a funereal perfume.

It was very cold.

Suddenly they were in front of him. He stopped. They approached him with the wariness of animals, sniffing. He looked okay, but you never could tell.

She stayed pretty well back, and let her two wolves check him out. Couple of boys with tooth-bud transplants, sharp canines protruding from lumpy jaws, and big clots of muscle implant in places the human body was not designed to have muscle.

"Wha y'here, guy?" the one on the right said. He wore trashed jeans and a T-shirt advertising The Pet Killers.

"Came to see the lady," Berg told him. "We're old friends, right?"

She moved forward then, tall and willowy, wearing what might have been a discarded wedding gown. The tattered lace moved like a windblown curtain as her face turned toward him in sunflower tropism.

Two huge eyes like saucers of blood. Infrared optical inserts. She operated as much on sound as on her shadowy kind of vision, and recognized his voice before she made out his dim outline.

She was a great lady in her world, and the two wolves would tear him into bloody shreds if she raised her finger.

"Hello, Lady," he said.

Her blind gaze sought his face. "Berg," she said. Her voice was surprisingly deep and strong. "You need something done?"

He nodded, then remembered she had trouble making out small movements. "Yeah. That's right."

She smiled, and for an instant her face looked wistful and sad. "Yes," she replied. "You usually do."

Then she turned businesslike. "So, what'd you bring with you?"

He grinned. "What I usually do," he told her. "I brought money."

When he got back to his condo, he accessed the Denver Deep and hung a message on one of the hacker bulletin boards there. The message was meaningless, but which board it was hung on conveyed information to those who knew. In this case, Toshi would get in touch with him as soon as possible.

Although the data-processing underground—the Deep—was a pretty tangled place, changing all the time, some of the corporate types knew their way around there, too, and he thought about finding a new way to keep in touch.

Then he poured some scotch into a glass, stuck a couple of adrenaline-seritonin analogs behind his right ear, and settled back to wait for a few answers. It had been a long day, and it looked as if the night would be longer.

I'm all right, Jack, he told himself, feeling the smooth high begin to hammer its velvet way into his skull. He sipped his drink and watched New Chicago flicker and burn below him in all the colors of a neon rainbow, and wondered how much somebody was paying to fuck him up. . . .

He propped one gummy eyelid open and wondered what had awakened him. The cheerful little Braun clock-holo at the foot of his bed snorted colored smoke rings that said it was ten o'clock in the morning. He heard the soft clink of glass on glass coming from the living room.

That somebody could enter his condo without his knowledge was nearly impossible. That somebody had, and that he was still alive, meant only one thing.

He pried open the other eyelid and yelled, "Hey, Toshi. I like my eggs poached."

The mellow, somber reply came instantly. "Yeah, massa, and cream in your coffee. I do walls and windows, too."

More clinking sounds. Berg chuckled, and began the laborious process of putting himself together.

Toshi most resembled a cartoon Japanese butterball. Since he could afford to look like anything from Superman to President Steenburg, Berg figured it was because Toshi liked the way he looked. One time Toshi told him the inch-thick layer of fat helped conceal all the Silicon Valley microcircuitry implanted throughout his body.

The morning sun stabbed bright, dusty lances into Berg's living room. Toshi was sprawled on a Weber sofa, his feet up on the one-of-a-kind coffee table Ralph Lauren had built for his own country place.

"I see you still know how to respect the finer things in life," Berg told him sourly.

Toshi grinned, his black eyes like two marbles in a glass of chilled liebfraumilch. "I see you still collect junk by anybody, as long as they have a social reputation," he replied. He glanced at Berg and added, "You know, Berg, you gain twenty pounds, get out in the sun every once in a while, and quit adding scotch to bizarre hormone compounds, you might not look like you spend all your time under a rock. You ever think about that?"

Berg padded across to the Tiffany coffee service and poured. Blue Mountain. Good. He sipped and sighed. "Tosh, I think I'm gonna live, but not if you keep trying to reform me. Besides, what's a guy that looks like Mr. Moto in a trash compactor giving me health tips for?"

Toshi shrugged. "I hear word your health—your future health, that is—might not be so good. Any truth in that, my man?"

It was Berg's turn to shrug. "Could be. You got my message?"

"I'm here, aren't I? Oh, and by the way, you need to rethink some of your defenses. It took me less than ten minutes to get in."

Berg drank some more coffee and thought about it. "How long for anybody else?"

"Couple of hours, probably."

Berg sighed. "Have to do," he said. "I don't have enough time to fix it right. Got another job on the table."

Toshi took his feet off the coffee table. He was wearing one of those appalling hawaiian shirts, the kind that look like pictures of lung cancer, white duck pants with about fifty pockets, and cheap plastic thongs. "You want to tell me about it? What other job?"

Berg lit the first of the day's sixty or so of Bolivia's finest, rode out the coughing spell, and poured more coffee.

Then he told him.

Toshi said, "Berg, you get mixed up with those people, it can get very tough. I think you may get yourself killed."

Berg grinned at him. "Yes, but is it *worth* it?"

Toshi rubbed his right ear. "Beats the hell out of me. All I am is lowly muscle, boss."

Berg poured more coffee. "Right. And at your lowly prices, we better get muscling. . . ."

\*      \*      \*

They were coming back into the lobby of Berg's building when Toshi touched his arm gently. Berg froze.

"Guests, Berg," Toshi said softly.

The wolf materialized from behind the shrubbery next to the elevators. He was wearing a furry, gray, floor-length coat that was hard to look at. The wolf nodded at Berg, but kept his eyes on Toshi.

"Theh ah p'pul in yah apt'mnt," the wolf growled softly.

Berg looked at Toshi.

"This a friend of yours?" Toshi asked.

"Yeah," Berg said. "I paid a lady to have my place watched. Among other things."

The wolf stared at them. "P'pul," he repeated.

"How many?" Berg asked.

The wolf held up three fingers. The fingers were ugly, clawlike things.

"Okay, thanks," Berg said. The wolf nodded and was suddenly gone.

"How does he do that?" Berg wondered.

"Mimetic carbon fibers in the fur," Toshi grunted. "He's over there behind us, doing an imitation of that marble wall. Listen, Berg, who is in your apartment?"

"I doubt if it's friends," he told him. "Shall we find out?"

"Sure thing," Toshi said. "Let's not take the elevator, though."

Toshi sighed as he stared at the black scorch marks on the fire door that opened onto Berg's kitchen. "Idiots," he said. "No finesse. They've burned out your entire system."

Berg glanced at him.

"It makes it easier for us, though," he said thoughtfully. "Listen, Berg, I think you better wait out here." He got a faraway look on his face and hunched over the lock. Berg heard a soft, metallic click, though Toshi didn't seem to have anything in his hands. The door swung softly open.

Toshi turned and winked at him. "Just take a second," he mouthed silently.

Toshi moved quietly into the apartment. Berg's hearing was very good, but there wasn't any sound. After a couple of minutes somebody tried to scream. Berg recognized the sudden sharp intake of breath, followed by—nothing. Except more silence.

Toshi's moonlike face appeared around the door. Berg jumped.

"Nerves, Berg?" Toshi said. "Come on in. It's all over."

Berg followed him through the kitchen and out into the main room. Just beyond the kitchen door they had to step over the body of a large, dark-haired woman. One of her arms was twisted at an impossible angle.

A small, rat-like man was crumpled against the window wall, his hands outstretched as if he had been trying to climb the glass. A trickle of bright red blood ran from one of his ears.

Both of these intruders were shabbily dressed, unlike the third man on the sofa, who appeared to be taking a short nap. He was tall and slender, dressed in an impeccable brown business suit. Wings of carefully trimmed white hair floated above his ears. He wore a gold signet ring on the little finger of his right hand.

Berg shook his head slowly. "Three bodies to get rid of, Toshi? What do you think I am, the garbage man?"

Toshi grinned. "Nobody's dead, Berg. It wasn't necessary. Besides, I thought you might want to talk to them."

"Oh, you inscrutable Oriental," Berg said. "You're smarter than you look."

"I'm smarter than you look, too," Toshi told him. "The one on the sofa is sleeping the lightest. Want me to wake him up?"

Berg appraised his visitor. "No. I've got some stuff that works better if I start while he's out. Come on, give me a hand."

When the guy woke up, Berg smiled at him. His

chiseled, aristocratic face was puzzled. He blinked quickly, twice, and then relaxed. He smiled.

"Mr. Berg?" he said. His voice was a clear, even tenor.

Berg glanced at Toshi. The visitor had recovered too quickly. He looked like any high-level corporate exec. But he wasn't.

Berg smiled again. "My name was on the door when you broke in," he told him.

"I apologize for that," the man said quickly. "I didn't think you would see me if you had a choice in the matter." He tried to shift his weight on the sofa, then stared at his legs in surprise.

"I gave you a spinal," Berg told him. "You're paralyzed from the waist down. You want to try anything else, I think my friend here can handle it okay."

Toshi grinned at him toothily.

A faint glimmer of disgust colored the man's expression. "You've had some work done," he said.

Toshi smiled. "Takes one to know one, dude," he replied.

"Listen," Berg said. "Right now you don't have any legs. Your two pals aren't going to wake up any time soon, either. Now, I've got some real interesting derms here, and when I slap them on your neck you're gonna tell me everything about this little episode. So can we cut the polite conversation and get to it?"

The man's gray eyes chilled suddenly. "Only if you want to talk to a corpse," he said.

"Oh," Berg said. "You're one of those." He sighed. "Okay, we do it the hard way, then."

"Is he wired?" Toshi asked.

"Nope. Bugged. Tailored bacteria that go toxic in the presence of certain drugs. Truth drugs, mostly. It's a new wrinkle."

"How about if I just cause him a whole lot of pain, while you use the retinal analyzer?"

Berg stared at his guest. "Might work," he said. "What do you think, buddy?"

The man began to look worried. "I think we might

have some grounds for negotiation. This is business, right?"

Toshi reached out and gently touched the man's shoulder. Cords exploded suddenly in his neck as his face turned into a pain-filled skull.

"It's really bad when it hurts that much and the nerve block won't let you scream, isn't it?" Toshi asked politely.

"Let go, Toshi," Berg said.

The man collapsed backward, breathing hard. Toshi winked at him.

"You here just looking, or you plan to kill me?" Berg asked.

"Actually, I had rather hoped to buy you. Or convince you," the man said.

"That what the two goons were for? What's your name, anyway?"

"Smith will do," he said calmly. "The two incompetent goons are bodyguards."

"Don't be too hard on them, Smith. You need more than competence to handle Toshi." Berg shrugged. "Not that it's relevant. How much are you going to offer?"

Smith turned his cool gaze on Berg's face. "Two million new. In the bank of your choice."

"A nice sum," Berg told him. "What are you offering it for?"

"I thought you'd know," Smith replied.

"Sorry. That much money makes me stupid. What's it for?"

"To drop your contract with Nakamura-Norton. Get sick. Take a vacation. Whatever."

Berg glanced at Toshi. Toshi winked again.

"Well, it's a nice offer. Who's making it?"

"Of course I can't tell you that."

"I think you can." Berg smiled carefully.

Toshi slowly reached for Smith's shoulder.

"No!" he said hastily. "What I mean is I don't know. Do you think whoever is paying this out would send me to a man like you if I had any actionable knowledge?"

Berg stared at his hands. Then he lit a Bolivian cigarette and blew smoke in Smith's face. Smith stared at him.

"Nakamura?"

No reply.

"Norton?"

Smith raised his beautifully tailored shoulders and let them fall.

Berg grinned. Then he walked over to the desk and replayed some readouts.

"You're telling the truth. *You* don't know. But your body thinks you're a Norton guy. And that makes absolutely no sense at all. . . ."

The hotwatch alarm on one of Berg's machines chimed softly. He looked at Smith, then brushed his fingers across the touchpad on his desktop. A screen lit up.

"ICEBERG," the letters danced. "COLLINS-WORTH, ALDOCCI, MARIE—THIMK—LOVE, ICE-BREAKER—ENDS."

Berg stared at Toshi, who cocked one bushy eyebrow. "Anything?" he asked.

Berg shrugged. "Love letter," he said. "From an old friend."

Cold.

A green, chilling taste, and the feel of vast space whirling. That was the first ride.

Later, it became easier. . . .

The office fit her like a black leather glove. She'd told the decorator, a thin young man who resembled a poolside matador, to make it look like a bruise.

The young man stared at her. "A what?"

"You know. Dark, soft. A little bit overripe, almost rotten. I don't want anybody to feel comfortable here. Except me, of course."

The desk was a ring of polished stainless steel, supported in thin air by a hidden array of magnets. When clients met her face to face, they saw her poised within the ring like a dart plunged into a target.

There were no windows.

"Ms. Calley," the visitor said.

She quickly ran thin fingers through her tangled, chopped mass of black hair and flashed a smile that left the man feeling as if he'd just been flipped a quick piece of identification. "Calley's okay," she said. "I don't need that Miz bullshit."

The office made him feel he was trapped in that part of a banana which lay just beneath the brown spot on the peel. Worse, he knew she was aware of his discomfort.

She propped her elbows on the ring of steel and said, "You're from Nakamura-Norton and you're buying. Fine. I'm selling. Let's talk about it."

His smooth face remained carefully impassive. "How do you know I represent Double En? Not that I say I do."

She leaned back suddenly in her chair, which made the sound of chains jangling. Her green eyes glittered. Her rough, tenor voice sounded husky and tired. "You came here looking for a pro, right? Why is it you corporate guys think you're the only people with computers? Your name is Frederick Oranson. You're a vice-president with Double En, in charge of security, and you report directly to William Norton's office." She snapped the smile on again. "You're a baby sitter, Frederick. You protect your employees and your machines from nasty people like me. It's my business to know all about people like you. Okay?"

He raised both hands, palms facing out. "I surrender," he said. "It's—this place. It's weird."

"You don't like my taste? Too bad, Fred. I didn't do it for you. Now do we talk business, or would you like the name of my decorator?" She stared at him musingly. "Maybe you would, at that. . . ."

It felt just like being mugged. Everything about this woman was an attack, an affront. In a few short moments she'd mocked his job, threatened his masculinity, exposed his minor secrets, and laughed at his taste. He shook his head.

"I see why they call you Icebreaker."

"Buddy, what you're thinking is ballbreaker, and no, you don't see at all. Which is beside the point. What's the job?"

Oranson reached inside the jacket of his corporate pinstripe and extracted a chip. "Here," he said. "It's standard. All the details." He placed the chip on her desk. She ignored it.

"Of course this is confidential," he said.

She stared at him. "You're an idiot," she said suddenly. "That's surprising—Bill Norton is supposed to be a very smart man." She stood suddenly, reached forward and took the chip.

"I'll check this out. Return codes included, I presume?"

"Yes." He rose slowly, controlling his anger. Everything about this made him want to tighten his big hands around her fragile, corded neck, except for one thing.

If he did so, he was afraid she would kill him.

Two hours later she sighed and watched a lazy, rising curl of cigarette smoke. The big jade ashtray next to her elbow was piled high with crumpled butts. "What do you think?" she said softly.

"It looks like a reasonable proposition. Straight-out attack on a major data center. What you're good at."

The reply seemed to come from the center of the room. She'd built that interaction program herself. She liked it all, hardware and software. To a visitor the voice would sound mildly familiar—until the visitor realized it was Calley's own voice, with all the rough edges filed off.

"The center isn't located," Calley said.

"Look at the size of it. There can't be many machines that big. And the storage is enormous. It's got to be one of the meatmatrix jobs. And there are only three or four of them."

"I'll bet Nakamura-Norton has this one," Calley said.

"Probably," the speaker replied. "They build them."

"So why would Bill Norton pay me to attack his own machine?" Calley said.

"Now that," her speaker replied, "is an interesting question."

The man was named Oswald. He'd once been bitten by a misengineered batch of oil-spill algae. The skin on his face looked something like thick, maroon velvet drapes.

His apartment was a vaulted explosion of junk. Steel

spines rusted quietly against oxidized copper pipes, against bits of glass, shards of broken plastic, chunks of burned wood. Things that had once tinkled, clanged, gonged. Things that still made odd, sighing noises as they rubbed against each other.

Oswald nested in the middle of this, his left eye like an oyster in its rumpled bed. His deformed cheeks glowed weirdly against the green backlight from the bank of monitor screens which circled him in a jerry-built wall of discarded hi-tech throwaway shit.

"Ozzie, you ever think about hiring a maid?" Calley said.

"What for?"

She sighed. "You're right. If you gotta ask, you don't need one."

"That's true about most things. Uh, you need something, little girl?"

"Sure," she said. "Don't I always?"

He made grunting, whuffling noises as he unfolded his lanky frame from the pile of twittering electronics. Standing in the dim, dusty green light, holes in the knees of his jeans, wearing a fresh T-shirt that read, "Zombies Make Quieter Lovers," he looked like some great, lost northern bird trying to figure out why everyone else had gone south. "And don't I always help?" he asked.

Calley pushed some trash from the top of some larger trash and sat down. "What do you know about meatmatrices?" she said.

It didn't seem to bother her that her small, clean, black-leather clad body was the only bit of human organization in the entire chaotic space.

Ozzie shrugged. "What everybody does. Bill Norton. Double En. There are, I think, six of them."

Her black eyes flickered. "I heard four."

He smiled, revealing perfect teeth, all the more startling in the ruined face. "NORAP has one, and the Lunies, too."

"The Lunies? Why the hell—?"

"They're doing some strange engineering up there

these days," he said, his eyes dancing with some frag-
mented madness. She wondered what Ozzie would
think was strange engineering.

"You know any more?" she asked. "Like how to
attack one?"

He turned and glanced at a pile of rust that had
started to vibrate on its own. "Might," he said.

"That's good enough for me," Calley replied.


Her eyes opened. It took her an instant to figure it
out. The shadows were sharp-edged and alien. There
was the taste of burnt iron in the air, and the smell of
rotted cloth.

"Mmm. . . ."

She looked down. Ozzie's hound dog face rubbed
gently on her breasts. "No, boy," she said softly.

He squinched his eyes shut and stuck out a probing
tongue.

Calley turned a little. "I said no," she said. She
pushed his head away. "We've got work to do."

He opened his eyes. "I'm horny," he said plaintively.

"You're always horny, and I'm the only one who'll
give you any. Why don't you get your face fixed,
anyway? God knows you've got enough money."

He peered up at her, his corneas faintly filmed.
"You don't mind my face," he said.

"Not really," she replied.

"Then it's okay with me," he told her. "By the way,
I think I figured a way to cobble it."

Calley slid all the way out from under and propped
herself up on both elbows. "Yeah?"

"I don't think anybody ever tried this one before,"
Ozzie said.

"All the better," she said.

Ozzie suddenly folded himself into a lotus position,
his bony ribs like scars down his sides. "Of course it
will cost a lot of money," he said.

"Everything costs, Ozzie. Spare the crap. Will it
work, and will I live through it?"

He thought a moment. "I guess so," he said.

"Then let's get to it."

Ozzie went manic when he worked. His fingers skittered like grasshoppers through the mounds of chips, the boards, the hunks of plastic and silver and gold wire.

"That's pretty clunky," Calley said.

"You want finished product, go to Sears," he told her. "Except they don't sell this quite yet."

She looked at the mound of gadgetry that was slowly taking shape beneath his knobby hands. "Run it by me again," she said.

He straightened up from his workbench. "You know, Calley, there's a whole world out there, a world of information. Corporations, governments, armies, even the billion or so PC users—data, and data some more. We pull it up on screens to look at it, but it doesn't really look like what we see on the screens. I got to wondering about that."

Calley scratched her right ear, just above the implant. "I work in that world all the time, Ozzie. I hear you."

"Your so-called real world doesn't look that way, either. You see a table, but it's only a whirl of electrons, protons, neutrons. Bits and pieces and mostly empty space. So why do we see a table—you and me both?"

She licked her thin lips. "I dunno," she said. "Never thought about it much."

" 'Cause your brain tells you it looks like that. So does mine. So does everybody's, except for a few crazies. It's the structure of the wetware, darling—it perceives what it can perceive. Some people think we're all in some kind of subconscious agreement. But that's not true. It's just the nature of our beast. So I figured this information world, it's just more electrons— but our wetware isn't wired to perceive them in any kind of structure. I put together some chips . . ."

She stared at the seemingly endless tangle of circuitry. "Some," she said.

He grinned. "Well, it got a little complicated, doing it, you know, but it's still simple. This thing just gears down all that input into a range where human wetware can handle it. Sort of like adding an extra sensory organ. And since it's the same circuitry for everybody, everybody should agree on what they perceive. See, I figure the matrices share a kind of common ground. Those brains are all grown from the same master culture, that Norton created at the beginning. Imagine if pieces of your brain were in separate places. I think there's continuous communication among them, probably a whole little world. The meatmatrices are individual brains residing in a greater world that includes all data processors—I think of it as a greater matrix, a *metamatrix*. And we should be able to access that common ground, maybe without getting into any individual matrix. You follow?"

He froze, then reached into the jumble and drew out a length of fiber-optic cable. The end of the cable was a common jack, the kind used by advanced programmers to hook directly into their big machines. Calley knew the jack would fit the plug beneath her right ear. "Here it is, babe," he said. "Hotwire to a new world."

She watched the cable as she would a snake. Ozzie was crazy as hell, but he was a genius. If he said it would work that way, it probably would. For a moment she tried to envision what the world of the meat-matrices—the metamatrix?—would be like. God only knew how much data was stored in that world, taken out, manipulated, put away. What would those storage bins look like? What would the great flesh machines, the massive files of the giant conglomerates smell like? Taste? Feel?

And what would it be like to actually be there, in that new place? For a moment she felt the one emotion that truly moved her, the one she could not let anyone ever see.

She shivered.

"If it works, you are going to be very rich," she said softly.

He smiled his startlingly perfect smile. "I'm already rich," he said. "If it works, what I'm gonna be is famous."

But she'd always known what drove him. It was her strength, that instinctive knowledge of root cause and humanity. On only one human had that knowledge ever failed.

"I think this means something," she told him. "I think it's serious as cancer, this little moment. Can't you feel it?"

He nodded. "Welcome to my world," he told her.

## 3

SOMETIMES IT WAS hard to keep it all straight. Today, for instance, the layout of the rooms seemed different. He paused for a moment, turned, re-entered his bedroom, and sat on the bed.

Yes. Hadn't it been a waterbed just the night before? Now it was a thick sheet of bodyfoam, just like the bed he'd had as a kid. And where had all the mirrors come from? Had they been there when he got up?

He shook his head slowly. None of it mattered, of course, but he really did appreciate order. His massive shoulders rose and fell once. He stood and left the room. He paid no attention to the wallpaper in the long hallway, walking head down until he reached the end, where he turned right and entered the breakfast nook.

He seated himself at the table and smiled.

His mother appeared, carrying a plate covered with scrambled eggs and two thick slices of ham.

"What? No pancakes?" he said.

She leaned over and ruffled his hair. He realized he was younger than he had been just seconds before. "You must be hungry," she said, the trill of remembered laughter bubbling just beneath her words.

"Sure, Ma," he said. "You know me. I'm always hungry."

Outside, chaos grew and waned, spawning intricate, precise geometries, but here was familiar; it would stay as long as he wanted—easy, when every wish was a command.

He settled back and waited for his pancakes.

As he ate, he watched his mother chop vegetables in the small kitchen off the breakfast nook. Everything was very warm and familiar. He guessed she was about thirty, which made him what—eleven? That seemed right. He remembered that his parents had married barely nine months before his birth.

The pancakes were very good. He forked up the last chunks, pushed them in a circle in the syrup, and lifted them to his mouth. How long had they lived this way, the three of them, in that small Los Angeles ranch house? He thought they hadn't moved till he was fifteen. That would have been—yeah—his dad had been laid off at the beginning of the Oil Stagflation, when they'd moved to Chicago.

"Hey, Ma," he said. "What was the name of the street we lived on when we went to Chicago? Up by the lake, remember?"

She turned, reached for a paper towel and wiped her hands. A strand of black hair straggled over her forehead. "Pine Grove," she said. "3515 Pine Grove."

"Right." He nodded slowly, ignoring the implausibility of his mother remembering something that wouldn't happen for another four years. He'd liked that house on Pine Grove. From there he'd attended the University of Chicago on a scholarship, and there he'd lived after his parents died, working on the project that eventually—

He forced the thought away. Chains of memories always led to this place, and he'd had enough experience with the futility of playing what that. Nothing else had happened, and all roads still led to his present estate.

The play on words cheered him mildly. The biggest, and at the same time the smallest estate any human had ever possessed. He noticed that everything had gone silent, and glanced at his mother. She was frozen, a still holo out of time, reaching forward.

"Stop that," he said, and with an audible click, everything started again.

"—Dad will be home soon, Billy. Did you clean up your room?"

He glared at her. "Go away," he said.

Her expression flattened and she turned and went into the kitchen again. When he left the breakfast nook she was still there, back to him, chopping vegetables.

He took another turn in the halls of his vast labyrinth and found himself in his Chicago office. The drapes swathing the glass walls were open, and he wandered over to look out on his domain.

It was always a shock. Before, his view had been over the dikes into Lake Michigan, the business towers of the NewTown spread out like so many diamond needles below him. Now the towers were gone.

The universe was there instead. He looked out on the clenched fist of light which was his home, and marveled. The other matrices were there, separated by velvet darkness, but somehow connected in a sort of cellular suspension. Data intrusions from other types of machines made hard, jewel-like clumps spotted here and there in the fleshy pudding, sharp-edged chunks of red and blue and green. The individual matrices which made up the greater metamatrix pulsed slowly in great organic pools of brilliance, and all of it floated serenely above a floor of diamond dust.

Impossibly straight lines in all the primary colors darted away from his cloud to other masses, and lines from them returned to him.

It was a strange, throbbing world, full of warped perspectives. Sometimes the lines all tended in a certain direction, and that made him feel as if he were rushing down a road with no end. He'd arbitrarily assigned "up" and "down" to his world, mostly based on the power of the various clumps of data. His own cloud was at the top, and not far below were five others of the same general type. One of those five was much further out than the rest. He knew it was the Lunie meatmatrix, and examined it carefully. Yes. There was some new construction there, and the matrix cloud had assumed a strangely warped shape. He wished for a moment he could find out what was going on out there. The Lunies had their own priorities, and they protected their secrets well.

He found it ridiculously easy to penetrate the other databanks, and to define the secrets of their megaprocessors. The Lunies were different, however—almost as if they knew something like him was loose in the metamatrix. Their programming had resisted his attempts to penetrate it—but he had found chinks, and knew it was only a matter of time. They might imagine something like him, but they couldn't *know*.

He turned from the window. When he turned back, the towers of Chicago ranged outside, their bases shrouded in fog off the lake. He judged it early morning, from the amount of light in the gray clouds overhead.

Time to get to work.

He'd personally taken a hand in the design of his office. When the Company had finally decided to build their headquarters in Chicago, he'd rammed through an appropriation to let him build any kind of workspace he could imagine. The result was this high-ceilinged room, un-walled and multi-leveled, wrapped in glass and space.

The office was unsubtle. It screamed of power, and knowledge, and secrets hidden. His desk was a slab of marble the size of a small swimming pool, unmarred by anything except a pair of touchpads, two screens, and two outlet slots for hardcopy. From that desk he ran an empire greater than Exxon or IBM had ever dreamed of, and even now the desk served a purpose.

It was his analog, his means of communication with the real world. He hated using such distinctions now, for he'd gained a more poignant understanding of those hazy generalities.

His thick fingers flickered across one touchpad. There was a faint chiming sound, and the left outlet slot began to spit paper.

He tore off the hardcopy and began to read. His expression thickened and darkened. The message was short.

DATALOSS IN L.A. BASE. TRADE WITH HONG KONG AFFECTED. WHAT THE FUCK ARE YOU DOING?

He wadded the paper into a ball and threw it on the floor. Data loss in the Los Angeles data base? It wasn't possible. He hadn't been anywhere near—

Or had he?

It was so hard to remember. Sometimes he forgot how fragile his world could be. He sighed and leaned forward, his fingers beginning to move.

REQUEST DETAILS DATALOSS L.A. BASE. CAN FIX.

He didn't add a signature code. He knew that none was needed.

## 4

HE APPEARED ON Berg's door monitor one windy afternoon, blonde brush-cut hair and die-stamped face, wearing creased jeans and a starched cowboy shirt. Ludicrous, Berg decided. He probably thought it was a disguise.

"Yeah?" Berg said.

He cleared his throat. "Mr. Jack Berg?" he asked.

"Maybe. Who are you?"

"May I come up? I have a message for you." He glanced around. "I can't talk in public."

"I'll bet," Berg snorted. "Who are you? General Electric Motors? RanData?"

He shook his head. "Please. Can I come in?"

What few pickups Berg had down there said he was okay, so he decided to check further. "Sure. First elevator on the right." Then he punched the buzzer.

It was a private elevator, and it was kinked about twenty different ways. By the time the visitor reached Berg's floor, Berg had even CAT-scanned him. He still looked okay. If he hadn't, of course, he would not have left the elevator alive. Maybe he knew. His face, as he came up, grew an uneasy coat of sweat.

Berg let him stand in front of the door for a final minute.

"I think you're all right," he told him. "About the only thing I can't check is some kind of bug you're immune to and I'm not. So understand: if I start to get sick, you won't leave this place breathing. Does that seem clear enough, Mr. Clean Jeans?"

"Perfectly clear, Mr. Berg."

Berg nodded. "Okay. Come on in."

He looked around the place, eyes slowly widening. Fifty stories above Lake Michigan, too high to see the floating pollution. Floor to ceiling glass. Polished antiques, rare pictures, hideously expensive furniture. Berg's public persona wasn't like that. The visitor didn't expect it, and it surprised him.

"Very nice, Mr. Berg," he said.

"Sure. Sit down, Clean Jeans. I make a lot of money, and I spend it on myself. Okay? Unless you want a tour, or something."

He sat on a genuine Corbusier chair. Berg figured it was Clean Jeans's salary for at least a year.

"Mr. Berg, I came to offer you a job."

Berg lit a Bolivian cigarette with an eighteen-carat Dunhill. "I didn't think you came to pick up the garbage," he told him. "Who do you work for?" He paused, then added, "And try to practice honesty. You think you can? If not, I've got a laser-driven retinal analyzer aimed at you. If the truth is a problem, we can sort it out. But you won't like it."

Christ. Berg could tell he missed his pinstripes, just like career soldiers feel naked when out of uniform.

The visitor took a deep breath and let it out, slowly, almost managing to look calm. Berg glanced at the readouts inlaid into the top of his desk. Yes. Pulse up, respiration a bit rocky. And sweating like a pig.

"I represent Nakamura-Norton, Mr. Berg. We have something we'd like you to do for us."

While the urban cowboy talked, Berg did some checking. According to the sanitized company histories, Bill Norton had been struck, more or less by the hand of God, while tinkering in his California garage, and had immediately invented bioelectronics. The truth was Norton was broke, barely enough to keep him in the two quarts of Detroit vodka he was drinking every day, when he accidentally induced a chunk of detached chicken brain to undergo mytosis, probably by dumping some of the vodka on it while in the midst of another process entirely. Regardless, it was the first time anybody had been able to grow nerve cells at that level, and once he sobered up and duplicated the procedure, he began to get very rich. Nobody much said whether he still liked his vodka, but his reputation was that of a hard man who wasn't afraid to use his power.

Nakamura Shigeinari, by virtue of selecting his parents properly, grew up with a great deal of Japanese yen and enough smarts to know an opportunity when it came knocking drunkenly at his door. Thus was born Nakamura-Norton, a marriage of particular luster, whose offspring spread the flaming red N/N lightning-bolt logo over most of the developed world.

Berg considered this while Clean Jeans made his offer. That was how it started.

"LOVE, ICEBREAKER."

Berg stared at the cryptic message. It had been two years, and a part of him thought he'd forgotten. Now, staring at the hard-edged green letters, he knew he would never forget.

"Toshi?" he said absently.

"Yeah, boss?"

"Take out the garbage, would you?"

Toshi nodded. "You want me to wrap it first?"

Smith's eyes darted, suddenly alarmed. Berg shook his head. "Not necessary," he said. "Just return to sender."

Smith relaxed. Toshi sighed and stood up, a small gray oval suddenly in his right hand. He walked over and pressed the hypospray against Smith's neck. Berg ignored the short hissing sound, his eyes focused on the screen, his thoughts far away.

He didn't look up until Toshi hoisted Smith's limp body to his shoulders. "I'll be back," the Oriental said.

"Just dump them somewhere. All that shit'll wear off in a few hours."

Toshi grinned. "You want me to look into some

systems for you, Berg? Those wolf friends of yours are okay spotters, but I can whip some crap together that'll do a little more. Unless you like guests?"

Berg nodded. "Yeah," he said. "Better do that. This is gonna be harder than I thought."

Toshi nodded, wearing Smith like a stole. "Told you so," he said.

"Yeah, well maybe you should go into the fucking clairvoyant business, you know?" Berg said.

"Already am," Toshi replied cheerfully.

Berg got up and began to wander slowly around the bright room, touching things. The set of Cartier candlesticks. The holophoto by Beltaque. The perfectly formed, cobalt-blue Chinese jar with the dragon curling round its sides: all things *she* had given him.

He hadn't had an attack for more than a year, but he could feel it coming on. Something he'd begun to call *Scenarios From Lesser Hell*.

Like this:

She threw the drink at him in slow motion. He moved and the glass bounced off the wall behind him, showering him with Glenlivit. A part of him wondered why it always had to be the good scotch.

"You know what, Jack? You're an asshole."

"You knew that when you married me," he said.

"Not really, pal. Nobody likes to think the worst of the man they love."

"You know, it's too bad you're beautiful," he told her. "If you were ugly then you wouldn't have to spend so much energy proving what a smart lady you are."

"Fuck off," she said. "You talk good. But I know the nasty part of you, the part nobody can crack. Not even me."

"So why do you want to crack it? I'm that way. You didn't think you were going to *change* me after we were married, did you? I gave you credit for more brains than that," Berg said.

She paused, her hands twitching slightly. He knew the signs. She was looking for something else to throw.

"Throw the frigging bottle," he told her. "I don't give a damn."

"I'm smarter than you are. I don't need cheap condescension. For that matter, I don't much need you, either."

"Sure you don't," he said.

She threw the bottle.

Silence.

"I love you," she said.

"Sure you do."

Maybe there should be a test ban treaty for emotional weapons, Berg thought suddenly, and noticed that his slender fingers were shaking.

He stared blankly at the shining glass wall and tried to put it together. First, a simple commission from Double En, protection work for a new machine and some techs connected with it.

Then three people dead. His condo invaded by men who appeared to work for the company already employing him. And finally a strange, occult message from his ex-wife.

A warning, then. And how was dear Gloria, the Icebreaker, mixed up in all this?

But that, after all, was what he was good at: figuring out shit. He put his fingers together and slowly popped each knuckle. Then he moved back to the desk.

Fine, he told himself, forcing the unwanted memory away. When it was all said and done, no matter how many assholes were involved, he was still the Iceberg.

And that was the best there was.

After two hours he noticed that the sun had risen past the shadowline, and his room had turned a cool, pearly gray. His stomach made soft complaining noises.

He rose and went into the kitchen. There were eggs and some leftover chicken. He chopped the chicken into small pieces, dropped it into a skillet with butter, and added scallions, garlic, a little burgundy. Stirred idly at the food, not really seeing it.

The pungent odor of the garlic finally brought him back. He took some salsa from the fridge, stirred it, spooned a bit into the chicken. Then he cracked three eggs over the whole thing.

The food helped. His stomach quieted and his head began to clear. Repeat, he told himself, that was the key: keep repeating. His great strength was filling all the holes. Other operators might be smarter, might be faster, but in his experience they generally missed something. There was always an *i* left undotted, a *t* uncrossed, a barn door unlocked until the herd was over the horizon.

He never did that. When he finished, all the details were covered, and nobody had ever penetrated one of his seamless creations.

He specialized in the software, the application/protection systems that were the hardest things in the world to design. But he had done some live work, too, the esoteric kind of high-corporate bodyguarding that megacompanies found useful in their ceaseless quest for each other's knowledge. Often that knowledge, that *ability* resided only in one person's skull, and that person, therefore, became as valuable as real estate or stock portfolios or a new process to the company involved.

Basically, he knew that he built jails, outlined the walls, sketched in the bars, designed the defensive weapons. As he slowly spooned up the hot eggs, he thought about the first lethal feedback system he'd devised—an ugly thing, designed to freeze any hotrod hacker into a trance, while nerve shredder programs crept through the circuits and into the neural pathways.

Nobody had ever done that before. He wasn't sure if he was proud or not, but that one thing had made his rep—and somebody had to pay for his tastes.

He rubbed his eyes. He hadn't jacked into his computer for one simple reason. He wanted to let his mind work the data over on its own, without the direct interface to the machine. That would come later, after his intuition had a chance to chew on the data.

Already certain impressions were becoming clear. The possibility that coincidence was involved in the deaths of Collinsworth, Aldocci, and Marie seemed unlikely. There had to be a connection with the contracts he had placed at the office of his San Francisco bodybroker. Either the broker had sold him, or somebody had cracked the broker's files.

Then there was the botched attempt to buy or kill him off the contract he'd accepted with Double En. Berg was familiar enough with the workings of conglomerates to understand the ceaseless interplay of corporate microcultures within the greater macroculture of the company. Who had sent those thugs? Double En? Somebody who just wanted it to look that way? Or was it fallout from some hidden upheaval inside the great company, something he might, or might not, ever discover?

Finally, the message from Gloria. He could call her and ask. That would be the simple way. But he was too familiar with her shifting, steely methodology to try something that uncomplicated. His ex-wife was hard to predict; he'd finally learned that even he couldn't do it. Better to discover Gloria's involvement without letting her know. If he could. It nagged at him that she also liked to play three moves ahead.

He glanced at the time readout. Just two days left—two days to find as many answers as he could, before he went out to suburban Oakbrook and stepped inside the miles of chainlink circling Double En's R&D facility. Or decided not to, and paid the massive kill fee attached to the contract he'd accepted.

Collinsworth, Aldocci, Marie. The thought hadn't escaped him that it would have been simpler to just kill *him* instead.

Fuck it, he thought slowly. I'll have to play four moves ahead.

# 5

**T**HEY CAME INTO the lower part of the metamatrix. At least it felt that way. Calley discovered that point of view was difficult here. Ozzie
was with her, a comforting presence just off her left
shoulder.

"Jeezus . . ." she breathed.

"Yeah, isn't it just," Ozzie replied.

Ozzie was running the application program, a simple thing designed with many branches, a glorified
"turn right, turn left, up, down" travel guide and
steering wheel. She knew his fingers were dancing
across the touchpad, altering the program as they went.
It seemed to her an awesome display of skill, one she
could no longer be without.

It was her third ride. The first had been formless,
chaotic, as her brain adjusted to radically different
input. "Just getting online," Ozzie told her cheerfully.

Now the new world arced about her in all its ab-
struse glory. There was a green, glowing light to everything. Down on the bottom things just sort of faded
away to a fine dust peppered with sparkles of white
light. Here and there the sparkles congealed into shimmering puddles.

"What are those?" she asked softly.

"Individual PCs hooked into loose datanets. The
pools are close linkages—bulletin boards, the Deep,
like that."

"Oh."

It was a paradox, a place of flowing rigidity. It
reminded her of the things she'd seen under a micro-

scope in school, great networks of slow-pulsing cells, but made of light instead of flesh. She sensed that everything was connected somehow. Quivering lines of color shot through the liquid dark, leaping from one giant construction to another.

"What the fuck—" Calley muttered.

She sensed that Ozzie's fingers were moving frantically. "Let's see," he said. "I'll get us up in it."

She was no longer aware of the chill that had cut through her bones at the beginning, nor did the absolute silence bother her. As her sensoria adjusted to the new world, she began to appreciate its huge green serenity, the ordered pattern of the moving lines, the intricate complexities of the clumps and chunks of data she began to perceive. The thing coming up, for instance. . . .

Big.

Ozzie brought them right up to its base, so it was a wall of color extending on either side and up out of sight. As they moved close, the original burning orange of the construct slowly began to shift as long, jagged patterns of bright blue light cut through its skin.

Inside, she could dimly make out constellations of white light bursting and fading. It reminded her of laserholo simulations of what human neurons looked like, firing and firing again.

Now she noticed that these explosions had begun to cluster close to the skin. More and more, until a solid ball of pulsing light hung there, radiating a strobing fan of blue, curving lines.

And dissolved into a pure pink beam which pierced the translucent skin, changed colors as it left the construct, and became an achingly clean arrow bound for places over the green horizon.

"My God," she said.

"I've never seen it do that before," Ozzie said. "It must be some kind of databurst. Didn't it look like it concentrated there before it left, all of a sudden? I think it's a squeeze transmission."

Calley's retinas burned from the departed arrow. "What the fuck is this, do you think? A meatmatrix?"

Ozzie laughed. "Naw. You know what this is? It's your friendly neighborhood telephone company."

Calley giggled suddenly. "No shit?"

"Nope. I sussed it out a while back. Looks nice, though."

"I guess," she said. She sighed suddenly. "It's so big, Ozzie."

"Bigger than anything," he agreed. "And the hardware, the cores, you could probably put in a single room. Or less. Big and small."

"I want to see a meatmatrix," she said suddenly.

His slow drawl was doubtful. "You sure? I never been that high before."

"High?"

"Yeah. They're way up at the top. I think this place is arranged according to processing power and storage capacity—the bigger it is, the higher. Just the opposite from gravity and the real world."

Calley pondered that. "But this is real, too, Ozzie. Isn't it?"

"Bet your ass," he agreed.

"So let's go look at the big ones," she said.

"Right. Hang on," he replied, and they took *off*.

Ozzie took them straight up the side of the data constructs, a wild roller-coaster ride that shot them laughing and yelling into the glittering upper reaches. From this vantage point she looked back and saw the bottom of the metamatrix dotted with a thousand thousand individual vortices of shining color.

"Straight ahead," Ozzie mumbled.

Six of them. She stared. Finally, she said, "They don't look like the stuff down below."

"Yeah," Ozzie said. "It's got to do with the way they organize data storage and manipulation," he said. "That is wetware, my dear. I think the other stuff is access perception. The matrices see it, and communicate with it, so it's there. They look different 'cause they're organic. That's what gives them that fluid, shifting shape."

Calley ran over what she knew about meatmatrices, the great clumps of engineered nerve cells that supposedly equaled the human brain in complexity, but possessed far greater storage capabilities. Rumor had it that the largest of the matrices massed over ten kilograms of tailored nerve tissue.

Still, it was hard to equate ten kilos of gray flesh with the massive, throbbing clouds of light which hung like leashed galaxies over the roof of the metamatrix itself.

"Six, like I told you," Ozzie said. "See that one way out there? That's the Lunies. And if Double En had any sense, they kept the best for themselves, so that one right at the top should be them. What do you think?"

She was still mesmerized by the awful size of the matrices. Now she began to make out hard cliffs of color which clung to the sides of the clouds.

"What're those things?" she wondered.

"Probably organized core storage," Ozzie said. "Maybe hardware implants of some kind. I sorta suspect they use the wetware more for processing capability, and use standard chip arrays for control factors. Simpler that way, and capacity is unlimited. That's what I mean about the Lunies."

"What's that?"

"Look at it. See all that shit bulging from the side of it? Kinda looks like tumors or something?"

Now she saw what he was talking about. Off one side of the Lunie meatmatrix were great clumps of vivid blue and red construction.

"Right," Calley said. "That *is* weird looking. It almost unbalances the whole cloud. You got any idea what they're doing out there?"

"Babe," he sighed, "I haven't the foggiest. But I'd sure *like* to know."

She considered quickly. "You never were able to write decent attack programs, Ozzie, you know that? Maybe we can do a deal, like, you help me with this, and afterward I'll lend my talents to your little prob-

lem. Who knows—maybe we can steal some stuff from
the Lunies. Bound to be worth something to somebody, right?"

He yanked them to a sudden halt. She luxuriated in
the glittering silence. finally, he said, "I never thought
about actually stealing shit. . . ."

She grinned. "We're going to make a lovely team,"
she told him. "Your brains and my larcenous heart
and—fuck, Ozzie, we're the only ones out here. Famous? Hell, we'll be legends!"

Slowly, he started them forward again, then picked
up speed. "Legends?" He paused. "You know, I kinda
like the sound of that."

As they approached the highest matrix, Calley noticed that it had begun to change colors, just as the
telephone complex had done. "Look at that," she
said. "Some kind of film over it—you see?"

His slow drawl was close. "Uh-huh. I don't know
what it is. A kind of membrane?"

In the slow, rhythmic contractions of the cloud she
began to feel something else, almost like a heartbeat.
There was still no sound—the metamatrix remained
silent—but she felt a pressure, a dim, barely perceived
warning signal.

They were coasting up to the huge mass when she
said, "Ozzie. Stop."

Obediently he brought them to a halt.

"Over there, almost to the edge. What's that?"

"Got me, babe."

A fiery red globe was beginning to form there,
growing and twisting even as they watched. The globe
began to throb—sickeningly, it reminded her of an
exposed human heart. Now abstract patterns of pink
and yellow began to chase themselves over the huge
mass of the matrix, flickering across the membrane.
Again Calley felt an ominous, watchful presence.

"Ozzie, could that thing know we're here?" she said
nervously.

"Don't see how. We haven't even touched it yet."

The red globe expanded suddenly, shifting form until it was a hollow cylinder pointing directly at them. Calley shivered. It was like looking down the barrel of a gun.

"Ozzie. I think you'd better back us up a bit. . . . I don't like this thing at all."

"Whatever you say—"

The red cylinder expanded all at once, like a camera shutter clicking, and surrounded them.

"Get us out of here!" Calley shouted.

"I *can't!*"

And then she felt it: the slow, heavy grinding of paralysis, a seeping cold that froze her fingertips and worked inward. Dimly she was aware that her teeth were chattering and her jaw was locked.

"Calley, what's going on?" Ozzie howled. "I've never—" His voice shut off. She felt his fingers scrabbling over the touchpad, seeking a way out.

And she knew what it was.

Berg. She recognized the feel of the program. "It's a lethal feedback routine," she said. "We've got to break it or we're dead."

Ozzie remained silent. She thought furiously. How had Berg built those things? A closed loop, feeding on itself, intensifying the synaptical surges.

"Ozzie, don't try to talk. I'm going to open up to it. That may distract it long enough for you to pull the plug. That's what you have to do—pull the jacks out of our heads. You pull yours first, then mine."

"Calley—" Ozzie's voice was weak.

"Don't argue," she snapped. "Just *do* it!"

The tube's inner surface began to spin in long, jagged spirals. The motion seemed to pull at her, like watching blood swirl down a drain. She forced herself to relax, to give into its insistent motion.

And felt herself begin to freeze, begin to revolve slowly like a top, like a tiny chip of wood caught in a typhoon. And down to where the liquid darkness waited, down—

Woke up and Ozzie was sitting on top of her, his face a twisted mask of fear. He slapped her.

"What—?"

"Oh God, Calley, you're alive. I didn't know what. . . ."

Every muscle in her body ached.

"You were vibrating like a bandsaw, Calley. Some kind of seizure—I thought you were gone. You quit breathing."

Weakly, she pushed him away. "I'm all right," she said. "I'm okay, Ozzie. Don't hit me again."

They stared at each other. His oyster eyes were rimmed with blood, shot through with lines of neon red. He looked like some kind of monster.

"What was it?" he breathed.

"That," she said softly, "is what I am being paid to attack."

They took a shower together. It was one of those funny old bathtubs, the big kind with feet, and Ozzie had rigged a hose up into a showerhead nailed to the wall.

The hot water soothed her. "Here," she said finally. "You soap my back, then I'll do yours." She arced against the rough gentleness of his big hands, letting him knead the tension from her shoulders and spine.

"It almost got us, you know," Ozzie remarked quietly. "It was all I could do to yank the plug. I kept going in and out of things—it felt like a continuous electric charge."

She nodded. "Ozzie, what do you know about my ex-husband?"

"Berg?" he asked. "Not that much. I don't think he liked me. You notice I stayed away after you got together?"

"Yeah. I used to wonder, then I figured the same thing. Berg didn't like you, and you picked up on it."

Ozzie's voice was carefully neutral. "How come he didn't like me? Jealous?"

She sighed. "I know you think you're being funny, but yeah, that's the head of the nail, all right. Berg was jealous—oh, not of your handsome face, but. . . ."

Let's just say he figured out how smart you are, something like that. Berg is a very wary person. It's one of
his strengths. The Iceberg, y'know, the great defender.
He's always on the lookout for anything, a potential
attack. Maybe he thought you didn't like him."

"I didn't," Ozzie said.

"Yeah? How come?"

" 'Cause he married you, Calley. Maybe I was the
jealous one."

"Oh, shit," Calley said. "Is it going to get complicated now, Ozzie?"

His hands stopped their slow movement. "No, Calley,
it isn't. This is business. I'm scared shitless about what
happened out there, and I'm gonna need your help.
Strictly business, you understand? I can't do it by
myself. And maybe I can help you, too."

Calley smiled faintly. "Rub my back, Ozzie. Don't
stop just yet. What jumped us out there was a program written by my ex. I don't know how Double En
got hold of it—bought it, stole it, who cares—but I
know a lot about those kind of programs. I should. I
cracked the first six he wrote, before he finally got
the system straightened out."

Ozzie's fingers had somehow worked their way
around to her soapy stomach. She leaned back into
him. "We're going back there, Ozzie, I promise you.
And this time we'll be ready."

Ozzie bit gently at her neck, his hooked nose pushing at her ear. "Whatever you say," he whispered
softly.

Calley let herself go limp, the last dregs of tension
finally falling away. "The sonofabitch may be the Iceberg," she told him grimly, "but I'm the Ice*breaker*."

# 6

THE OFFICE WAS the usual huge size dictated by corporate ideas of face, but there was a different aura to it. The great windows were covered with white wood-and-paper screens, so that the light in the room was pearly, almost like moonlight. Fully half the floor was covered with a carefully raked rock garden, so that as the sun moved behind the opalescent screens, shadows shifted and lengthened across the perfectly tended gravel, forming mysterious patterns.

The furniture was antique Danish, what once had been called "modern." The slender, graceful lines of the pine and maple pieces seemed to blend with extended shadows from the garden, forming a symphony of calm reflection.

Behind the garden a tiny brook flowed, filling the room with the sound of water over stone. To the right of the garden was a small desk, and behind the desk a small yellow man.

At first glance, in the dappled light, the man appeared quite young, but when he grimaced at the bank of remotes behind the desk, a lacework of fine wrinkles appeared like a magician's trick, and his true age became apparent. As he watched the information slide down the monitor screen, his displeasure became more obvious. His black eyes began to snap, and he bared a mouthful of small, perfectly white teeth. He hissed softly.

He turned back to his desk and touched a button.

"Get Fred Oranson in here," he said. His voice was
soft, a clear tenor that betrayed, through long training, absolutely no emotion.

While he waited, he tapped his manicured fingertips
together. He appeared quite composed, but to those
very few he allowed to know him, it would have been
obvious that Shigeinari "Shag" Nakamura was pissed
off.

Frederic Oranson was large and blond and going
just a bit to fat. He looked like an over-the-hill foot-
ball player and had, once, been a star tackle for the
Oklahoma State Cowboys. He'd been cut in his tryout
with the Denver Broncos, however, and quickly realized that if he was ever to get a clawhold on the big
money, he would have to find another use for his
native size, strength, and shrewdness. Business had
welcomed him with open arms: he'd been Double En's
Chief of Security almost fours years, and viewed that
position as merely a steppingstone to bigger and better
things.

Shag Nakamura despised him but, never wasteful of
the tool at hand, used him unmercifully.

Oranson came softly into the room, his normal
buoyant personality carefully throttled. "Yes, sir," he
said.

"Fred, what has that asshole done now?" Nakamura
asked.

Oranson hated those kind of questions. He knew
lots of assholes, not the least of which was the man in
front of him. So he thought for a second, then finally
decided there was only one asshole that mattered to
his boss.

"Mr. Norton? Nothing, that I know of," he said
carefully.

Nakamura pointed at the monitor behind him. "Half
the fucking database in Los Angeles appears to be
inaccessible. It's there, but we can't touch it. Did your
people do it?"

Oh, Lord, prayed Frederick Oranson. He walked
over to the screen and began to read quickly. After a

moment he turned as said, "Nope. Not our guys, sir. You're probably right—it's Mr. Norton again."

Oranson had learned to be extremely wary of the little man who held the reins of the third-largest privately held conglomerate on the face of the earth. So he said just that, and nothing more. Mr. Nakamura would do what he would, and Fred Oranson had an acute idea of his own place.

Nakamura made a small, sucking sound. He brushed his palm over his mouth. Then he said, "I wish we could just kill the bastard and be done with it."

Oranson nodded. "That would be the best solution, but we can't do it," he said.

"I know it!" Somehow, Nakamura contrived to put an explanation point on the sentence without changing his tone in any way whatsoever. Oranson shivered at his intimation of the rage leashed in the smaller man.

"Bill has always been a suspicious—no, a paranoid—man," Nakamura continued. "But a genius. And if he says he can fry our entire data system, I have to believe him. It would cost billions to replace, if we could do it at all. Which we can't. So he gets to sit in that fucking tank, at least his body does, while he frolics like a lunatic Caesar in ten kilos of augmented chicken brain."

Nakamura slowly forced himself to calm. He stared at a particular jagged chunk of granite in the middle of the garden, willing himself to partake of its serenity. Finally he sighed.

"Okay, Fred. Get your people on it. I'll do what I can from here."

"Yes, sir," Oranson replied.

Shag Nakamura waited until the security man had gone, then turned away from his desk and began to work the touchpad behind him.

He no longer understood exactly what his partner had become or was still becoming, but at least he would talk to the sonofabitch.

Carefully, he typed. "DATALOSS IN L.A. BASE.

TRADE WITH HONG KONG AFFECTED. WHAT THE
FUCK ARE YOU DOING?"

With infinite patience, Nakamura sat back to wait
for a reply.

It took him a while to figure it out, but finally he
decided it must have been the dream. He had dreamed
of cells, of circuits and endless etched pathways—but
in his world, dreams could be real. He dealt with
analogs, manipulated them, and was in turn manipulated, to some extent, by them.

Of course it was a stupid analog. The process by
which his consciousness had been maintained, even as
his brain grew into a riotous pudding of cancer cells,
was extremely complicated—the kind of thing available only to a man like himself, who sat at the very peak
of a pyramid of technology. His body lived, after a
fashion. His mind lived more surely, through the artificial extensions of twenty pounds of chicken neurons.
There were no circuits or paths involved, but still he
dreamt of them.

Thus he hadn't lied to Nakamura when he told him
he could fry the Double En data base. In a sense, he
*was* the data base. And when he touched the cells,
crossed the circuits of which he dreamed, strange things
happened. The matrix was too great to perceive as a
whole; he envisioned it as a cloud, or presumed he
did. Even then, he often became confused. Sometimes
it seemed to him that the cloud was his body. When
this occurred, he could deal with parts of the matrix as
he would his own fingers and toes, and thus was well
equipped to repair any problems caused by his own
carelessness.

It involved only a few concentrated moments to
restore Los Angeles. Then he ordered lunch.

The woman who brought his chicken salad sandwich
was a maelstrom of dark hair and green eyes. He
watched her warily. Something new. She entered the

office slowly, brought the sandwich to his desk, then retreated.

"Hello, Marsha," he said.

He had noticed that it was best to initiate conversation. Usually, if he didn't, the ghosts populating his world remained silent.

"Hello, Billy," she replied. Her voice was the kind you heard over telephone wires and fell in love with, and which always belonged to a fat woman with bad teeth.

"How do you happen to be here?" he said. He tried to forget that he had once loved her.

She shrugged. "You wanted a sandwich," she said. "I brought it."

He picked up the sandwich and began to eat. She watched him. Finally, he said, "What were you doing before I called for lunch?"

"I . . . don't remember."

He chewed some more. Now he could smell the familiar scent of her perfume: roses. He had once spent a young fortune having that fragrance brewed for her. Even today, one of his subsidiaries made a tidy profit from the sale of it. He felt himself responding to the smell of the memory, and to the sight of her.

"Marsha, come closer," he said, and put down the sandwich. This time she would not turn away. This time she couldn't leave him.

After, she smiled her perfect smile at him, straightened her clothes, and left. He finished the sandwich, brushed the crumbs from the desk—they disappeared before they hit the floor, but he didn't notice—and propped his chin in his hands.

What next? His shrink had warned him, before he had submitted to the endless process which had brought him here, that he might elude death only to find madness. Catatonia. This whole construct might end up a trillion-dollar microscope for ever deeper examinations of his own navel.

He sighed. There was truth to the prediction. Certainly ennui was the only force strong enough to threaten him here. Absolute power corrupts—what? Bullshit, he decided. Absolute power mostly bores.

He supposed that the shrink's dire predictions might have turned out to be fact, but for one thing everybody overlooked. He wasn't alone here. Not his constructs, not the flawed resonances from his past, or the bizarre creations of his imagination, but things truly other, not of his creation.

The incredible constellation of data through which his own galaxy swirled was not his. Ever changing, growing, a universe generated from *outside*, as the metamatrix sucked in and replicated all the data which flowed to it.

It kept him sane.

He was already a god here, and soon he would be a god in the real world as well. Reality depended totally on its machines, its glowing hot cores of information, and slowly, with great and cautious care, he was unraveling the secrets of those near-infinite storehouses.

The thought of it brought a certain warmth to this cold place. Slowly he rose from the desk, turned, and faced the windows overlooking his domain.

The laughter of a child. . . .

"Damn it!" he roared, spinning to face the door. He thought he almost saw it, the tiny familiar figure, but it was too late.

"Come back!" he yelled.

Silence.

The glass windows bulged outward. Flames exploded, devouring carpet, wood, stone. The building itself shivered, cracked, fell.

A storm, then, ravening and feeding, and at its heart . . .

"*Come back!*"

Tinkling laughter—

Darkness.

Nakamura spoke soothingly to the heavy-faced man on his screen. "I am aware of the situation, Arthur."

The two men were conversing in German.

"No, Arthur, Double En is not involved in some kind of data hijack. We've had our problems, too."

The sound was turned off on the monitor. Shag Nakamura was reading the other man's lips. He shook his head.

"Well, what do you propose? Certainly. Let's get some of the others involved as well. I'm sure you will agree that whatever it is, it's a threat to all of us."

He waited, then bobbed his head politely. "Of course. I'll set it up. Until then . . . ?"

And turned from the monitor, shaking with what the conversation had cost him. Got up and walked over to the rock garden and stood very still, until he was in control again.

The soft, sharp whine of the alarm brought him back to the remotes behind his desk. He stared in disbelief.

"Buddah," he said quietly, "that ratfuck has done it again!"

## 7

"**H**EY BERG," TOSHI said. "There's a wolf at your door."

"Yeah?" Berg said. "What else is new? With my creditors . . ."

The room was full of blue smoke, which caught the late afternoon sunlight in lazy whorls. Berg stubbed out the last of his second pack of Bolivian Extras, and keyed in his telltales and monitors. The wolf was waiting patiently in the lobby, standing in front of Berg's private elevator.

"One of the Lady's people," Berg grunted. After a moment, he added, "Looks okay." He thumbed open a voice channel. "Come on up," he told the wolf.

Toshi wandered over to the front door of the apartment. He interlaced his thick, stubby fingers and cracked each knuckle. Berg grimaced at what sounded like bones being crushed.

"I wish you could break that habit," he said.

Toshi grinned. "At least I'm not a human smokestack. They never had to develop gigabuck technology to handle cracked knuckles."

"They had to develop gigabuck cop systems to handle murder," Berg replied. "You check this guy out personally when I let him in, okay? Anybody with money can buy ogre implants."

"I hears and obeys, boss," Toshi replied. "You know me, always ready to please."

"Always ready to mouth off," Berg said sourly.

The doorbell chimed. As if on signal, the seven antique cuckoo clocks Berg had scattered about the room began to sound; the two men listened to a symphony of artificial bird calls.

"You really are weird, Berg," Toshi said.

"Let that sucker in," Berg replied. He looked down and saw that his right hand was hovering next to the heavy grip of the Colt AV15 weapons system—a long name for the short, ugly machine pistol clamped to the underside of his desk.

Toshi pushed the button which withdrew the mag-bolts from the edges of the armored door. The wolf came into the room, glanced at Toshi, and started to detour around him.

"No, fella," Toshi said kindly. "We gotta have a look at you first." He stepped up and expertly patted down the wolf. Stepped back and shrugged. "Clean," he said. "Except for this," and held up a chrome-handled switchblade. "Personal weapon, guy?"

The wolf stared at him, his thick pink tongue lolling across very sharp teeth. "Gi' back," he said.

"No, no," Toshi told him. "You can have it when you leave." He glanced at Berg. "How'd he get this past your systems?" he asked.

"He didn't," Berg said tiredly. "I figured you could handle one little switchblade."

"You could have told me," Toshi said.

Berg only grinned at him. "Come on over here," he told the wolf.

The wolf did a strange kind of shuffling dance forward, which allowed him to watch Toshi and Berg at the same time. Toshi clearly made the little monster nervous.

"Th' Lay, wanna see ya," the wolf said.

"Lady wants to see me?" Berg said. "Sure. When?"

The wolf shrugged. "Now. Ah take ya," the wolf told him.

Berg rolled his shoulders, feeling strained muscles stretch there. One more time he told himself that he spent too much time pounding a touchpad or jacked into a machine.

"Just have to get more exercise," he muttered.

"My ass," Toshi mumbled in reply.

"Come on," Berg said to the wolf. "Shut up," he said to Toshi.

The wolf moved out of his way. "Give him back his toothpick, Toshi," Berg said. Toshi smiled sweetly and returned the switchblade to its owner, who took it gingerly, then made it disappear with a quick movement. Toshi's eyes snapped once, but that was all.

"Quit spitting at each other and let's go," Berg said. "I don't have all day."

They went straight to the lobby, the wolf plastered against one wall of the elevator, as far as he could get from Toshi. The chubby Oriental kept winking at the wolf, and Berg stared at both of them in exasperation.

"Jeezus," he muttered as they went out into the lobby. The wolf turned sharply right, however, away from the pair of tall doors which opened onto the street.

"Thi' way," the wolf said, and led them to a door near the back.

"This goes to the parking garage," Berg said. "Why there? I don't have a car."

"Lay, sh' say thi' way," the wolf replied.

Berg glanced at Toshi. The Oriental shrugged. "Might as well," he said. "There's only this one, and the one by the elevator."

Surprised, Berg turned and stared back the way they'd come. "I don't see shit," he said.

"When do you ever?"

They clumped down three flights of concrete stairs, went through the door at the bottom and entered the echoing, dimly lit garage.

The wolf immediately scuttled down one aisle, leading them toward the far wall of the garage. Another door, heavily locked and plastered with several "Keep Out" signs, was their destination. The wolf bent over the locks for a moment. Berg heard several sharp clicks, then a soft, rasping groan as the wolf swung the heavy door open.

"Not bad," Toshi said.

Berg reached under his jacket and patted the comforting weight of the AV15.

The room was large, filled with pipes, generators, and a jungle of cables. Berg made out fiber optics, sheathed electric wires, communications nets—all hung from the ceiling in peeling webs, or stapled to walls in incomprehensibly looping patterns.

"Building core room," he said softly.

The wolf padded over to a rusty metal cover set into the floor. Carefully, he stooped and began to pry at one edge of it, but he wasn't quite strong enough to lift the heavy disk. Toshi sighed, bent over, and flipped the manhole cover like a poker chip.

"Nice little walk," he remarked, staring into the blank darkness below.

Berg stared at the wolf. "You want me to go down there? What the fuck is this, guy?"

The wolf said, "The Lay, sh' say thi' way."

Berg stared at him dubiously. "The Lady?" Finally he shrugged. "Keep an eye out, Toshi?"

"Naw, I thought I'd wear a bag over my head, boss," Toshi replied. "Asshole," Berg heard him mutter as he slid down the hole behind the wolf.

The group clambered down a ladder slippery with rust and mold. At the bottom they stood in darkness for a moment. Berg felt the wolf moving somewhere nearby. Then the cold blue of a portable fluorescent lit up the dank tunnel like an endless photoflash.

"Real pretty," Toshi said.

Berg stared at the area delimited by the hard globe of light. It was a tunnel, perhaps three meters at the highest point of its arch, made of ancient red brick. The edges of the brick had been worn smooth. The floor of the tunnel was newer—raw concrete, with a channel perhaps a meter wide cut down the middle. Liquid, thick and slow, pulsed down the channel in slow arterial waves. The stench was incredible, an amalgam of decay and corruption that could only have been achieved after decades of steady pollution.

"It's a sewer," Berg said.

"No shit," Toshi replied.

Berg laughed, a creaking, corroded sound. "A lot of shit, Toshi. Among other things."

The wolf began to lead them down the tunnel. Suddenly he paused.

"What—?" Berg said, and then he felt it, too. A deep rumbling, almost too low for human ears, accompanied by faint vibrations that he felt through his feet as much as anything.

"What the hell—?"

"Explosion," Toshi said tersely, eyeing the crumbling roof of the tunnel. "Not too far away, either. Let's get out of here. I don't trust this deathtrap."

Berg nodded. The group moved on, more quickly now.

The tunnel forked; they took the right-hand path. The way seemed familiar to their guide. He moved quickly and surely down the abraded concrete, a few meters in front of the other two. Toshi glanced at Berg. "Real adventurous, huh?" he said.

"Shut up," Berg replied. He was worried about the explosion. He was thinking about Collinsworth, and Aldocci, and Marie.

So his head was down and he wasn't paying much attention when they passed yet another branching way and something short, dark, and feral sprang out at them, a bit of pointed brightness in one paw.

Toshi *moved!*

A turning blur, augmented musculature erupting in smooth burst of power. Berg caught a glimpse of— light?—near the Oriental's chest, and subliminally felt an awful, punching force emanating from the tangle.

And it was over.

Their wolf skittered back, turned, then stooped over the crumpled, limp form which lay like torn tissue a few meters down the second tunnel. In the harsh light, they saw it was another wolf. To Berg, the chest of Toshi's victim looked badly misshapen, almost crushed.

The wolf straightened, a twin to his own switchblade in his hand. He showed it to Toshi, who shrugged, took the knife and broke it in one quick, clean motion.

Berg felt the shivering aftereffect of the adrenaline rush begin to turn his muscles to mush. "One of your buddies?" he asked.

The wolf snarled. "A trait'r t' th' Lay," he mouthed. His huge eyes glowed redly. He bent over and made a quick swipe with one bulky hand, and Berg realized for the first time what the retractable claw implants were really for.

They moved on down the tunnel. Berg listened to the sound of something thick leaking in the dark behind them. He shuddered.

After what was, to Berg, an interminable time, they climbed another withered, rotted ladder, passed two doors, and entered a large, concrete-ribbed space. Berg had the impression, somehow, that they were still underground. The walls of the warehouse-like space were leprous with ancient water scabs. The air was thick, moist, and chilly.

Glowsticks hung from the ceiling, casting a soft, mottled pink light over the area. Toward the center of the room were clustered boxy shapes, tended by fuzzy figures that did not much resemble anything human.

Toshi seemed unmoved by the recent violence. "You think I get a paycheck this week, Berg?" he said. He was wiping his hands on the garish robe he wore, and Berg looked away from the stains they left. He swallowed.

"Thanks, Tosh," he said softly.

Toshi nodded. "Ain't over yet, boss," he said. "Stay cool."

They approached the center of the room. Here, huge ventilator fans, apparently ripped from housings elsewhere, were spotted about the machines, sucking at the omnipresent damp.

She moved away from her people, willowy as a summer plant, and came to them.

"Berg, I'm sorry," she said.

"Lady," Berg replied. "I am, too."

She sighed. "No one is completely immune to money. Not even my little ones."

Berg shook off the fog which had slowed him for the last several minutes. He inhaled sharply, then let it out. "Lady," he said, "cut the shit. What is going on here?"

She glided past them, her blood-saucer eyes luminous. "Let's talk over here," she said, leading them away. "Berg, your friend here is holding a lot of firepower. It makes my little ones nervous."

"Damn well told," Toshi grunted.

She looked at him. "Hell, Toshi," she said. "It doesn't bother me. I know you're just a big pussycat."

Toshi stared at her in amazement.

She snorted. "Yes, Berg, I know. Enough fun and games. But keep Toshi with you, if you can. He can protect you for a while."

Berg clapped his hands together suddenly. The sound was muffled by the mist. "Lady," he said, exasperation thickening his voice, "what is this shit? Why am I here?"

"Simple," she said. "You hired me for some things. In the course of doing them, I discovered other things— that you should know about."

"So why down here? Why not my condo? Why not a simple message?"

"Berg," she said sadly, "your condo wasn't safe. In fact, your condo doesn't exist anymore."

"What!"

"About twenty minutes ago," she continued calmly, "somebody put several Little Man rockets through your windows, tipped with incendiaries. Your whole floor is gone."

Berg stared at her. "Gone?"

She nodded slowly. "I'm afraid so . . . and I'm sorry."

There was silence. Finally, Toshi said, "That was the explosion we heard."

When Berg spoke again, his voice was a clear, steely sound, stretched tight. "Okay," he said. "Okay—let's get this over with. I've got some killing to do."

She moved closer, reached out and touched his shoulders with gentle fingers. "Yes," she agreed, "there will be more killing. You are going on a journey, Berg, a long one. I can't protect you there—no one can—but I have something for you that might help."

Berg nodded jerkily. "How do you know all this? A journey? What journey? Who's trying to blow me up?"

She shook her head. "I only know parts, Berg. Some of my sources are—well, you would say unscientific."

Berg watched her silently, his small, lean body tense.

"Berg, you won't really buy this, but you have gotten mixed up in something involving—well, I would call it powers, or forces. Things not really human. Big things. And it's too late for you to get out of it. So. . . ."

"It's all bullshit," Berg snorted. "Powers. Forces. All bullshit. There's some big corporate scam going down, and I seem to be under the footprint. That's all."

Her shoulders moved slightly. "All right. Have it your way." She reached under her own robes, brought out a small package. "Here," she said.

Berg took the package. "What is it?"

"What I told you. Something that will help."

He hefted it. "Feels like microsoft."

She nodded. "You'll know when to use it," she said.

"This is all pretty much mumbo-jumbo, you know," he told her.

"Berg," she replied tartly, "there is more to the world than eyes can see or ears can hear. Whether you believe it or not. But that's your problem. Take the damn thing and get your butt on out of here. You are not a safe person to be around right now." She stopped, then added more gently, "I'd tell you to trust me, but you haven't trusted anybody since you were two years old."

Berg slipped the package into his jacket pocket. "Que sera, sera," he said. "Okay, I'm outta here, Lady. Uh, thanks. I think."

Just before the door closed behind them, Berg turned and saw her still standing there, silent, her saucer eyes watching them.

As the little wolf led them down dripping corridors, Berg said, "Toshi? It kinda looks like you stick with me, you might not qualify for life insurance. Maybe I should put you on hazardous-duty pay."

Toshi chuckled softly. "Oh, don't worry about that, massa. You already have. You just haven't got the bill yet."

## 8

"**I**T'S A SIMPLE concept, really," she told Ozzie. "Like epilepsy."

Ozzie scratched at the folds of his cheek. "Epilepsy's simple?"

"No, Berg's lethal feedback programs," Calley said. "Did you know that a strobe can trigger an attack in an epileptic?"

Ozzie had clambered up on the roof of his warehouse and scraped years of accumulated grime from the cracked skylight, so that a kind of smeared, watery glow illuminated the huge room. It was Calley's idea—and the result was a sort of cross between Amazon rain forest and South Chicago junkyard. Ozzie was pleased. He said it gave the place a better ambiance. Calley thought the room looked haunted.

"Yeah," Ozzie said, "I read about that once."

"Well," Calley went on, "when you're jacked in, Berg's program does something similar: it gets your brain's attention and starts a loop. The first thing happens is you freeze. Then while you sit there like a lump of ice, the feedback swings wider and wider until it chops you down. Works on the vagus nerve in the end: your heart stops."

Ozzie shivered. "I always knew there was a reason I liked your ex. Nice kind of mind."

"You're such a sweet boy, Ozzie," she said. "I kind of enjoyed the routines he came up with, though. Elegant." She paused, then rubbed her eyes. "The key to them is catching it right at the beginning. The damn things take time to work, and if you can break the freeze, you can get away. Now, the simple thing would be to rig your box to detect the loop and just shut itself down. He thought of that. For your box to be that sensitive, it would be turning itself off all the time. So what I came up with was a counter-program. When my routine encounters one of his, it sets up an arhythmic loop—just sort of slides right into his and starts vibrating it apart. Poof, no lethal feedback."

She grinned wryly. "The effect is sort of like driving a garbage truck into a concrete wall at eighty klicks per, but you walk away in one piece."

They'd worked all night, Ozzie quivering behind enormous amounts of methamphetamine isomers, which he washed down with frequent swigs from a bottle of Stolychnaya he kept next to him in a trash can filled with ice cubes. "The trick is to balance the dosage so that your brain doesn't blow up, but you don't pass out, either," he'd said.

"I'd rather stick red-hot needles in my eyeballs," she told him. Ozzie seemed to thrive on this chemical high-wire, though, loping through his reefs and shoals of hi-tech detritus like a bizarre hybrid of coon dog and praying mantis. As night melted into watery morning he began to slow down, and now they lay on his futon, talking and listening to the small wheeps and moans from the spiked wreckage which surrounded them.

"You said you cracked him six times," he reminded her. "What then?"

She sighed. "It's like a chess game. I cracked him one time. He added a shift pattern which detected my programming and moved his. Then I added one, and so fourth. The winner in a contest like that is the guy who makes the last move. After we'd gotten to what amounted to the sixth level, we decided there was no point—remember, as far as I know, nobody else has stuff like his. We both doubted that anybody who tried to penetrate one of his routines would come prepared to detect, recognize, analyze, and shift through six levels. And it's a pretty mechanical thing for him to keep shifting. In fact, if I know Berg, his new stuff probably has an automatic shifter built into it by now. Which is the nut I've been trying to crack while you did whatever to that pile of hardware you've been screwing around with all night."

Ozzie brightened at the mention of his nocturnal labors. "Hey, Calley, I've done some neat things with that big old box of mine."

"Yeah? Like what?"

His filmy gray eyes moved shyly. "Well, I gave that trap we ran into some thought myself. One of the things I considered was a mechanical programmed cutout, like you said, but I gave up on it for the same reason—if it was any good, it would be too hair-trigger for any practical use. But then I thought of something else. For one of these things to hurt you, it has to affect you physically, right? So I just rigged up a couple of biomonitor cutout circuits. If your heartbeat moves beyond a safe range, or you start to show major anomaly in your EEG, the box automatically pulls out of the circuit. Shuts down. Do you think something like that would work?"

Calley yanked suddenly at her jumbled mop of hair. "Ozzie! You little darling. I knew there was a reason I liked you. Why didn't I think of that?"

He shrugged. " 'Cause you like to attack things, I guess. You wrote an attack program to counter his defense. I just came up with another defense."

She stared at him. "Yeah, maybe," she said. "I see what you mean. Sometimes I wonder, you know. I'm not wired to think that way. It seems cleaner to me, to just . . . charge right on through stuff. Stick a knife in it and see what comes out."

They were lying on their backs, staring up at the bleary skylight. Her head rested on his left arm. He flexed, and pulled her closer. "We're opposites, darling," he said softly. "You know what they say about that."

She blinked. "Uh-huh. But nobody was more opposite than me and Berg, and that didn't work out. It was even better, because we were such a match for each other. He's a lot stronger than you, Ozzie—no offense—and tougher, too. A lot like me, maybe, that way. His talents were just different than mine."

Ozzie quivered slightly as sweat dried from his naked chest. He was wearing a ragged pair of cutoffs and a pair of high-top sneakers. "He's a defender and you attack," he said slowly. "Maybe you should have left well enough alone."

Calley shook her head, a short, brutal motion. "Not in this world, laddie. I've never backed away from anything, and I wasn't about to start with Mr. Jack 'Iceberg' Berg. No shit, why do you think I took back my maiden name? I never was all that fond of Calley, but that was what I went by before I met him. You know what he called me all the time? Glory—for Gloria, I guess. Now is that sickening, or what?"

" 'Glory,' " he mused. "I don't think it's so bad."

She exhaled slowly. "So what do you know? You can't even get your stupid face fixed."

"Hey, Calley," he said.

"What?"

"Why are you crying?"

"Shut up, dammit."

The gummy skylight glowed a thin, bilious pink from the backwash of the city lights. Down below, they sat within the circle of Ozzie's constructions, phosphorescent ghosts in the green fluorescence of the monitor screens.

Calley was already jacked in. She wore a red T-shirt and a pair of baggy white shorts. Ozzie still wore nothing but his cutoffs and sneakers. She sat in a full lotus, drumming bitten fingernails on her muscular thighs.

"Nervous?" he asked. His long fingers were busy with final adjustments.

"Naw," she said. "Just impatient, that's all. I want

another crack at whatever kind of fucker it was that
zapped me in there. If somebody bought a bunch of
Berg's programs, they had to spend a lot of money.
That kind of money is protecting something, and I
want it. Besides, the routines I wrote for this are kind
of intriguing. If my gimmicks can crack Berg's stuff for
real, then that's worth cash, too."

He stopped what he was doing and let his shoulders
slump. "That's it, I guess," he said. "I can't think of
anything else—it'll have to do."

"You don't sound very confident," Calley told him.
Carefully, she reached out and began to squeeze the
back of his neck with two fingers.

"That feels good," he said.

"Just relax. You're all tense. Don't worry, mom-
ma's packing a real big gun this time."

He rolled his head. "Better be, darling. That fucker
scared the shit out of me."

"Well," she said, pulling away, "let's go scare
the shit out of it." Then she chuckled. "Listen to
me, babbling like that stupid program is alive, or
something."

Ozzie ran his fingers tentatively over his touchpad.
"You never know." he said.

Then they went.

They entered the metamatrix from below, as usual.
"Hold it," Calley said. Obediently, Ozzie froze them
just above the glittering, milky floor. "I want to see
what you look like."

"Sure, darling," he said. She tried to swivel her
point of view. She knew he was somewhere just behind her left shoulder.

The world swirled around her, but she couldn't see
Ozzie. "Where are you?" she said.

"Just behind you," he replied cheerfully. "And you're
just behind me," he added.

"What?"

"I can't see you, either," he said. "I think it's because we're jacked into the same box."

"Oh—well, it doesn't make any difference, I guess. I just wanted to see."

"Right," he said. "Now what?"

"I'd like to sneak up on the big guy," she said thoughtfully. "Can you take us up, but sort of keep other stuff between us?"

"You think that cloud has eyes or something?"

"I don't know what it has. If Berg's been playing with their defense systems, the goddam thing could have a nose, for all I know."

It was ghost silent, the matrices glittering and popping like a city of burning jukeboxes. Ozzie began to pick his way out and up, slithering up slides of congealed light, always keeping something between them and the bloated galaxy hanging over the metamatrix.

"That's enough," Calley breathed. They hovered at a point just below the tip of a gigantic magenta pile, the tallest thing at their level. Above was vacant space, ashimmer with the neon message lines, and higher still, the chandeliered glory of the meatmatrix.

"Awful far away," Calley muttered.

Ozzie sighed. "It ain't gonna get any closer, darling. What now?"

"Go ahead and run my programs," she told him.

After a moment he said, "Up and on, kid."

They waited. Gradually, then, it began to appear. "Oh, wow," Calley said.

Something like a butterfly first unfolding from its chrysalis. A wing. A sail of many colors. And another, beautifully curved, a reach of fragile turquoise. Still another, softly amber, transparent. . . .

Until they were surrounded by wave after wave of them, a hundred refracting shards of light.

"So that's what it looks like," Calley said. "I never realized that—"

"What?" Ozzie said.

"This is a beautiful world, isn't it?" she said.

"Right. It just about chopped us up last time, this beautiful world, darling. You think all that diaphanous bullshit is going to help this time around?"

"Only one way to find out," she said. "Take us up there. And step on the gas."

There was no wind, but as Ozzie headed out and screamed for altitude, the wings began to elongate, stretching and fluttering and turning. Slowly their leading edges coalesced into a hook, a twisted barb of ruby glare. As they approached the meatmatrix, Calley saw it once again, the same pulsing crimson globe and then, quickly, the cylinder formed, swinging around to track them.

"This better work," she said.

She was vaguely conscious that Ozzie was pouring on the power, that their speed was increasing. "That's right," she muttered, "ram the sucker."

The cylinder exploded into a whirling funnel, reaching out to catch them in its ravenous embrace—

Their sails snapped suddenly rigid. Fitted like spinning vanes equidistant around the mouth of the glittering tornado, slowly beginning to spin with it.

In the center, everything stopped. They felt frozen, caught like insects in the center of a hurricane. Their sails began to flash in different colors, red, blue, and finally an insane emerald color.

Colors that had no names at all.

Spinning, whirling, turning.

Began to gently strobe.

To delicately shred the funnel into torn pieces of light.

They came through.

"I dunno," Calley said. "Are we alive?"

"I think so, babe," Ozzie replied. "Jeezus, would you look at it!"

Below them spread an endless field of white fire. As they raced across its surface, vast pools yawned, shifted, burst wide in glistening sprays. Here and there, in momentary eyeball flickers, strange, insectile structures appeared and vanished, leaving nothing but a trail of sparks in memory.

"Slow us down," she said.

Their motion faltered, then stopped. Directly ahead a blue core burned, surrounded by an infection of ominous orange rings.

"What do you think?" Calley asked.

"Hardware," Ozzie told her. "Implants, controls, you name it."

"Can we access?" she said.

"Well, that's what I built this box to do. Let's see. . . ."

He brought them close to the blue construction, and she sensed that his concentration was elsewhere. She imagined his fingers skittering madly over his touchpad, feeding in the instructions that slowly brought them next to the coruscation of cold blue radiance.

Suddenly she felt a silent click, and a steady stream of bright pink balls arched from the core and disappeared into space behind her left shoulder.

"What's happening?" she asked.

"Cracker program," he said shortly. "I tapped into it, whatever it is. The box is sussing it out now."

The process continued, and Calley took a moment to glance around. Everything looked cool, except—

She went rigid.

"Ozzie," she said.

"I'm busy," he replied.

"You better hurry up," she said. "Something's coming. I don't know what it is, but it's *big*, and it's moving fast. I hope that fucking cutout system of yours works, 'cause—oh, Jeezus!"

The thunderstorm of bruised light that grew from nowhere came down on them like the heel of God.

She screamed.

She had a few fleeting impressions: laughing lips, thick, heavy, covered with scabs. View of a great room full of diamond light. A rusty knife, blood-stained. Two small dogs, both brown, both dead. An empty metal box. Berg's face, strained with fatigue. A small Oriental man wearing an iron mask. A great wheel, turning, rushing forward.

Crushing laughter.

Midnight.

They came out of it together, on the futon, inter-twined like sticks of kindling.

"God," she said carefully, "my head hurts."

Ozzie lay on his back, mouth open, breathing heavily.

"Are you okay?" she asked, leaning over to brush his damp forehead.

"Uh. Uh, okay," he managed. Then, finally, "Yeah. I'm gonna live. I think." He tried to sit up, moaned, then lay back down. "I think I'll just rest for a minute," he said.

Her head throbbed, but she remembered something. A piece of what she'd caught before the wheel stomped them flat.

"Yeah, you rest," she said. "I gotta make a call." Carefully, she got to her feet. Paused for a moment until the dizziness passed, then moved on wobbly knees to Ozzie's commlink.

Stood for a moment putting it together, then leaned forward, punched in the codes, and typed, "ICEBERG—COLLINSWORTH, ALDOCCI, MARIE—THIMK—LOVE, ICEBREAKER—ENDS."

Then she half-staggered to the bathroom, put her head over the stained toilet, and puked for five minutes.

## 9

AT FIRST HE thought it was Nakamura. William Norton had not become the fourth richest man in the world through cherishing any illusions about his fellow man, and he knew that in Nakamura's peculiar position he would be doing his best to remove the persistent thorn which resided at the heart of his irreplaceable data handling systems. But as the storm which had repelled the anomaly subsided, he began to have second thoughts.

He caused the light in his high-ceilinged office to subside, willed the great doors to swing shut, and settled himself behind the slab of marble he used for a desk. Then he slowly turned and stared out into the silent, glittering void.

Man is a time-binding animal, he considered, but man here is . . . something else. As he watched, the scene began to replay itself.

Ah! So that was where it began. His point of view suddenly expanded, darted forward to the source of the first disturbance. In this altered state, he was part of the metamatrix itself, and his whole universe became a wave of changed perception. He smelled the point of intrusion as a nostalgic whiff of bacon frying. As the tiny star appeared, at first one tiny point among the giganumbers of individual PCs caught in the great nets, he fancied he heard the pop and snap of crisp meat cooking.

Now he watched carefully. What he saw was strange.

The tiny point of light grew until it was about the size of a baseball. He had the idea there was something dual about the small globe, but he couldn't quite figure out what it was.

One moment the globe was a part of the scintillating fabric of the massnet and then, with an audible click, it separated and began to move away. Intrigued, he followed.

Almost as if it were some kind of tiny animal, the globe darted to the protection of the nearest data construct. Norton knew that core—Chicago data base for General Electric Motors—and for a moment wondered if that vast conglomerate could be involved with this. But the globe only paused there before making the short leap to Midwest Ameritech's switching systems.

Getting into the spirit of the thing, he envisioned himself stalking the globe, the hunter on tippy-toe following the unknowing rabbit. Hippity-hop went the globe; hoppity-hip went the hunter. Finally they reached the point of the Matsushita U.S. central core, above which floated only the spectral outlines of the meatmatrices.

What was the damn thing?

He pursued more closely, coming right up on the small sphere, but still couldn't make out any details. Just as he was deciding to try a probe, the first sail flickered out. Startled, he jerked backward, so that the second sail narrowly missed brushing him with its tip. He kept his distance until the process was complete, and the entire diaphanous construct had begun the sudden leap toward his home.

He flipped back to his office.

From this comforting vantage point he watched the attack once again. The—sailship?—dove in, met his massively lethal defenses, broke through them. That gave him pause and he replayed the whole scene one more time, slowly, and this time made out the precision with which the vanes of the attacker snapped rigid in the teeth of his defense programming.

"It's an analog, idiot," he muttered to himself, tapping his square, heavy front teeth with his index finger. He turned to his desk and began to work the touchpad there, seeking information.

One of the screens began to scroll data, and there he found what he sought. Nakamura-Norton had bought, through an untraceable subsidiary, the series of lethal feedback programs from a man named Jack Berg, who had designed them to fit parameters that were carefully doctored to conceal the existence of the metamatrix. The programs had then been de-engineered by Double En's own techs, and modified to fit the peculiar requirements of biodata logic handling systems.

Jack Berg? Why was that name dimly familiar to him? Perhaps he had dealt with the man in the distant past, when he still had flesh to call his own? He shook his head. Already that time was fading, becoming less real, as his memory base slowly expanded across the shifting hugeness of the metamatrix.

He sighed and punched in a search routine keyed on the man's name. If Nakamura-Norton, in any of its thousand facets, had ever touched the man, he would soon know.

"I am no longer certain of my own power," he said aloud.

"I know," his wife said.

He looked up, startled.

Carefully she shut the large door behind her. "Hi, Bill," she said quietly.

"Sarah," he said, rising. "This is a nice surprise."

She was as beautiful as ever, her straight blonde hair impeccably styled in a simple bob, her clear green glance measured and cool. The black silk Balmain reconstruction fit her perfectly, its simplicity accentuating the lushness of her figure.

She walked toward him with the strides of a trained model, her chin high. He kept on smiling, but wondered what had brought her here. He hadn't seen her for a very long time.

"How are you, darling?" she asked. Her voice was

somewhat high-pitched; he remembered that she had spent a lot of money on training it, but hadn't achieved any noticeable results.

"I'm fine, dear," he said, reaching out for her, but the sudden low chime of the search program announcing its success caused him to look away for an instant. When he looked back she was gone.

He sat down, staring at the space where she had been. His world was haunted, and he was the head ghost. He wondered if she still looked like that, back in the unreal world.

His desk chimed again. He leaned forward and began to read. Yes. The details of the man's history. Fairly well-known, but there was no evidence they had ever met face-to-face. And yet—he stopped, rereading an intriguing piece of data. For some unknown reason, Double En had caused the deaths of three of Berg's compatriots. Quite recently, in fact.

He studied the names. Collinsworth, Aldocci, and Marie Theroux. Interesting. He wondered why Nakamura had done that.

A plot, no doubt. And no doubt in some way directed at him. It would take him a while to find out, but he would unravel it in the end. There was nothing Nakamura could truly hide.

Which left only one thing. Where had the storm come from?

Shigeinari Nakamura settled down in the plush chair and rested his elbow on the fake onyx tabletop. The lights in the bar were low; on one wall a holo of skiers attempting the more interesting black runs at Vail gave the place a subdued vibrancy.

The waiter smiled at him. "What for you tonight, Shag?"

Nakamura checked the Cartier tank on his wrist. "Louis XIII, Kenneth. Water back."

"Coming right up," the waiter said. Within a few moments he was back, carrying a large crystal balloon with about half an inch of dark liquid inside. He placed the drink on a napkin next to Nakamura's elbow, added a heavy tumbler of ice water, and straightened. Nakamura eyed him suspiciously. "You didn't do anything stupid like heating the brandy?"

The waiter's handsome features flickered indignantly. "Of course not," he said. "Ruin great shit like that?"

"Good," Nakamura replied. He handed over his credit chip. "Add a C for yourself," he said.

The waiter smiled. "Thanks," he said.

Nakamura watched him go, then lifted the balloon and inhaled deeply of the thick, dark aroma. Finally, his head aswim with the heavy fumes, he sipped delicately, held it, then let the incredibly expensive cognac slide down his throat.

The fiery little bomb hit his stomach and exploded in a burst of relaxation.

"Ahh," Nakamura said softly. He closed his eyes.

"Mr. Nakamura?" the man said.

Nakamura opened his eyes. "Oh. Simmons—sit down." He gestured to a chair on the other side of the table. Somewhat hesitantly, the man who headed Double En's research and development division obeyed the invitation.

Once again, as he studied him for a moment over the rim of his cognac balloon, Nakamura was reminded how life often put people in strange roles. Nathan Simmons was a world-class scientist. His background was flawless, a spectacular rise through the esoteric West Coast world of Berkeley and Stanford and what had once been Silicon Valley, culminating in his appointment to one of the three or four premier research positions on the planet. On paper the man was perfect. Yet, as Nakamura regarded his hired genius calmly, he wondered what drove the man . . . for Nate Simmons had the perfect, chiseled good looks of a professional model. From the black wave of hair which looped across his broad forehead to the wide blue eyes and handsome, squared chin, Simmons was about as far from the runty, four-eyed scientific ideal as he could be. Could physical attractiveness ever be a handicap,

Nakamura wondered? Did other scientists downgrade this man's abilities because of his spectacular appearance?

In all other aspects, however, Nate Simmons hewed to the norm. Slow and careful in his speech and painfully shy in his dealings with other people, the man was a paragon of respectability. If only he didn't have that perfect smile, Nakamura mused.

"You have followed my instructions to the letter?" Nakamura asked coldly.

"Yes, sir," Simmons replied. "Not one bit of this had come near any computer. Although that has delayed us greatly. I've had to use extremely primitive methods of calculation."

Nakamura shrugged. "So did Einstein," he replied. "But you now have results?"

Simmons sighed. "Well, yes, of a sort."

"What does that mean?"

Simmons spread his hands. "The results are ambiguous."

Nakamura made a short, exasperated clicking sound. "Just tell me what you know. I'll worry about ambiguity."

Simmons nodded. "We don't really understand the connection between Mr. Norton and his body anymore."

"Yes?"

"Well, the body is still in suspension, and the tumors are still multiplying—that is, the flesh lives. But all our scans show brain death. Everything we know how to measure is flat. The man is dead."

Nakamura shook his head. "The man is not dead, I can assure you," he said.

"Well, then," Simmons said. "If he is alive, it's not anything we can understand. Although that's not so strange, either."

Nakamura toyed with his drink. "How so?"

"We never have understood the mind-body connection." Simmons paused, looked up and motioned to the waiter. "Do you mind?" he asked Nakamura.

The Oriental shook his head. Simmons ordered a

glass of white wine. Then he continued. "For all our research of the past years, particularly into the biochemical aspects of the brain, we still have never proven, one or the other, exactly what part is played by the 'self.' That is, identity may be only a chemical function, or the brain may be some kind of biological machine operated by another force which we call, for lack of better terms, the soul, the self, the consciousness. I must say that our experience with Mr. Norton is beginning to tip the scales in favor of the second theory'

"Why is that?"

"Because the man's brain is useless for anything!" Simmons exploded. "It's a tub of cancer cells. If Norton is still alive, as you say, then it has nothing to do with his brain."

Nakamura contemplated this for a moment, tapping his fingertips together. "Um," he said. "Are you saying that if something happens to Norton's body, it might not affect Norton himself—his consciousness—inside the meatmatrix?"

Simmons winced. "I don't much like that name," he said. "I prefer 'biologic system.' "

Nakamura kept his voice even. "Doctor, I don't give a rat's ass what you prefer. I don't pay you for your preferences, only your knowledge. Which you are at the moment singularly unhelpful in supplying. Can you give me a straight answer? Do we have to destroy the matrix in order to do anything about Norton?"

Simmons shook his head slowly. "I'm sorry," he said. "I just can't tell you. I don't know."

The oriental lifted his cognac. "Very well, Doctor. If you don't know, you don't know. Which means the path becomes simplified."

The scientist regarded his own drink. "And that means . . . ?"

"We take the safer path. As usual," Nakamura replied.

The two men finished their cocktails in silence.

Nakamura inclined his head slightly when Simmons rose and took his leave, but didn't speak.

What a shame the man was so beautiful, but such a twit otherwise, Nakamura thought.

"I saw pretty boy leaving," Frederick Oranson said as he slid into the chair Simmons had just vacated.

"Yes," Nakamura replied. "Doctor Simmons was not particularly helpful."

Oranson snorted. "Guys like that never are. Their idea of pr_matism is deciding to wear socks in the morning."

Nakamura's nostrils flared slightly. "But you are much more practical, aren't you, Fred?" he said softly.

Oranson had enough wit to merely nod.

"Good," Nakamura said. "So you will tell me now how our little project is doing?"

The security man paused, then said, "A minor problem or two."

"Nothing truly debilitating, I would hope," Nakamura said.

"Somebody blew up Berg's condo," Oranson said flatly.

"Ah." Nakamura examined the back of his hand. "And who did a thing like that?"

Oranson shrugged. "Don't know yet. It was a pretty straightforward job. Probably garden-variety hired muscle. We're on it."

"Perhaps an enemy Berg picked up on a previous job?" Nakamura suggested.

Oranson stared at him. "I didn't know you had taken up a belief in coincidence," he said.

"Yes. There is that." Nakamura sighed. "Very well, follow up. What about Gloria Calley?"

"She's been laid up with a weirdo named Oswald Karman," Oranson said. "Nothing much happening—they've been screwing, it looks like. She hasn't accepted our offer yet."

"The deadline is day after tomorrow, is it not?"

"Yes," Oranson agreed. He raised his hand for the waiter, but Nakamura stopped him.

"That won't be necessary, Fred," he said. "You won't be staying. Too much to do, isn't there?"

The security chief swallowed. "Right," he said. "Well, I'll be going, then."

Nakamura watched the butterfly exploits of the skiers for a while, wondering if he himself had gotten trapped on a similarly wild downhill flight. After a few moments he was conscious of another presence.

"I brought you another, sir," the waiter said, placing a second balloon of cognac on the table and removing the pair of empty glasses. As he did so, his fingers brushed lightly across the back of Nakamura's left hand.

Nakamura smiled gently. The night had been kind. The waiter, like the cognac, was a commodity.

Nakamura understood commodities.

# 10

B E IT EVER so humble, there's no place like home," Toshi said.

"Yeah, big mouth, and you get to wash the dishes," Berg told him.

It was a single large room. The one window on the far wall was covered by a slatted steel screen painted hospital green. The ancient wooden floor was deeply scarred, as if heavy machinery had been anchored there and then dragged away. The walls had been replastered three or four times, and each layer, like an archeological dig, revealed where mold had eaten chunks of it away.

It was very damp, and smelled like an abandoned harbor, of waterlogged wood, rusted iron, and decomposing fish.

"I think we'd do better to pitch the dishes out the window," Toshi said.

One entire wall of the room was covered with a scrambled web of hi-tech outlets, monitors, and boxes of several different varieties, including a small mainframe. The equipment was neat and sparkling. It looked incredibly out of place.

"How long was this place under water?" Toshi asked.

Berg grinned. "About two years," he said.

On the wall opposite the equipment was a table, its top covered with an intricate mosaic of rings, burn marks, and deep scratches. In the center of the table was a rusted hubcap filled with ancient cigarette butts. Three rickety chairs completed the set; and next to it sat a broken-backed rollaway bed topped with an un-

made mattress crusted with brown stains. A sink–
stove–fridge combo of archaic design completed the
amenities.

"I wonder why they bothered to pump it out," Toshi
said.

"Officially, they didn't," Berg told him. "As far as
the city is concerned, this place doesn't exist."

Toshi wandered over to the window and cranked
open the slats. "Nice view," he said.

"The Toadmothers run things down here. They have
most of this building," Berg said. "In fact, they're my
landlords. I pay a lot of rent."

"I'll bet," Toshi grunted. "Get anything for it?"

"It'll be tough for anybody to sneak down here with
a Little Man rocket launcher strapped to his back,"
Berg said.

Toshi snapped the shutters closed. "Right," he said.
"So what next?"

Berg plopped himself on the greasy mattress, lay
back, and knuckled his eyes. "Tosh, I'm in a bind," he
said.

"I'd say," Toshi agreed.

Berg exhaled slowly. "Besides getting blown out of
my apartment," he said. "First Collinsworth, Aldocci,
and Marie get snuffed. Then I get a mysterious visit
from some bozo who wants me to do unspecified defensive programming for Double En. Then more mysterious bozos, a whole team of them, who don't know
who they work for, but appear to work for Double
En. Next my condo gets blown up, the Lady goes all
mystic on me, and I still don't know what the fuck is
going on."

"Berg, Berg," the Oriental said. "You've got two
choices. Blow off the contract, or take it. Or—" He
paused."—You could stay here for the rest of your
life, I guess."

The smaller man sat up. "It must be nice to have
that kind of mind, Tosh, but you've missed a few things.
It'll cost me a fortune to trash that contract—even
though somebody wants me to, and is willing to go to

great lengths to make it happen. I could end up broke or dead either way. I need more information, is what." Berg got up from the bed and went over to the table. "So, I figure I've got a day or so, and all that shit on the wall there, it wasn't cheap." He sat on one of the spindly chairs, lit a cigarette, and pulled the hubcap ashtray close.

"It's time to get to work," he said.

"I thought so," Berg said.

The bed creaked as Toshi shifted slowly out of a full lotus into a roll which brought him flat-footed onto the floor. "Ouch!" Toshi said. "Frigging splinters—!"

"I told you to wear something on your feet," Berg said mildly.

"Your advice is noted," Toshi said. "And what is it you think, bubba?"

"You're even more disgusting in your Jewish mother persona," Berg replied. "Take a look at this."

Toshi was wearing a loose pair of white muslin pants. His hard, round belly overhung the drawstring, and bounced slightly as he came to the touchpad where Berg had crouched like a manic spider for almost two hours. "All I see is words," Toshi said.

"So learn to read," Berg told him. "About a year ago I did some work for a little company I'd never heard of, Tapco. Anyway, it was expensive work, and the parameters they gave me were for something big. Defensive stuff. So I got to thinking about it, and I did a full search on Tapco. This is what I found. Interesting, isn't it?"

Toshi leaned over and peered at the monitor screen. "Um. Tapco is owned by Genext, which is a blind subsidiary of. . . ." The Oriental scratched his upper lip. "Um, uh-huh, yeah—oh. Jackpot. Double En owns Tapco, through the usual thicket of corporate hide-hole bullshit."

"Right," Berg said. "Double En bought my stuff, and that makes sense. What I put together was a lethal defense system for a very large machine—too big for a shrimp company like Tapco."

"Didn't you think about that at the time?"

Berg grinned. "Their credit was good, they paid on time, what's to think?"

"Good logic, Berg," Toshi said disgustedly. "Tell it to your interior decorators when they rebuild your condo."

Berg ignored him. "I wonder if I've already built stuff for their meatmatrix without knowing it?"

"Is there any way to check?"

Berg shook his head. "I could always ask," he said. "Or there's one other way, but it's not what I'd call safe."

The Oriental shrugged his massive shoulders. "You pays your money, you takes your chance," he said.

"Always the philosopher, aren't you?" Berg told him.

"I've written a couple of new things that should help," Berg said. "But you are my backup, Tosh. You sure you understand what to do?"

The two men were seated in front of the input remotes for the small mainframe. A fiber optic ran from one remote to the plug under Berg's right ear. Toshi was balanced on one of the ruined chairs, just behind Berg's left shoulder.

"Simple enough," he said. "You start to shake, or breathe funny, or pass out, I yank the cable. That all?"

Berg sighed. "That's it," he agreed. "Just be sure you do it. I wrote those programs and I know what they do. They kill people."

"So do I," Toshi told him. "It's no big deal."

"Right, samurai," Berg said. "So let's get to it."

His fingers gently began a farrago on the touchpad.

On the monitor screens, brightly colored forms began to appear, a scrolling stream of elongated shapes interlaced with an endless rush of lines and numbers.

"I'm using a business code I cracked from one of Double En's coast branches," Berg muttered. "Just following the river back to source. Oops!"

"What?" Toshi's hand was on the cable.

"No, nothing—a tricky littly cutout there. I'm back on track. . . ."

Slowly, Berg felt the old sensations return, the give and play as he maneuvered up the gossamer chains of data, seeking a source. The screen became his world, his fingers forgotten as they automatically punched in new instructions, made choices, pursued possibilities.

"Getting close now. . . ." he mumbled, his pupils the size of small dark coins. Toshi watched him carefully.

"Ah. . . ." Berg became immobile for one frozen instant, then exploded in frantic movement. "I'm engaged with the defenses," he said. "There's something—no, that not it—"

Toshi shifted around Berg until his thick fingers were only centimeters from the cable running into the smaller man's skull.

"No, I'm . . . *that's not mine!*"

Berg's back arched like a drawn bow, then snapped forward. His head crashed into the screen, cracking the tough plastic. Toshi's hand moved in a single lightning motion and came away, holding the jack end of the cable.

Still Berg convulsed.

Toshi hauled him away from the box and stretched him on the floor. Berg's fox-like face was distorted, his eyes rolled back until only the yellowish whites showed. His mouth stretched slowly into an obscene yawn.

Then his teeth began to grind.

Toshi reached into Berg's mouth and pried his jaws apart. A quiet metallic sound overrode Berg's rattling breaths. It was the noise a ratchet wrench makes as it adjusts to fit. Toshi heard it clearly, realized what his reinforced hands really sounded like when they were cranked up high.

Finally Berg gave one last heaving shudder and collapsed limp on the floor. He began to snore.

Toshi removed his fingers, examined the gnawed

skin, shook his head, and lifted Berg from the floor in one smooth, powerful motion. He carried him to the bed and laid him down gently. Then he waited.

The single portable glowlight near the ceiling cast a weird, halidic glare over the room. Berg still lay on the bed, half-sitting, his back against the wall.

"I don't know," he said for the second time.

"You ever have an epileptic episode?" Toshi asked. "Any history like that?"

Berg grinned tightly. "What are you, the family doctor?"

"No, asshole, but I do have a medical degree somewhere in my checkered past."

Berg regarded him with new interest. "Yeah? I didn't know that."

"Which is only a small part of the many things you don't know," Toshi told him sourly. "I never practiced, but I know grand mal when I see it. You were a spring-loaded mess. You remember anything?"

Berg shook his head slowly. "Nothing," he said. "I was just getting past the feedback shit, when everything went blank."

"Getting past? I doubt it," Toshi said.

"No, really, it was my own stuff. I recognized the sequencing. It was modified, but not enough that I didn't know what I was doing. No shit, Toshi, I had it cracked. Something else hit me, but I don't remember a thing."

Toshi stared at him. "All this is not good, Berg," he said. "I pulled the plug and you just went right on flopping. You weren't connecting to anything when you did that fish dance."

Berg spread his hands. "I said I don't remember. I was just breaking through. . . ." He paused.

"What?"

"I wonder if the computer got anything," Berg said.

"What are you raving about?"

"The box, you mongoloid idiot. My mainframe was programmed to smash and grab. I *know* I got through the defensive crap. Maybe the box picked up something!" He started to roll off the bed.

"No you don't," Toshi said, his big hand flat against Berg's scrawny chest. "I'm the doctor, and I prescribe rest. For a while, at least. If your electronic voodoo machine picked up anything, it'll keep. You need some sleep," he said firmly.

Berg wriggled. "Toshi, you meatball, let me—"

And stopped, as Toshi's fingers found a nerve and Berg slumped instantly into oblivion.

The first thing he noticed was that the steel slats were open a bit, admitting a few wan rays of watery light. The next thing he saw was Toshi's face turned toward his own, eyes closed, next to him on the bed.

"Hey, sleeping beauty," he whispered.

Toshi's eyes snapped open. "Morning," Toshi said. He propped himself up on one elbow. "How you feel today?"

Berg grinned. "Doctor, if I can survive your version of anesthesia, waking up six inches from your ugly kisser isn't going to hurt me."

The Oriental nodded, then rolled off the bed. "You got any coffee in that fridge?" he asked dubiously.

Berg laughed. "You look, you just might find some Blue Mountain. There's a pot and cups and shit in that box next to the stove."

"Blue Mountain in this dump?" Toshi said. "Berg, you continue to teach me new dimensions of decadence. Or hubris. Or something."

Berg sat up on the bed. "Did I ever teach you how to make coffee?"

"Fuck you," Toshi replied calmly as he rummaged in the fridge. He got the pot boiling on the stove and threw in a double handful of the rich, dark grounds. The celestial aroma filled the dingy room like a blessing.

"I think I'll keep you," Berg said.

"Let's wait and see how it turns out," Toshi replied.

Berg held the heavy ceramic mug with both hands

as he sipped the mellow brew. "Is this gonna be a habit, you feeding me coffee after rough nights?" he asked.

Toshi set his cup down. "Noblesse oblige, boss. Us civilized Oriental races owe you barbarian round-eyes the lessons of our sophisticated culture. Yellow man's burden, I guess."

Berg snorted. "I thought that was 'yellow peril.' "

"Either way," Toshi said. "You know, without throwing you into that tricked up elevator of yours for a quick CAT scan I can't really tell, but I think you're okay. So, yes, you can drag your skinny ass out of bed and start beating that devil machine of yours. I won't stop you—but do me one favor. Don't plug in without telling me first."

Berg shook his head. "No intention, pal. In fact, I'm just going to dump it all to hardcopy. It struck me that certain visuals can induce epilepsy. . . ."

"Me, too," Toshi said.

Berg sipped again from his mug. He turned and put both feet on the floor. "Shit!"

"Splinters?" Toshi asked.

Berg picked something out of the ball of his right foot, then tried again. This time nothing bit him and he padded over to his setup, only the faintest hesitation evident to Toshi's trained eyes.

He sighed, seated himself, powered everything up, and tapped in a series of piped commands. Near the end of the bank of gear a highspeed printer suddenly whirred into operation. With jaundiced eyes, Berg watched the flimsies drop into the basket.

"If I got through," he said, "there'll be something about it here."

The printer abruptly stopped. Berg retrieved the hardcopy, picked up his coffee, and climbed back onto the mattress. For a while there was nothing in the room but the sound of coffee being slurped and the occasional rattle of paper. Finally, Berg grunted. "I thought so," he said.

"Thought what?"

"I did get through. I was in the meatmatrix itself."

"You sure about that?" Toshi asked.

Berg waved the wad of hardcopy at him. "It's all here, sushi-breath." Suddenly he looked tired. "I got through all right."

Toshi stared at him. "But if you beat the feedback program, then what triggered the seizure?"

Berg's drawn face was somber. "I don't know," he said, "but whatever it was, it looks as if my ex-wife designed it."

Berg cranked the shutters closed for the last time. He paused and glanced around the nasty little room. "Well, that's that," he said. He was wearing a thick, waist-length black leather jacket with several zippered pockets, faded blue Levis, and a pleated dress shirt. Toshi was bundled up in a shapeless brown overcoat which bulged suspiciously in odd places.

"You sure you want to do this?" Toshi said.

"I'm tired of dicking around," Berg said. "This whole slimy ball of shit is tied up with the corporations. I can smell it, I swear to God I can. And I can't hide from those guys forever. Or run from them, either. You think you can keep me alive till we get there?"

Toshi shrugged. His movement caused the coat to emit a muffled symphony of metallic sounds. "Maybe. Probably, if we both use up our ration of luck for the next ten years."

Berg walked over to the door and opened it. "Well, what the hell," he said cheerfully. "Let's go see what that fucking drunk and that feral nip at Double En have in mind."

"Watch the racial slurs," Toshi told him.

## 11

I T WAS A small restaurant, and cheap: not a human server in sight. But in the distant past somebody had capitalized on the collapsed roof in the back room, cleaning the rubble out and planting ivy which crawled up the aged, naked brick walls in pleasant, dark green patterns. Overhead, a few large stars managed to penetrate the pink glow of the city.

"Romantic, isn't it?" Ozzie said.

"Well, it's dark enough," she admitted. "You think you could get this candle lit?" She pointed to the stub of wax encased in a cracked glass jar.

He fumbled for a moment, then came up with a book of matches. "Wait a sec—there. . . ."

"Matches," she said. "You ever think about that, what an anachronism they are?"

"Naw," Ozzie said. "A near-perfect solution. Cheap, easy, effective. The wheel never goes out of style."

"Philosophy," Calley said. "That's nice."

"You okay, woman?"

"Why don't you call me girl, Oz? Make me feel all young and innocent?"

"You *are* romantic, aren't you? But what about your stature as an individual, free forever from dominating male influence?"

She stared at him. "Are you kidding?"

"Sorry," he said. "It was a thought. Girl."

Her tense, dark features softened. "See if one of those obsolete machines knows how to make espresso, okay?"

He nodded amiably, rose, and shambled off into the

shadows. After a time her returned, balancing two styrofoam cups. "You want sugar, cream, like that? Costs extra, though. . . ."

"Black's fine," she said. "Jeez. Plastic cups."

He grinned lopsidedly. In the dimness of the candle-glow, his monstrous, misshapen face looked oddly appealing. She thought for a moment of some dog-prince in a forgotten fairy tale.

"Well, here we are," she said.

Ozzie sipped carefully at his espresso. "Um. Hot You want to talk about it yet?"

Her eyes flickered. "About what?"

"You didn't tell me, but you picked up something you didn't like on that last run. Well, my hardware grabbed some stuff, too. I'll trade."

Now her decadent elf features became intent. "You didn't tell me," she said accusingly.

He shrugged. "You weren't talking much. I figured it was better to wait. Have we waited long enough, yet, Calley? What was that message you sent just after we came out?"

"Oh, that." She placed her cup on the tabletop. "It was to Berg."

"Berg? The arch-daddy? I thought you two weren't speaking. Wasn't there a divorce, little girl?"

"I take it back. Don't call me girl."

"Sorry. You get my point, though."

"Ozzie, even though Berg and I decided to split it doesn't mean that I hate him—well, not really, only sometimes. But I picked up something that concerns him. I let him know. That's all."

"I thought you said he engineered the systems that zapped us. Doesn't sound all that friendly."

She sighed. "Oz, just because somebody builds a fence, and later somebody else gets caught in the barbed wire, doesn't mean the fence-builder has it in for you specifically. Those were Berg's defenses, sure—though there was something very funny, very un-Berg about them—but they weren't set up for us. It wasn't his fault we blundered into them. If we did. The second time I thought my eyes were wide open." She stopped for a second, toyed with her espresso. "Besides, it wasn't Berg's shit that stomped us in the end. I got us through that, remember? We were in the matrix. What finally dinged us for real was—something else."

Ozzie shifted in his seat, plainly puzzled. "I admit I didn't see much of it, but I thought it was just more of the defensive system."

She shook her head. "No. It had nothing to do with programming. It was almost like the matrix itself came after us."

"And that, darling, is plainly impossible," Ozzie said. "It's a hunk of fucking chicken brain. It does what it's told to do. This thing is messed up enough without you bringing in wizzy stuff like that."

"Oz, I told you, *I don't know*—but I do know enough about programming to tell you that shit wasn't like anything I've ever run into—or even heard about, for that matter."

Ozzie slowly rearranged his gangling limbs on the chair until he looked like some elongated, nodding insect on its perch. "Okay," he said. "You don't know. I don't know, either. So what did you send to Berg?"

Carefully she smoothed her chopped black hair. "When that godawful thing squashed us, for a few instants I picked up a lot of impressions. Just flashes, garbled pictures, but I saw three people. A guy named Collinsworth, another one named Aldocci, and a woman I knew as Marie. They were all dead—I got that much—and they didn't die of what you'd call natural causes. I don't know what I was tapped into there, whether it was memory or planning or whatever. I couldn't tell if this was past or future stuff, is what I mean. But Berg was involved. Those three were people he used to hire for touchy stuff. Very high-class muscle, bodyguard types. I didn't know what it was all about, but I figured maybe Berg did. So I just sent him their names, and a little warning. Maybe he knows. If not, maybe he can figure it out." She shook her head suddenly. "Like I said, babe, I'm in the dark."

"Does it strike you that we seem to be running into Berg just about everywhere we turn? I thought I had discovered the metamatrix all by myself, but every time we go exploring lately we come up against your ex-hubby."

"I'd given it some thought," Calley said. "And this, too: Do you get the feeling that we're mixed up in something that's ongoing—something big, and somehow we fit into it, too?"

Ozzie lowered his head in thought. "Yeah," he said finally, " 'Cause I brought some stuff back, too. At least my box did."

"I wondered if you were gonna get around to telling me," she said dryly.

"Um. Well, I didn't know what to make of it. Still don't. Remember when I cracked into that chunk of what I thought was hardware? That chain of little balls I grabbed?"

"Uh-huh."

"Well, it was hardware. But very strange. It seems to be the control and command center for some kind of life-support system."

"Maybe for the matrix?" she asked.

He shook his big head. "No, outside. I don't know what it is, but for some reason the great chicken brain in the sky is devoting a lot of effort to keeping a corpse—well, not alive, but at least kicking."

She stared at him, her dark eyes narrow. "Something new? Double En has gotten into life support, something like that?"

He wadded his styrofoam cup and tossed it expertly into an overflowing wastebasket against the far wall. "I dunno. I gave it some thought, but I don't read it that way. Some of the data I got shows cancer. Why bother with that? I mean, do you buy Double En taking up massive charity for one carcinoma patient?"

"No," she said, "not very much. Not with just one corpsesicle. I wonder who Bill Norton cares enough about to spend gigabucks to keep the body warm?"

"That might be something we don't really want to

find out," Ozzie said. "They seem to feel that way about it."

She grinned suddenly. "Oh, no, laddybuck, exactly wrong. We care very much about finding out." She chuckled suddenly. "Or don't you believe in blackmail?"

Later they sprawled on Ozzie's futon in the middle of his slowly oxidizing technoswamp. Calley had brought the candle from the restaurant; its guttering flame made the shadows even wider than usual.

He passed her the plastic jug of California vin ordinaire. "Not bad," he said.

"None of it is, after the first liter or so," she agreed. She expertly tilted the bottle on her arm and swallowed.

"Hey, Calley. . . ."

"Mm?"

"You never talk about Berg much."

She passed the jug back. "Maybe 'cause I don't want to."

"Yeah? That says a lot, too. How come everything happened?"

"Everything? You don't want much, do you, boy?" She stretched slowly, her rib cage a patterned, twisted ladder. "Shit, Ozzie, I don't know. Maybe it's this romantic atmosphere, the fine wine, candlelight, your comfortable, half-inch futon, the ambience of your lovely pad—what the hell. I met Berg just after I set up shop with DataPunchers. . . ."

". . .the worst was right at the end," she said. Her voice, fuzzed down slow with wine, hung in the night over the viscous puddle that marked where the candle had finally sputtered out. The sharp, gingery odor of cheap burgundy filled the air. Their two forms were indistinct shadows in the hard-edged geometries of the big room.

"I'd already started another company—Smash-n-Grab—'cause I guess I knew the end was nigh. But I just couldn't fucking give up without one last try, you know. So I put on a frilly nightgown thing, real short, and arranged myself on Berg's most comfortable sofa."

She fumbled for the wine bottle, but it was empty. "Damn," she said. "Anyway, he walked in through that forest of defensive hardware, the little hubby home from a hard day building data walls, and I took my best shot."

"Hello, Jack," Calley said.

He just stared at her. "What's this for?" he said at last. "Is it Halloween or something?"

"Oh, shit," she said. "I knew this was doomed, but you scrawny fucker, we gotta talk."

"Hey, you're serious, right?" He walked over to one of the antique end tables and picked up a lighter. "Okay," he said as the light flamed at the end of his cigarette, "I'm game."

"That's not it, buddy," she said. "It's not a game. We're getting a divorce."

He sat down on the sofa, careful not to touch her. "Yeah. We already decided that, didn't we? The last time, when you tried to carve your initials on my liver with a laser-pick."

"Do we have to go all through it again? I don't want to waste time picking all those scabs. They *hurt*."

"So what do you have in mind?" he said.

"I want to try again. This shit doesn't have to happen."

He shook his head just a little. "Glory, Glory—it's been two years. We're both grown up now. You really think we can forget everything and start over?"

"Damn it, maybe you can't. Maybe I can't. But we could agree to try."

He sat there for the longest time, not moving a single muscle, and she watched the smoke curl up in front of his face. Then he looked at her with those flat dark eyes and said, "Okay, babe, you win. Whatever you want. I'll do it."

And that's when she knew it was terminally over.

"I don't understand that scene at all," Ozzie said.

"Yeah? I don't understand it either. Some thing'

you don't understand at all. You just recognize them
when they happen, like plane crashes or slum fires.
Things that always leave a lot of casualties behind. When
Berg said that I won, he was telling me I lost. Berg
can never lose and still be Berg. I can't lose either, not
that way. What we needed to do was work out something that didn't involve winning or losing, just living.
But he told me we couldn't do that. And he was
right."

She inhaled heavily. "I guess he was right."

Ozzie touched her hair gently. "If you still love him
that much, why not go back?"

"Oh, Oz, you just don't catch it, do you? Love and
divorce have nothing to do with each other. I love him
all right, but I can't live with him. How's that for an
ultimate cliché?"

"Clichés get that way because there's truth in them,"
Ozzie said. "How about me? Could you live with
me?"

She regarded him levelly. Finally she said, "Oh,
yeah. I could. For a while."


"Here's how I see it," Calley said.

It was raining in the city, thick, heavy pellets hitting
the skylight like BBs, splattering and smearing the
heavy glass. From one corner a thin stream of water
dripped into a large bucket on the floor.

Calley was dressed in a chamois jumpsuit that fit her
like the skin of a grape.

"I'm supposed to give Double En an answer today.
I don't know what they want me to do, but I'll bet it
has something to do with their big meat. And I want
to know everything about that particular chunk of
chicken neurons. So I'm gonna take their job."

Ozzie's lank brown hair was matted from the shower
they had taken together. He yanked at it with a comb
missing several plastic teeth. "Just like that, huh? The
thing almost fried your brain, darling."

She tossed her head back and forth, letting her own
cut settle. "They don't know that. All they

know is I'm good, and they need me for something they think I can do. Well, they're gonna get me, with bells on. Berg is mixed up in this somehow, and I don't think mixed up good. He's in danger, Ozzie, and even after everything, I can't just walk away from it."

"Woman's intuition?"

"I got your woman's intuition right here, asshole," she said.

"Uh, right," Ozzie replied. "So you're just gonna walk in wearing your innocent lamb costume and see what happens, huh?"

"You got a better idea?"

"Well, you could take me along."

"Oh, my crooked little prince charming, I'm way ahead of you. Of course you're coming along. Just not the way you think, is all."

She sat behind the knife chrome desk in the bruise-colored office and stared at the chip with the tiny lightning bolt Double En logo etched in one corner. Finally she sighed and inserted the bit of silicon into a reader and punched it home. Barely thirty seconds passed before her commlink monitor lit up with the smiling face of Frederick Oranson.

"Ah, Miz Calley," he said jovially. "You've decided to accept our offer?"

"Remember what I told you about the 'Miz' bull-shit?" she said coldly. "But yeah, I'm gonna take you on. Subject to a few contract revisions, of course."

His face retained its smile, but his eyes chilled. "Oh? Well, contracts are made to be changed. What did you have in mind?"

"I think there's something kinky about this deal," Calley said. "If you're involved I can almost bet on it, Oranson. So I want the money doubled, and I want a danger premium. That's not okay with you, then find somebody else."

She stared at the monitor. Oranson laughed suddenly. "No problem, Calley. Done and done. Welcome aboard."

She smiled then, and his smile widened. "Okay, Oranson, it's a deal."

"Good. We need you at our R&D center sometime this evening. Can you make it on your own, or you want us to send a limo?"

She thought about it. "A limo sounds nice. What time?"

"Say four o'clock?"

"Fine," she said, and clicked him off.

She kindled a cigarette with her fingernail lighter and sat for a few minutes, smoking in short, rapid puffs. Finally she stubbed the butt out and punched another number.

"Yeah?" The monitor remained dark.

"It stinks on ice," she said.

"Well, you're the boss," the disembodied voice replied.

"That's right," she said. "From here on out, be sure you keep it in mind."

"For sure," the voice said.

After she switched off, Calley put her booted feet up on the desk and leaned back in her chair. She closed her eyes and began to whistle softly.

It was an old tune: "You Can't Always Get What You Want," by the Rolling Stones. After a few bars she stopped.

"Why the hell not?" she wondered aloud.

## 12

I T WAS SINGLE-FAMILY prefabs clear to the flat horizon, a die-stamped rash of plastic Fuller-domes, each with its smaller, bubble-covered swimming pool. Two million people lived here, caught in their middle-class webs, getting up each day to drink coffee and turn on their remotes and manipulate the trillions of data bits which made up a commerce about which Adam Smith had known nothing, but would have understood. In terms of physical luxury they were the most privileged group of people who had ever lived, and they spent an inordinate amount of their time bitching about the barrenness of it all.

The sun rode high, casting drifted shadows from a few popcorn clouds on a sky as clear as the eye of a hunting bird.

Berg rode the A-train down a gentle slope and began to make out the plain green scar of Double En's research fortress in the fuzzy distance. "Coming up," he said.

Toshi peered over his left shoulder. "Big sucker," he said. He held his overcoat tightly closed and scanned the nearly empty compartment every few seconds.

Amazingly, the interior of the car was untouched by gang graffiti. Berg stared at this phenomenon, then realized it was a directline suburban train—and out in the burbs, they were handing down ten-year sentences for defacing public property.

He pressed his face against the cool plastic of the

window and let the smooth, bone-quivering hum of
the magnetic rail soothe his tired brain. Dreamlike,
the endless bubbles flowed past, and he wondered
what it was like to live in one. Here and there he
spotted an occasional tree, carefully tended in a circu-
lar concrete ring, and on one barely glimpsed specimen, a swing juryrigged from a large tire and a rope.

The anachronism jarred him, and for a moment he
just wanted to close his eyes and become somebody,
something, else. It made him tired to even think about
it. Somehow Gloria was tied up in all of this, and he
dreaded facing her again. She had never known, but
his personal defenses, those carefully tended walls of
pain and denial, were no longer proof against her own
special brand of emotional larceny. That was what had
destroyed their marriage, the slow crumbling of the
roads to his innermost heart—and now, for her, the
way lay open and naked.

God help me if she ever finds out, Berg thought
slowly. Perversely, another part of him whispered exactly the opposite, and at last he did close his eyes, but
the pictures never stopped.

There were three uniformed guards at the entrance
of the facility. The cabbie who dropped them off didn't
linger, but screeched all three of his tires in a high-G
departure.

"Doesn't seem like a popular stop," Toshi observed.

They stood outside a tall, chain-link gate, the only
opening they saw in the fence that stretched away
from them in twin curves as far as they could see.

"See those slots?" Toshi said. He nodded at a pattern of rectangular indentations in the black-topped
road that wound from the gate and up the hill behind
it. Berg nodded. "Tank trap," Toshi said succinctly.
"This shit is all for show. Bet you twenty newdollars
the real ballbreakers are behind that ridge."

"You out there!" It was a brazen, metallic hooting
that came from a cluster of loudspeakers on a pole
next to the armored guardhouse behind the fence.

Berg felt the sun pounding on his bare head and sweat beginning to bead at the tip of his nose.

"Fuck this," he said tiredly. He raised one hand, middle finger extended, and grinned at the three dim forms he could see behind the smoked glass of the chunky little building.

There was silence. He listened to the sound of unseen birds, the occasional humming pass of an insect, and waited. He was good at waiting.

Finally, out of sight, a door slammed open. They heard bootsteps crunch on gravel, and then two smartly uniformed guards marched around the corner and quick-stepped down to the gate. Both guards, one male, the other female, carried Bausch laser carbines at port arms.

Berg waited until they had stopped. Then he said, "Listen to me, you fuckers. My name is Jack Berg. Check your rosters, or whatever you look at to find out what's okay for you to do, and then open this fucking gate. Or not, I don't give a shit. But hurry it up, 'cause it's hot out here, and I don't plan to wait all fucking day. In fact, I don't plan to stand here even two more minutes, so that's how much time you've got."

The two guards ignored him completely, their globular helmets and dark green face shields looking a lot like a pair of matched eyeballs from some dimly remembered childhood horror video.

Thirty seconds went by like this. Berg listened to the sound of his own raspy breathing, half hoping that his deadline wouldn't be met and he could turn around and walk away from all of this. There was a sick certainty growing in his gut that something disastrous was beginning to yawn nastily open in front of him.

A sharp, high-pitched buzz sounded from the gate locks. The woman stepped smartly forward and pulled the right-hand gate wide. "So come on in, asshole," she said.

They walked through. Toshi grinned at the female guard. "Nice talking to you, too," he said.

She shoved the gate shut and rejoined her companion. "Follow us," she said, turned, and led them up toward the blockhouse.

It was dim and cool inside. The air smelled faintly of leather and machine oil. Two interior walls were covered with ranks of monitor screens, most showing scenes of empty fence. The third member of the team, a middle-aged man with a receding hairline, sat in a chair which swiveled to cover all the monitors. He wore a crisp white jumpsuit and black leather boots. A thick plastic ID badge was pinned to his chest. He appeared entirely harmless, until Berg got a good look at his blank green eyes. He'd seen eyes like that before, and knew that such stares concealed an interest in nothing but death.

"Mr. Berg," the man said softly. "My apologies for delaying you like this, but we have our rules. I understood you would be coming alone." He glanced at Toshi.

"My bodyguard," Berg said shortly. "It seems I have a few enemies this week."

"Ah. Well, it sometimes happens." The little man smiled briefly, a yellow flicker that Berg thought probably caused him some pain. "Of course, now that you're here, you won't require his services. You are perfectly safe under our protection."

Berg stared at him. "Right now, I don't know if I'm perfectly safe anywhere. So Toshi stays with me."

The man's green gaze swept Toshi. "Mr. Berg," he said, "your guard is heavily armed. Our monitors pick up a number of weapons, some of them quite esoteric. I certainly can't permit this—"

"Do you have trouble hearing?" Berg asked. "I said Toshi stays with me. The flip side of the coin is that I walk the fuck out of here. So get on your telephone or whatever and tell your boss the situation. And while you're doing that, you got anything to drink around here?"

The supervisor stared at him briefly, then nodded. "It will take a moment," he said, and spun his chair to face the wall. Berg heard a gurgling sound, and the male guard handed him a plastic glass full of water. Berg sipped the cool liquid and smiled.

"Just right," he said. He reached into his jacket and withdrew a slim, elegant silver flask, and poured a hefty slug of its golden contents into the glass. He tasted carefully and smiled. "Ah," he said to Toshi, "Glenfiddich. You want a taste?"

"Don't mind if I do," Toshi replied, and took the glass.

The supervisor turned. "It's all right," he said. "But your man has to be disarmed. I can't let him go any further with all that stuff he's carrying."

Berg looked at Toshi. Toshi nodded. "It's okay," he said. "I haven't seen anything yet I'd need even a pair of chopsticks to handle."

Both uniformed guards stirred at this, but remained silent.

"Here you go," Toshi said, and began to disgorge an incredible amount of weaponry.

"You brought all of that shit?" Berg said in wonder. "What were you planning? A war?"

"You never know," Toshi told him.

The man in the white jumpsuit waved a hand scanner in Toshi's direction. He didn't seem entirely pleased with the result, and repeated the process. Finally he shrugged and said, "That's it, then. If you'll wait a moment, a car is on the way to pick you up."

Toshi handed the scotch and water back to Berg. "Not bad," he said. "Now if we could just find a better class of people to drink it with."

Berg recognized the man who opened the door of the small, luxuriously furnished office-library, but noticed that he no longer had the faintly servile air he'd displayed before.

The room smelled of the leather bindings of real books that covered three walls. The fourth wall was dominated by a single painting, an excellent copy of Picasso's *Guernica*—surely it was a copy—and in front of that, a beautifully carved oak desk of the Empire period that Berg figured probably cost about twenty thousand new dollars.

"Mr. Berg," the man said, "pleased to see you again. My name is Fred Oranson." He offered his hand.

Berg ignored it and walked past him into the room. "Oranson," he said. He seated himself in a beautifully kept leather club chair which faced the desk, and motioned for Toshi to join him in its mate.

"What is this shit, Oranson? I'm very curious about all this shit, Oranson. If that is your name. Maybe, Oranson, you owe me for a decorating job."

The man came over and stood by the desk. His face was set in a determined smile. " 'Decorating job,' Mr. Berg? What are you talking about?"

Berg pushed himself back in the big chair. "Maybe you don't watch the news. I do. The story about my condo getting blown up made all the channels. You probably missed it, I guess."

Oranson's fingers stroked the polished top of the desk unconsciously. "Was that your place? I didn't know—the news people didn't identify the owner."

Berg massaged the back of his neck. "Yeah, you're probably right. I doubt if you could tell it was the place you visited from the pictures. There wasn't a lot left. I thought maybe you would have remembered the address."

Oranson spread his hands, palms up. "I'm sorry, Mr. Berg. I really don't know why you're asking me about all this. You could say all I do is run errands."

"Oh? You have a real nice office. Running errands must pay pretty good these days."

Oranson pulled his hand away from the desk. "Office? Oh, this isn't my office. Mr. Nakamura will be joining us in a minute. He left me to greet you. And I apologize—can I get you or your friend something? A bit of Glenfiddich, perhaps?"

Toshi spoke softly. "Laphroaig for me, Mr. Oranson. If you don't mind."

Berg nodded. "I'll stick with my brand, thanks. Nakamura, you say? Would that be the second letter in your logo, by any chance?"

Oranson did something complicated to one of the bookcases, which swung away to reveal a completely equipped bar. He busied himself for a moment, then brought two heavy crystal tumblers to them. "Yes," he said. "Mr. Nakamura is the man who hired you."

The tumbler was cold and heavy. Berg lifted it to his lips, sipped, and clicked his tongue in appreciation. "The Scots do one thing well," he said. "So what's keeping my employer?"

"Mr. Nakamura never enters any situation which might involve personal danger for him," Oranson said smoothly.

Jack Berg didn't quite catch it, but Toshi did, and came out of his chair with one hand raised. A thin needle of yellow light exploded from his index finger. Oranson screamed, a high, thin sound. Berg smelled burning meat. Toshi was halfway across the desk when the sizzling green glare of the lightblade took off his right hand at the wrist.

"Berg—*go!*" Toshi roared, and tried to turn. Berg heard the sound of something heavy striking flesh, saw Oranson, his face contorted, fall away from the desk, and smelled the faint odor of violets.

Darkness. . . .

Far in the distance the city burned. He watched the flames devour great buildings, watched towers crumble in vast sparkling conflagrations, but all of it seemed apart, had no effect, as if viewed from darkness in a brightly lit room across a nameless street.

He woke up.

The cubicle was dimly lit by the small nightlight he faced as he lay on the bed. Thick, bloodshot explosions pounded behind his temples. When he raised one hand, the movement sent shafts of momentary pain, like brilliant icepicks, deep into the recesses of his brain.

He grunted. After a while the agony began to subside. He waited. Tried again. This time he was able to
prop himself up on the pillow and turn away from the
light.

Toshi. He began to remember.

It came to him that they would not kill him. Not
yet, or he wouldn't be alive at all. So they needed him
and all this had been a ruse. He had tried to play their
game and keep a move ahead, but the vast corporate
apparat had picked him off like some annoying but
valued insect.

Very well. He needed them, too. The memory of
Toshi's severed hand—had those fingers actually burst?
—haunted him. He needed him very much, he decided. Only the living pay debts of blood, for only the
living bleed.

He sank back on the pillow. Rest, he thought. Rest
until it goes away and you can function again. Rest
until Shigeinari Nakamura comes for you and reveals
his weakness.

They always do, he promised himself.


When he woke the second time, the Oriental man
was there. He sat in a chair beside Berg's bed and
watched him blankly. Berg opened his eyes and saw
him, and for a moment thought he was facing—
still in a dream—the statue of some ancient Japanese
war god.

He licked his lips. "Nakamura?" he said.

Nakamura's black gaze flickered slightly. Then he
said, "You gave me quite a time there, you little
bastard. I thought we were going to lose your ass."

"What happened?" Berg asked.

The Japanese man shrugged. "We had to disarm
your companion. Psych profiles said he wouldn't leave
you, and he had enough off-brand tech shit implanted
in various places to take down half this complex. So
we took him down instead."

"Dead?" Berg croaked softly.

Nakamura raised his shoulders and let them fall.

Berg sighed. "What the fuck did I ever do to you, you shithead?" he said.

"Nothing," Nakamura replied. "It's what I need *you* to do."

Berg noticed that his vision was growing clearer. "What's that?" he asked.

"I want you to—shall we say—dispose of my partner," Nakamura said simply.

The door to the room opened, and a small, elfin face appeared, framed with a mop of ragged, choppy black hair. Berg stared at the visitor.

"Oh, fuck," he said.

"You got that right," Calley replied.

The small library had changed slightly. Berg noted with satisfaction that a jagged scar, raw and new, was burned across the face of the Picasso. He sat in the same chair as before, but it was pulled away from its twin, which Calley now occupied. Shag Nakamura sat behind the antique desk, his face impassive. Fred Oranson stood at the side of the desk, facing them, a polyresin cast encasing his right shoulder. Beneath the clear covering, Berg could see an angry wound, and felt even better.

Not enough, you bastards, he thought to himself, but it's not over yet.

"To make things simple," Nakamura continued, "my partner, Bill Norton, has managed to become an intolerable nuisance. I have decided to remove him, and every analysis we've made says you are the people to do it." He paused and looked down at his neatly folded hands.

"Why us? I'm not some kind of hired gun. You want Norton murdered, use somebody like that thug next to you," Berg told him.

"Oh, you misunderstand," Nakamura replied. "I don't want anybody murdered. It would be impossible anyway. My asshole partner is already dead."

"Berg," Calley said suddenly. "Just listen to what the man has to say."

"Fuck off, bitch," Berg said.

"Well," she replied. "Some things never change, do they?"

"The fee," Nakamura said, "is one billion new-dollars "

# 13

THEY STARED AT each other. Each wondered what the other saw.

"I'm gonna have to find a way to snuff you," Berg said quietly.

The faint web of lines at the corner of her eyes deepened slightly. "As usual, Berg," she said, "you have it all screwed up."

His teeth remained tightly together. The words came through as if filtered by stone. "I don't understand," he said. "I didn't think—what did I do, for you to hate me this much?"

She shook her head. "I don't hate you, Berg. You're a miserable, rotten, selfish sonofabitch, and you fucked me up good, but I don't hate you."

"Then *why?*"

"What the hell are you talking about?"

He rubbed his cheek heavily, pulling and tugging at the pallid skin. "Collinsworth," he said. "They had to use three bodybags for him. Aldocci. Him they picked up with a suction hose. Marie. I bet there's still a little bit of Marie ground into the concrete in front of the Illinois building."

"They're dead? For sure?"

"Fucking right they're dead," he snarled. "And your slimy fingerprints are all over it. Who else would know me well enough to take them out just because I hired them?"

"Berg, you asshole, I didn't have anything to do with it."

He watched her lips. "Then what was that message all about?"

She considered. "I can't tell you. I ran across some information involving them . . . somewhere else." She shook her head suddenly. "A different job, their names came up. I thought you might be involved. So I sent you a warning. A friendly gesture, nothing more."

"You expect me to buy that vague garbage? They'd been dead three days when your love note came in. Which, by the way, happened while I was entertaining some legbreakers that were probably hired by this company."

"Berg, you want to slow down, try to make a little sense. You think you can do that? What legbreakers?"

"They blew up my condo," he said bitterly.

She stared at him. "They what? *Who* blew up your condo?"

"I don't *know*."

"Oh, Berg, Jeezus. I'm sorry. I really am. What happened?"

"Are you telling me you don't have any idea what I'm talking about?"

Her voice was rough with exasperation. "That's exactly what I'm telling you, you dumb shithead. The only thing I know a little about is those three corpses, and—"

"And what?"

"And that you've been writing killer programs for Double En."

He stared at her. "Now how in the fuck would you know a thing like that?"

"I can't tell you that, either."

He glared at the tip of his smoldering cigarette. "Is there anything," he said levelly, "that you can tell me, that might let me trust you just a little bit?"

"Sure," she said. "I still love you. A little bit."

"Oh, fuck me," he said wearily.

"Well. Not here," she replied.


They sat in a vast, empty, echoing cafeteria, two small figures hunched over coffee at a table by windows overlooking a stretch of manicured greenery.

"How long have you been working for Double En?" Berg asked.

"How long have we been here? Three days? That's how long."

"You think I believe that?" he said.

She pushed her coffee mug in a small ring on the Formica tabletop. The smell of the dark liquid was sharp in the carefully filtered air. "Berg," she said, "I really don't give a damn what you believe. And I'm not gonna keep on trying to convince you of anything. You ask, I'll answer. What you do after that is your own frigging business. As usual," she added sourly.

He inhaled slowly. "All right. I'll just pretend that you're not a vicious, murderous bitch, and we'll try to talk as if there's some kind of sense to all this."

She lifted her coffee mug. "Fine by me," she said. "One vicious murderer to another."

He looked at her oddly, but let it pass. "Okay—how long have you been working for that warped little Nipponese monster?"

"I told you, three days. His people made contact with me in the usual way: Old Freddy, the guy your bodyguard fried, dropped by the office with an offer and a chip to back it up. And by the way, he wasn't very clear, so I thought he was speaking for Bill Norton. Old Shag has been something of a surprise."

"No shit," Berg replied. "What was the offer?"

She stared out the window at a pair of techs walking across the lawn. "A lot of money to do a job."

"What kind of job?" Berg asked patiently.

"The kind I'm good at," she replied. "Smash and grab. Break into a big machine—unspecified—and destroy some data—also unspecified."

"And you took it? Just like that? What happened to your normal healthy paranoia?"

She tilted her head back and let her breath out slowly, her chest falling. "Oh, it functioned, Berg. I checked him out good. Everything seemed like it was straight. They even sent a limo."

"Smash and grab, huh? They wanted me to design

some defenses, but they weren't very specific, either. Something experimental, they said. Has anybody tried to kill you lately?"

Her eyes popped open. "Kill me? Not so you'd notice," she said.

He told her about the three strongarms who had broken into his condo, about the Little Man rocket attack, and about the wolf who'd tried to stick a knife into him.

Calley listened intently. "Somebody sure as hell doesn't like you," she said. "You turned the burglars inside out?"

He grinned tightly. "My habits haven't changed all that much. And what I got made no sense. The guy's numbers went off the chart when I mentioned Bill Norton."

"Well," she said slowly, "Bill Norton's dead. Or so we're told."

He nodded. "Uh-huh. But what if he's not? It wouldn't be the first time some corporate disagreement degenerated into blood and guts."

She tilted her empty coffee mug, set it back down. "So play it this way. Norton isn't dead, but old Shag has him crowded out somehow. Still, everybody knows Norton was the technical brains behind the company. Nakamura's nothing more than the usual variety of voracious Jap business thug. Let's say Norton is waging some kind of guerilla war that involved their meatmatrix. It's got Nakamura scared enough to take action that involves us. Norton still has his own friends, he decides to take us out. How does that play?"

"Why do you bring up the meatmatrix?" he asked.

"Just a thought. It's new, and it's big enough to provoke that kind of brushwar. You think they hire— hell, kidnap—people like us to fix the secretary's word processor?"

He pushed back his chair and stood up. "You want more coffee?"

"Sure." She watched him walk away, her eyes half-closed in thought. When he returned, she faced him squarely.

"Berg? How come you did a bunch of lethal feed-back programs for the Double En matrix?"

She noticed how thin his bony fingers were as he carefully raised his mug. His dark eyes peered over the rim at her. He sipped delicately and swallowed. "What makes you think I did?" he asked.

"I think so," she said. "Leave it at that."

"More secrets? My, we're getting trustful. Good relationship, just like the old times."

"More than you know," she told him. "Answer the question."

His eyebrows arced. "Simple," he said. "I didn't—at least I didn't know I did. They suckered me. Some dipshit subsidiary, paid good, they owned it. A little de-engineering and presto—their matrix had lethal feedback for about one-tenth what I would have charged if I'd known." One side of his mouth curved up. "Standard business ripoff."

"Oh. When was this?"

"About a year ago," he said.

"We made a good team," she said.

"What?"

"If I'd still been around, they wouldn't have ripped you. You never could design a cracker program for shit. I would have turned that little contract inside out for you."

He rubbed the tabletop slowly with the palm of his right hand. "Well, they've put the team back together. More or less."

"That they have, laddybuck. That they have."


Nakamura had a small private dining room next to his office. Berg presumed that the little corporate potentate kept an entire suite there.

They sat on either side of a polished teak table, and Nakamura lounged at the end. The remains of their meal were being cleared away by a young waiter who had served them without speaking a single word during the entire meal.

Nakamura lit a cigar. "They still remember how to

handle tobacco in Havana," he said with heavy satisfaction. He tilted one thin eyebrow in Berg's direction. "Join me?"

"Thanks, no," Berg replied. "I like my Bolivians."

The waiter returned carrying a silver tray on which he balanced three crystal snifters and a heavy, faceted decanter. He placed this at the head of the table, on Nakamura's right, bowed slightly, and went away.

Nakamura lifted the stopper and sniffed. "Ah. Janneau Grand Reserve. Do you like Armagnac, Mr. Berg?"

"I have a taste every now and then," Berg admitted.

"Excellent." Carefully, with surgical precision, Nakamura measured out three snifters and handed two of them down the table. He waited until Berg and Calley had nodded approval, tasted his own drink, and leaned back.

"Well," he said, "do you think we can work together?"

"I don't think that is the question, Mr. Nakamura," Calley said suddenly.

"Oh?"

"No, not at all. It occurs to me that our position here is tenuous, to say the least. We've had a murder committed in front of us. You've given us information about your company that would be explosively valuable to your competitors. Other killings have been done, which may or may not be linked to you. In short, there is every reason to dispose of us, and very few for you to keep your end of the bargain."

Nakamura bared his teeth slightly. "It's even worse, young lady. The process we wish you to undergo is very dangerous. You may not survive it."

"So?" Berg said. "Calley has some good points, Nakamura. Where is the motivation?"

The Japanese laced his fingers together and looked at them over the resulting tent. "One billion dollars is the motivation, Mr. Berg. Here is why. First, you haven't seen a murder committed. Mr. Nakasone—Toshi—isn't dead. Oh, we weren't able to save his hand, but the prosthetic is quite advanced. Better even than some of the implants he already had."

"Toshi's alive? I want to see him," Berg said.

"Impossible, Mr. Berg. For obvious reasons, your bodyguard is no longer at this facility. He is recovering, and undergoing stringent programming which will erase all memory of this episode. He will come out of it with a lot of money, and a perfectly reasonable explanation for it. As for the other killings, they are, as you point out, hard to attribute to any specific agency. Come now, Berg—three hired bravos? Double En can protect itself from any rumors involving them. Finally, the information to which you refer *is* explosive. That's true." He grinned widely this time. Then he folded up the grin and put it away. "But if you are successful, the situation will no longer exist. Nothing explosive there."

He took another birdlike sip of his Armagnac. "The danger is real. It involves the process itself, and your mission. You might not live through it. I tell you this honestly—so you'll understand what it is I'm paying for."

"Kidnapping, extortion, brain-burning—what a lovely picture you paint, Nakamura," Calley replied.

"Business, Calley," he said. "No, you must understand exactly what your position is. You are in no danger if you succeed. There will be little you can do to hurt me, or Double En, and less reason to try. If you fail to live through the commission, all questions are moot. But if you refuse even to try, then yes, I am afraid my options become narrow in your case." He nodded once. "Quite narrow."

Calley glanced at Berg. He raised his eyebrows.

"Right," Calley said. "When do you want a decision?"

Nakamura rocked slowly forward, then back. "No hurry," he said. "Tomorrow morning will be fine."

He came to her room that night and knocked softly at the door. "Come in," she said.

He closed the door behind him and sat on the edge of the bed. "What do you think?" he said.

She reached out and took his right hand in hers. Her fingers began to tap quickly on his palm. He was rusty, but in a few moments their old touchcode came back fluently.

"Berg," she tapped, "do you trust me?"

"Stupid question," he replied. "Of course not. It doesn't matter, though. It's gonna take both of us to get out of this alive. Unless you believe the logic of that oily-tongued motherfucker."

In the faint glow of the nightlamp, her skin was the color of gold under water. She smiled faintly. "He talks good, but I'd say the odds we end up in an industrial food processor are very high. Why waste a billion bucks?"

"So what do we do?" he tapped.

"We go along," she told him. "Way I see it, the only way we are reasonably sure of getting off this merry-go-round is to burn the matrix itself. Nakamura's got nothing to do with it."

"What about Norton?"

"If you believe the Jap, no problem. If Norton really is alive, still no problem. Destroy Double En, you get Norton as part of the package. Their own competition will take care of it for us."

They were silent, their fingers unmoving for a moment. He stared at her face. Finally his hand began to jitter on her palm again. "They've got into me too heavy," he tapped. "Toshi, the other three, my condo. Somebody's got to pay. Yeah, we'll take down their fucking chicken brain."

"That's my boy," she replied. "That's the vindictive sonofabitch I knew and loved."

"You said you still do," he tapped slowly.

"You already know you can't trust me," she said, and pulled him down.

Berg and Calley were eating breakfast in the cafeteria when Fred Oranson, still pale but minus his cast, slid into an empty chair at their table. The big room was full, and the noise level from hundreds of technicians riding a caffeine high was nearly deafening. The smell of bacon frying and coffee perking surrounded them like a fog.

"Fuck off, ratface," Berg said calmly. "I'm trying to eat, and you aren't good for my digestion."

Calley forked up a piece of ham and smiled cheerfully. "You already know what I think," she said. "And absence hasn't made the heart grow any fonder. Raped any children lately, buddy boy?"

Oranson swallowed twice, hard, before he was able to choke out the words. "Mr. Nakamura sent me," he said. "He wants to know if you have reached a decision."

"We have," Berg replied, "and we'll be happy to tell Mr. Nakamura about it. Not his idiot flunkie, however."

Oranson's face was the color of a ripe plum. "He told me to get the answer," he said finally.

Calley glanced at him. "You don't speak English, maybe, asshole? We'll talk to the great man himself, thanks. Now beat it. I have a stronger stomach than Berg, but there are limits." She turned back to her plate.

The security man sat rigid for a few more moments, then slowly stood up. Berg and Calley ignored him. He started to walk away, then turned. "Is that little shrimp any kind of a good screw, bitch?" he spat out.

They both looked at him, spellbound with astonishment, and then burst out laughing simultaneously.

"Better than you'll ever know," Calley chortled. "Way better than you'll *ever* know."

It was a good sized room, white-tiled, brightly lit, and chilly. The air had the sterile taste of massive refrigeration and filtering apparatus constantly at work.

A large mainframe filled most of one wall. Berg recognized the massive array of miniprocessors that once had been called a "thinking box," when the concept had first been advanced near the end of the twentieth century.

"Are you using that thing as some kind of inter-face?" he asked Nakamura, puzzling over its odd configuration.

"Exactly, Mr. Berg," the Japanese replied. He was immaculate in a black pinstripe suit that appeared to have been stitched to his body.

The remainder of the room was taken up by banked monitors, readouts, and printers, all surrounding four coffin-like white tanks. Heavy cables connected the four, which were the locus for a web of complicated piping. On the first tank a series of colored telltales winked off and on in intricate patterns.

Two technicians hovered by this tank. They stepped away when Nakamura led Calley and Berg up.

"I think this may help you understand what is in-volved," he said. He turned to one of the techs and snapped, "Do we have interior video monitoring?"

"Up and running," the tech replied crisply.

"Good," Nakamura said. "If you'll just watch that big screen over there," he said, pointing to the far wall.

The monitor jittered green static for a moment, then cleared suddenly into full color.

"Oh, my God," Calley breathed softly.

Berg just stared.

"Allow me to introduce my partner, Mister William Norton," Nakamura said.

## 14

CALLEY TURNED AWAY from the churning mass on the monitor.

Nakamura smiled. Berg thought the man's teeth were much too large, and whiter than they should be. Those teeth made him almost as nervous as what he saw on the screen.

Black. His first impression was of a jumbled, inky brew, something he imagined a squid might eject in terror and flight. Then he began to see the highlights: a shining, filmy sheen to the stuff, unhealthy, with hints of colors no living thing should wear.

Finally he began to discern something even more horrible. The shifting, slimy mass had a *shape*—and its form was obscenely reminiscent of a human skull. As he watched, he could dimly make out eye sockets, the shadowy outlines of a nose, the faint sketch of a jutting chin.

What appeared to be bone chips dotted the devil's pudding here and there. "What *is* it?" he asked.

"Norton's head," Nakamura replied. "It's completely carcinomic now. Nothing left you could really call a brain."

Berg looked at the screen one last time. Something soft and rancid was stuck in his throat. "That's enough," he said. "Turn it off."

Nakamura nodded and raised his hand. Mercifully, the monitor went blank. "That is what is left of my partner, at least on this earthly plane," he said. "Appetizing, isn't he?"

Calley raised her head and stared at him. "Is this some kind of joke?"

The oriental man shrugged. "Life is a joke, sometimes, Calley. But there is nothing funny about this."

"Bullshit. You go to all the trouble to get us here, and now you tell us a bunch of cancer cells is the enemy? That pile of garbage can't do anything to anybody."

"I wish," Nakamura said, "it were as simple as that."

For the first time, Berg felt himself oppressed by opulence. The Picasso behind Nakamura's desk had been replaced by another: a white bird diving—to Berg, his mind filled with hideous imagery, a killer bird stooping to prey, to eat. The small office smothered him with expensive gimcracks. He longed for a breath of fresh, unfiltered air, and a wide blue horizon.

"Why don't you just disconnect . . . him . . . from the matrix?" Calley asked.

Nakamura placed his small hands palms down on the oak desktop. Berg was conscious of the odor of sandalwood.

"Let me start at the beginning," Nakamura said. "There are questions involved that go beyond mere physical considerations, as you will see."

He looked calmly at his manicured fingernails, his eyelids lowered. To Berg, he appeared to be practicing the opening stages of meditation.

"Bill Norton," said Nakamura slowly, "is a much greater genius than anybody ever gave him credit for. I recognized it when he came to me blowing breath you could strip paint with, and showed me something absolutely startling: the beginning of his neural growth process. Because of that I put an enormous amount of money into our new company. As we grew, Bill saw that it was to his advantage to remain mysterious—the scientist owner who might or might not be a hopeless drunk. He was content to leave me in the forefront of things. Even then, paranoia was his driving force. And, in fact, he was right. At that level he became the center of the universe for many people, and a target for many others. Paranoia, in a sense, became fact. They *were* out to get him."

Berg blinked. For a moment, he saw that rotted skull again.

"Then, when they diagnosed cancer, Bill really went crazy."

Calley shifted in her chair. Her hair had jagged fingertracks through it. "Cancer? Cancer is curable."

Nakamura shook his head. "Not the tailored kind. Not the kind you get when somebody accidently scratches the back of your hand at a dinner party, and two months later your brain starts to dissolve."

Berg felt the hair on the back of his neck start to stand up. "Somebody did it to him, you're trying to say? Somebody infected him with that shit? The fucker wasn't paranoid, he was absolutely realistic."

Nakamura smiled enigmatically, and seeing those large, white teeth again, Berg suddenly knew who had arranged for that dinner-party scratch.

He sighed. "Big business must be wonderful," he said.

Nakamura moved his hands slightly. "Don't horse-shit me, Berg. I don't think you will qualify for saint-hood any time soon."

"Yeah," Berg said. "So Norton came down suddenly with this bad case of cancer?"

"Uh-huh. His medics gave him a about a year. It was too long."

Calley got up from her chair. Her white overalls looked limp and wrinkled. "You got anything to drink around here? I bet you do," she said.

Nakamura nodded. Berg didn't see him move or touch anything, but suddenly the young waiter was in the room. Probably a few guards with narrow-band lasers watching, too, he thought.

Calley smiled at the young man. Don't bother, Berg thought tiredly. You're not his type.

"Stoly on the rocks," she told him. He bowed slightly and turned to the bar hidden behind the books.

"Anybody else?" Nakamura asked.

"Glen Grants," Berg said.

Nakamura glanced at the waiter. "I'm glad we share a taste for the single malts, Berg," he said. "I keep twenty-seven of them in stock."

"That's nice to know," Berg told him.

"One for me, too," Nakamura told the boy.

After the waiter had served the drinks and left, Calley said, "What do you mean by 'too long'?"

"It gave him enough time to figure out a new setup and save his life," Nakamura said. He raised his glass to his lips and sipped. Berg listened to the soft, sharp clink of ice against crystal.

"What we saw in the other room," Berg said.

"Yes. Exactly. I told you he was a genius, paranoid jerkoff and all. He came up with a way. I'm not a scientist, but it involved a method of holographic encryption utilizing memory 'models,' which allowed him to transfer himself into a suitable holding environment. . . . We'd been developing the matrices for some time. He decided they could be modified to accept a human personality, and he was right. He could lay up there until we learned how to cure his body."

"Which," Berg said slowly, "you haven't been able to do."

"Oddly enough, no," Nakamura said. His smile flicked out again, and Berg repressed a shudder. To be condemned to choose between life in a chicken brain and life in—*that*. . . .

Nakamura saw the look on his face. The Oriental's dark eyes hardened. "Don't presume to judge me, Berg. We play a different game, with far more stringent rules, than you've ever dreamed of. My partner understood that, even if you don't—as you will see."

"Don't mind me, Nakamura. My stomach is a remarkably adaptable creature," Berg said.

"Pour more scotch on it," Calley suggested.

Berg gulped the smoky liquid, shivered, and felt it warm him a bit. "So, it still seems simple to me. Just turn off that godawful tank and let him die."

Nakamura shook his head. "Fine, except we are no longer sure that's what would happen."

"I don't understand," Berg said.

"Norton's personality may have nothing to do with his body anymore," Nakamura replied. He paused, lifted the lid of the onyx humidor on his desk, and extracted a long, thick cigar. For a moment he busied himself with cutting, trimming, and lighting the thing. He inhaled, then slowly exhaled a thin stream of white smoke.

"Comment?" he asked.

"It's crazy," Berg said. "You kill the body, you kill everything. Personality, memory, all of it."

"Prove it," Nakamura said simply.

"Well—" Berg stopped.

"Yes," Nakamura agreed. "A whole lot of religions will inform you that you're dead wrong—but that doesn't bother me. What does bother me is that we don't know. We don't even know for sure if the brain has anything to do with personality—call it consciousness, soul, whatever—or if it is just some kind of meat machine which another force manipulates."

"Pretty fucking mystic, Nakamura," Calley said.

Nakamura sighted down the cigar at her. "Too mystic for me, Calley," he replied. "But Norton has added another chip to the game. He says he has rigged a gimmick to wipe the matrix—which just happens to contain our entire data base—if his body is attacked in any way. The matrix constantly monitors the tanks, of course. And his reaction time is far faster than ours. My people tell me he can do it."

Berg glanced at Calley. She nodded. "You *are* in a bind, aren't you?"

"Couldn't happen to a nicer guy," Berg said.

Nakamura glared at him. "I don't give a fuck whether I make your Christmas list or not," he said. "All I

want is for you to do what seems necessary, and I
don't think you have a hell of a lot of choice."

"And what exactly is necessary?" Berg asked.

"You and that woman over there go into the matrix
after my partner," Nakamura said, "and when you get
in there, you kill him." He stopped. "*Then* I turn off
that ghastly tub of shit."

Nakamura had not invited them to dinner. They sat
in their usual spot in the cafeteria, making the best of
what the machines offered that time of night. Outside,
flickering insects danced low above the shadowed lawn,
and in the distance, slightly haloed by the night mists,
street lamps glowed.

"We go into those tanks," Calley said.

"Looks like," Berg agreed.

She shivered slightly. "I don't think there are any
good guys involved in this."

"When are there, ever?"

"Oh, sometimes, Berg. Sometimes you don't need a
scorecard to tell the difference."

"I think Nakamura has what you'd call a warped
sense of humor."

She stirred her plastic bowl of something that had
been labeled Chicken à la King. "What do you think
it'd be like?"

"What's that?"

"Being out of your body. Being in a hunk of chicken
brain. . . ."

Berg shifted uneasily on the hard surface of his
chair. "I don't know. What Nakamura showed us. All
those tapes of Norton's messages. He seems okay."

"Electronic impulses, Berg. That's all, pixels lighting up on a screen."

"So? What's the difference? Your eyes don't see.
Your brain does. And hears and smells and tastes and
touches. It's all electronic impulses, kiddo."

"It scares me, Berg."

He looked at her suddenly, blinking. "Scares you,
Calley? I didn't think anything scared you."

"Which shows how much you fucking know. Quit trying to fit me into your nasty little defensive paradigm, Berg. It ruined us once, and it can screw this up, too."

"What? Are we back together or something? One fast clitoral rub doesn't a marriage make, Calley."

"God, you're nasty," she said. "I didn't mean that. But Nakamura has us slotted as a team. You know the word? We used to be one, and it looks like we're gonna have to do it again if we want to come out of this alive."

"You think that's in the cards? Survival?"

"The show ain't over, Berg, till the fat lady sings. You taught me that."

He grinned slowly. "Yeah, I did, didn't I?"

"So what about all our big plans? Destroy the matrix, all that?"

"It looks like what he wants us to do."

"No, he just wants Norton," Calley said. "Not the matrix itself—that's his family jewels."

"Uh-huh," Berg said. "One thing he missed, though."

"What's that?"

"If he's right about Norton, then the same applies. Once we're inside, he doesn't dare do anything to us. If he fucks with our bodies, maybe we end up stuck in his data base, too. And there's nothing he can do about it. I don't think he can take the chance."

She considered, chewing carefully on a mushy chunk of preformed chicken analog. "You think he missed all that?"

Berg stared out the window. "No," he said at last. "But I don't think he considered all the ramifications."


Nakamura ate alone in his small dining room. Several elaborate lacquered boxes of sushi were placed at his end of the table. The waiter hovered near, clearing the empty containers and keeping Nakamura's glass topped off with a Haut-Brion '19.

A musical tone chimed in the silence. The waiter

looked at his boss. "Let him in," Nakamura said. "I'm almost finished."

The waiter moved lithely to the door and opened it. Nakamura watched him, an enigmatic expression on his face.

Frederick Oranson entered the room. "Yes, sir," he said. His face was still tanned, but an obvious pallor underlay it. New wrinkles fanned from the edge of his eyes, and the set of his broad shoulders held an element of—? Fear, Nakamura decided.

"Come in, Fred. Have a seat." He motioned to the chair at the far end of the dining table. "Some wine?"

"No, thank you," Oranson replied.

Nakamura nodded. "Have you anything to report?"

Oranson's features twitched unhappily. "Yes," he said.

A moment. "Well?" Nakamura said. "Who has been trying to kill our obnoxious little guest?"

"We have, sir," Oranson replied softly.

"Really?" Nakamura carefully placed his carved ivory chopsticks on the top of a bowl and stared at the security man. "What are you talking about?"

Oranson sighed. "In every instance—the thugs who tried to strongarm him, the rocket attack on his condo, the assassination attempt in the sewers—I've traced the initiator back to Double En. For instance, Berg's uninvited guests: hired by an advertising agency which is subbed to one of our branch companies in California. The wolf with the knife: bought by a crooked cop who is in the bag to one of our political reps. And the rocket attack: terrorists from a British camp we've supported for years."

Nakamura examined his raw fish. "That doesn't seem possible," he said.

"Oh, it's possible, all right. As is usual in such cases, all documentation was destroyed, but each order came, with the proper authorizing codes, from Bill Norton. In one case he commissioned the account in person—well, face to face, by monitor."

Nakamura felt a cloud of darkness rising behind his

eyes, threatening to engulf him. With control he didn't know he possessed, he fought it down. "You understand what this means?" he said.

"Yes, sir, I'm afraid I do. Somehow Norton has gotten wind of our plans, and is taking action on his own. He's operating through the entire Double En data base, probably."

Nakamura shook his head up and down sharply. "Exactly. And that means the miserable fuckhead has all the power of the company behind him. As much as I do myself."

Oranson licked his lips. "Yes," he said. He was fascinated by the visible effort Nakamura was expending to maintain his composure.

Nakamura glanced at Oranson. "Is there any evidence he has taken other action?"

The unspoken question hung naked in the air between them.

Oranson shook his head. "Hit teams headed for you, sir? No. No evidence whatsoever. But then, there wouldn't be, would there?"

Nakamura's face didn't change at all. "No, there wouldn't," he said finally. "Okay. Keep on it."

Oranson nodded and rose from the table. "Of course," he said. But as he left the room, he was careful to disguise any physical manifestation of the new idea that had suddenly bloomed inside his skull.


Nakamura finished his meal in silence, staring blankly into the middle distance as his waiter carefully cleared the last of the dishes.

"Some of the Louis XIIIth, please," Nakamura said. He lifted the snifter from the silver tray and tasted. "Fine," he said. He got up and walked slowly to the door which opened into his office.

At his desk he thumbed the hidden latch which rolled back the oak desktop to reveal the remote data system hidden beneath. He tapped several codes onto the touchpad, waited a moment, then began to enter his message.

The screen lit up. A thick, brutal face topped by a short brush of white hair appeared. The man seemed surprised at receiving a message from Nakamura personally.

"Yes, sir?" he said. His voice was extremely thick, almost garbled. Nakamura noticed the heavy, livid scar running from the man's right ear, down one side of his throat, and on into his shirt collar.

"Frederick Oranson. Security Director, Double En," Nakamura said.

The man nodded. "I'll get right on it. I can handle it myself."

"Good," Nakamura said. "But don't initiate. Not yet. I'll tell you when."

"Yes, sir," the man replied.

Nakamura switched off his machines and waited until the polished desktop was back smoothly in place. He turned, the crystal balloon in his hand, and stared at the plunging white bird frozen on his wall. He raised his glass.

"Good hunting, you sonofabitch," he said.

## 15

A WIND BLOWING down from Minnesota muffled their words, tugged at the standard-issue jackets they wore as they idled around the stretch of lawn dotted with corporate Henry Moore-cloned statuary. They paused before a particularly awful example of heroically curved bronze.

"I wonder why it always looks like it's swallowing itself?" Calley said.

Berg shrugged. "Fecal obsession," he replied. "That's why the business types love it."

She laughed. "Berg, only you would make a connection between conglomerate art and eating shit."

He pointed. "Come on," he said. "Tell me it isn't inescapable."

She laughed again and this time he joined her. He moved to the concrete base of the statue and carefully brushed off a spot. "You think this thing is wired?" he asked.

She examined it more carefully, then shook her head. "Hollow, and probably vibrates like a tuning fork. Feel the wind. I think it's okay."

He sat down on the base, sheltered by a massively arced overhang of metal. "Come on," he said, holding out his hands.

She joined him. "I feel like I'm being crushed by some kind of industrial womb," she said.

"Womb to grow?" he asked.

She punched his shoulder. Hard.

"Ouch!"

"More where that came from, buddy." She settled back against the statue, her shoulder digging into his side. "Mm. Comfy. Out of the breeze, at least."

They were silent for a moment, savoring the illusion of freedom. Overhead, a few clouds, like vast heads of cauliflower, drifted ponderously across the sky. The air smelled of grass, of fresh moisture, and just a tang of onrushing autumn.

"Snow coming soon," she remarked.

"Do we care?" he asked.

She turned away, watching distant figures move slowly down the network of roads and walkways which surrounded their sculpted nook. At the edge of the park, the banked windows of the cafeteria watched them blankly.

She snuggled a little closer to his thin, wiry body. "Serious time, is it?" she said.

He nodded. "Time," he said. "What we don't have a lot of, I'm afraid."

"Another week," she said.

"Uh-huh. How you coming on your routines?"

Her reply was interrupted by the high, thin scream of one of the lunar shuttles slicing across the Illinois sky toward touchdown on the new Midway field. She watched the shining needle pierce one knobby cumulus, her eyes tracking its downward slope.

Finally, she said, "I'm doing okay. It's mostly simple virus stuff, you know. I'm modifying it to handle the peculiar storage configurations of wetware. The seeker instructions are the hard part—I've got one of Nakamura's mainframes busy synthesizing piped series of them. Brute labor. But if we're gonna just clear Norton out of the system and not take the whole thing down, we gotta be selective."

He took her left hand in his right. "Save it for the directional mikes," he tapped. "You think we're being watched?"

"Lip readers, more likely," she said.

"So you're gonna use a virus approach? I've got

some ideas along that line—like a shadow program that'll make it look like standard input . . . until some keys go off. We can do it in stages—first Norton, then the rest. After we've collected—"

"Their people are gonna vet our programs pretty good," she tapped.

"Sure. Which is why not all of it's going in with us. I've got an idea. ... ."

Later, they held hands as they walked across the sod toward one of the concrete paths. "This isn't too bad, is it, Berg?" she said.

His pale face wrinkled in smile lines. "No. This part never was."

She didn't look at him. "Always something, though, right?"

He didn't reply. They walked on.


The problem was the bands. Berg lay on his bed, the nightlight set as low as it would go, and stared at the ceiling. The only other illumination in the cramped cubicle was the faint luminescence from his monitor screen, hanging like a green ghost over his touchpad.

He lifted his right arm and stared at the thin plastic strap with its ceram-sheathed monomole core which encircled his skinny wrist. Right in the middle, like an antique wristwatch, was the flat lump of the locator biomonitor. It sent a steady stream of information to a mainframe somewhere, reporting on his location, and the presence of certain enzymes in his bloodstream. Monitoring those enzymes was supposed to reveal if his emotional state was unstable—as it supposedly would be if he were trying to escape. The computer would compare location with enzyme count, and if the correlation triggered any danger pattern in its files, it would call for human help.

There was no way to remove the wristband that he could think of. Even if he could, the interruption in the biomonitoring process would in itself be a danger signal.

And all he needed was a few moments with that mainframe interface in the tank room.

He dropped his hand and stared into the gloom. It would come. He was the Iceberg, after all—and some-day these fuckers would understand what that meant. . . .

Calley sat at her own touchpad and monitor, checking the complicated series of serial commands which would initiate the spread of the virus sections which were the heart of her own killer program. She was dimly conscious of the vast complex, now lethargic in the grip of early morning, which slumbered around her.

"Assholes," she muttered to nobody in particular, as she watched the stream of symbols scroll quickly down the screen.

In a horrible way, it felt good to work with Berg again. She knew she had her own weaknesses—the irrepressible urge to attack, and attack again, battering down whatever stood in her way, was only one of them. He smoothed out that urge, pointed out where she'd left herself vulnerable, where her attack could fail through lack of simple caution. Though, she considered, it worked the other way, too. Berg's programs sometimes had a disconcerting tendency to just sit there passively, waiting for an attack, and totally open to any unanticipated thrust. It was how she'd cracked his first lethal feedback routines: simple shifts into levels of entry he'd not prepared for.

Suddenly she turned away from the screen. The routines were right—she'd been over them a dozen times. She leaned back in her chair, feeling tense vertebrae pop, and closed her eyes.

Did she want him back?

It was a question that had dogged her ever since she'd seen his angry face in the small infirmary, felt the anger and hurt and betrayal which animated his dark eyes. Their relationship operated much like their programming skills. She was the emotional ravager,

the penetrator—for a moment a series of particularly
nasty Freudian cliches drifted into her consciousness—
and he the stolid, impenetrable emotional bulwark,
ever protecting something unknown, perhaps unknow-
able, at the very core of his being.

But did she want him back? Or was it just an urge
to avenge the only real defeat she'd ever known?

The flickering screen held no answers. She sighed
and slapped at the touchpad. The screen flashed, then
went dark except for the single pulsing note of the
cursor.

It would be a long night.


Shag Nakamura lay sleepless on silk sheets, feeling
the gentle support of the warm jellybed beneath his
muscular spine. The waiter, Kenneth, had gone, but
the strong, erotic smell of his sweating body remained.
Suddenly Nakamura was sick of it all. Nothing helped.

If he'd only known what Norton *really* had in mind
when he'd first outlined the meatmatrix development
process. If only he'd understood the absolutely fero-
cious survival drive which truly animated the man. He
had no children, and would not have, for his particular
brand of sterility had resisted every effort of even the
greatest of the hospitals—and so Norton had succumbed
to the siren lure of immortality. As many before him
had done, but none of those had possessed both the
raw genius and the unsurpassed resources of a company like Double En to implement their intuitive leaps.

In retrospect, Nakamura saw it all. Now he understood why Norton had insisted on transferring their
entire database to the matrix. Yes, it was faster. Yes,
it was more efficient. Yes, it gave them a business
advantage that was, within the limits of obsolescence,
insurmountable.

And yes, Bill Norton now held a knife to the heart
of the empire.

Nakamura wished he could leave this place, these
small rooms, and return to the clean space of his
office, or to the ordered existence which permeated

the great country house almost nobody ever saw. But events demanded his presence. More was at stake here than the problem of William Norton and his paranoid presence.

Others were now involved. After the first crashes, small, exploratory feelers had been extended from Double En's competitors. Arthur Kraus, the blunt, stocky head of Salingen, Krupp, was already sniffing around. If the rest of the great magnates discovered what Norton had done, they would unite to destroy Double En for the sole purpose of eradicating the meatmatrix and its poisonous contents. Could Norton invade their own databases? Nakamura didn't know— but in Arthur Kraus's position, he would take no chances either.

It was up to him. Centuries of *giri*, the iron notion of duty bred into every Japanese of his class, demanded that he atone for the errors which had caused this intolerable situation.

Which he would do. If he could just keep everything under control for a little while longer.

He made a short, gutteral hissing noise, rolled over, and tried once again to sleep.

Berg gave up. It was early in the morning. His exhaustion-fogged brain just didn't seem to function any more. He kept cycling through the problem, but couldn't find a solution. He couldn't get to the computer because of the wristband, and he couldn't remove the wristband without alerting the computer.

Maybe sleep. . . . He rubbed his eyes hard. No. One last thing to try. Two heads—and the best head he'd ever known was just down the hall. He stood up, let the momentary dizziness pass, and shambled out into the light.

"Mm . . . what?" Then she was awake. "Berg? What do you want?"

"Wake up," he whispered. "Want to talk."

"Oh." She came all the way up now. "What is it?"

"Got a problem, babe," he said. "Thought maybe you could help."

She reached out and took his hand. "Our rooms have more bugs than an ant colony. What's bothering you?" she tapped.

He told her as quickly as he could.

"I see," she muttered aloud. She lapsed into silence. Berg fancied he could almost hear her finely honed instincts savaging at his dilemma. Finally she nodded minutely and took his hand back.

"Simple," she said. "We gimmick the security computer. I bet I can do it from here."

He dropped her fingers and stared at her. "I knew there was a reason I loved you," he said.

"You what? What did you say?"

He stopped, his fingers frozen against her palm.

"Fuck it," she whispered. "Come here. . . ."

"I wonder if anybody will notice where you slept last night," Calley said.

"Probably," Berg replied. "That asshole Oranson seemed to have a pretty good grip on it, the time before."

"Someday I may have to do something about him," she mused.

"You'll have to stand in line," he told her. "Someday. . . ."

"Yeah, there is that," she replied. "Well, what do you think?"

She scrolled the new program she'd been working on all morning. He watched the ranks of instructions, checking them against some notes of his own.

"Okay," he said. "It should work."

She nodded. "Well, do I run it or not?"

"What the hell," he said. "Go for it, kid."

She keyed in the entry routine. They sat back and waited, watching the screen.

"God damn, you did it!" he said.

"Gutted like a Christmas goose," she agreed, a note

of satisfaction in her rough voice. "From now on, any deviation from normal routines will be marked by the computer as an unexplained glitch in its subprogramming. It'll spend its time gazing at its own navel."

He hugged her suddenly. "I wouldn't have thought of it," he said.

She wiggled against his wiry arms. "I know," she told him.

"Bitch."

"That, too," she replied. "Anything else?"

He released her slowly. "Naw. I can take it from here."

She stared at him. "Okay, Berg. Ride 'em, cowboy."

He nodded, his face suddenly somber. "Yeah," he said. "Ride 'em." He left her room.

She stared at the door, her eyes narrow. Then she turned back to her touchpad and slowly began to punch.

"I gotta go to the john."

Berg peered around the doorjamb, crouched low to the floor so the movement wouldn't be noticeable at eye level. The two tank-room techs were on the far side, one horizontal on a cot, the other standing over him.

"Mm?"

"Wake up, asshole. I gotta leave for a while."

The reclining tech cocked open one eye. "So, leave," he said.

"Don't go back to sleep," the first tech warned. He was holding a small hand reader, and a compact minidisk.

"Yeah, sure." The second tech propped himself up on one elbow. "Go ahead, I'll keep an eye open, your highness. You still reading that goddamn space epic?"

"It's good literature," the other replied.

"Right." The tech whose nap had been interrupted watched the other leave the room. He snorted. "Jerkoff," he said. He rolled back on his stomach. Berg waited tensely. Within a couple of minutes, soft snoring filled the room.

Berg whispered a small prayer of thanks for the liberal policies of Double En's infirmary, and the sedatives they'd supplied him to help him sleep. Three of them in the sleeping tech's evening coffee in the cafeteria were having the desired effect. The other tech had not been there, and Berg had been waiting for something to take him out of the room for almost an hour.

He knew it was shaky—but then, all of it was.

After a few more moments, he sighed, stood up and walked into the room. The remotes servicing the interface mainframe were equidistant from his door and the cot where the technician lay sleeping soundly.

Quickly, Berg brought a remote on line and began to slot chips. He worked quickly, one eye cocked on the door to the john.

It only took a few moments. Finally, sweat dripping in his eyes despite the chill refrigeration of the room, he stood up and fumbled in his coveralls. The small package was there. Quickly he unwrapped it to reveal a single microchip.

"If you say so, Lady," he muttered, his lips barely moving, and slotted the final bit of input. The screen lit up suddenly, flashing red, black, and red again. Large letters streamed across the screen: UNAUTHORIZED INPUT—UNAUTHORIZED INPUT—INSERT REQUIRED CODES—

Berg froze. There was no sudden alarm, but he could imagine warnings being flashed in every monitoring machine in the complex. Quickly he reached for the touchpad, trying to think of an abort command that might work, when the screen suddenly cleared.

A new message flashed, this time in cool blue: INPUT ACCEPTED.

Berg started to breathe again. Hurriedly, he retrieved the chip given him by the Lady and slipped it into a pocket. He could hear dim footsteps beyond the far door, and the sound of someone humming quietly.

He glanced one last time at the screen before shutting down the remote, and suddenly broke into a wide grin.

One more message flashed briefly. THINK NOTHING OF IT, BREAKER.

He was still grinning when he reached his own room. He paused, then went on down the hall. He knocked quietly at her door, then pushed it open.

"Okay?" she said.

"Very okay," he replied. "I got the whole program in and covered. At least when we go into the wild black yonder, we'll have a few surprises up our sleeves. Uh, you saved my ass back there. . . ."

She grinned. "Somebody had to."

He moved close and touched her cheek. "Maybe I do need you around."

She put both hands on his shoulders and pulled him down. "For more than that, buddy," she said. "For more than that."

## 16

BERG STILL COULDN'T shake the chilling idea that the tank resembled nothing so much as a hi-tech coffin.

One of the technicians was pointing to the complicated gear occupying the space where his head would rest. "That band right there holds your head steady," he said.

"Am I supposed to move around a lot?" Berg asked hollowly.

The tech grinned. He was a tall, round-faced man. Berg remembered that he had been asleep most of the last time he'd seen him. "No, you should be still as a corpse—well, that's not a good analogy."

"Damn right," Berg muttered.

"It's for the insertion process, actually. We use fifteen hairline lasers to drill the holes—then we insert the needles which feed the coated molecular chains directly into your brain."

Berg nodded. "Is there any pain involved?"

"Not really. You'll feel a faint pricking sensation, more of an itch, actually." The tech's meaty lips curled up at the corners. "Of course, you won't be able to scratch. . . ."

There was a jaundiced cast to Calley's gamin features. "Why can't we just use our plugs?"

"Plugs? Oh, you mean your opti-fiber cable jacks? Different thing entirely. Those just let you interface with a computer—communications really. You aren't *there*, if you understand my meaning. The molecular chains bond with RNA molecules in such a way as to mirror-image the holographic memory function. They 'take a holo,' if you will."

Berg nodded. "So there really isn't a transfer. You move a duplicate. My own mind remains untouched, there in the tank."

The tech looked uncomfortable. "Well, it's not as simple as all that, but yes, that's the general idea."

Berg shuddered. Buried alive. . . . "We don't remain conscious in the tank, do we?"

The tech shook his head. "No. We put you way down. Of course, brain function does continue, and we monitor it. I suspect it's rather like going to sleep."

"You don't know?" Calley broke in.

Nakamura glanced at her. "No," he said, "we don't. Only one person has undergone the process, and he didn't make any reports."

Calley looked aghast. "You mean Norton?"

"I'm afraid so," Nakamura admitted.

"Not that his report would make any difference," Berg said. "The part of him in the matrix would have no knowledge about what had happened to his original 'self,' would it? I mean, he is now two separate individuals, right?"

Nakamura looked at the tank which held Norton's body. "If you want to call that an individual. . . ."

Berg looked at Norton's tank, then looked away. "Bottom line," he said. "Is there any connection between the tank and the matrix personality?"

"We don't know," the tech admitted. "At first we operated as if there was—we still do, for that matter. The RNA duplication process is continuous—we feed data from the tank to the matrix on an ongoing basis. But our situation here—well, there's no support structure left in Norton's brain for the nucleic acid formations. Really, no detectable brain function at all. So we just don't know."

The chilly room seemed unbearably warm to Berg, and yet he shivered. "It's nice you have such an un-

derstanding of the process we're going to risk our lives
on."

Nakamura smiled grimly. "A billion dollars worth
of risk," he said. "Now you know why."

"Right," Berg said.

If it was a coffin, Berg considered, at least it was a
comfortable one. He lay on the molded jelly support
bags, feeling the warmth of the stuff seep into his
bones. The band around his forehead was barely felt—
and the short episode of the needle insertion remained
only as a faint memory.

"Watch it, motherfucker!" Calley snarled from the
next tank, and Berg grinned faintly.

He wondered how Toshi was doing. Nakamura had
every reason to lie to him about that. Toshi could
easily be dead. But somehow he didn't think so. Toshi
had always seemed to him as close to unkillable as
possible. But then, he'd always had a strong sense of
his own immortality, and look where he was now.

Nakamura's craggy features swam into his view. The
Oriental man smiled down at him. Berg blinked.

"Not long," Nakamura said. "They are inserting
your programming into the interface computer now."
He paused. "I'm risking a lot on this, Berg. All of my
company, for one thing. You think it will work?"

This sudden uncertainty on the part of the man who
had up to now shown only absolute faith in his own
machinations shook Berg, but then he realized what
was bothering him.

Nakamura was now forced to depend on someone
else to get the job done. He'd done everything he
could to ensure loyalty and good performance, but in
his own mind, nothing could substitute for his own
skill. Yet he had to trust everything to Berg and Calley.
It must be grinding him up inside, Berg thought slowly.

"Nakamura," he said.

"Yes?"

"How come you aren't going?"

The little man's black eyes clouded over. "If I could,

I would. Believe it. But I don't have the skill. . . ."
Nakamura shook his head. "Only you and Calley can
run those programs. You designed them. Just. . . ."

"What?" Berg asked.

"Just don't let me down. There's more riding on this
than you know."

The statement set alarm bells clanging in the recesses of Berg's mind, but already the sedatives were
taking hold, and gradually the foreboding receded to a
dim, nagging tingle.

"Don't worry," Berg heard himself say, mildly astonished at how distanced he felt from his own words.
"I plan to come out of this okay," he said.

"Not the same thing," Nakamura told him. "But
better than nothing, I guess." He smiled one more
time, and then his face moved out of Berg's foggy
vision.

The cover of the tank came down, and with it,
darkness. Berg was barely awake now, but the audio
inputs were still hooked up, and he could hear the
countdown. A babble of words—somewhere in the
distance a buzzer sounded—more words—and just before he went down, somebody barked, "Insertion!"

And there was.

Light.

It was fast, no more than a few seconds. He *felt* the
invisible forces shearing in, wild planes bent at impossible angles, as light exploded in great gouts around
him, and something—conscious—malignant—*quick*—

Reached in over the glittering universe and touched
Calley.

Was gone.

It was all there, every bit of it, just as it should be.
Berg ignored the faint tick of uneasiness—something
*wrong*—and walked to the windows. "Open, says me,"
he said, and the thick, hand-woven wool drapes slid
smoothly back.

He clasped his hands behind his back and looked out over the city. Further down the lakeshore the Illinois Building thrust its jeweled spire into the night, a quick-frozen steel firebomb. Something about the building made his uneasy feeling worse—something forgotten.

It soured his usual pleasure in the view. He turned away from the glass wall, ran his tongue over his teeth nervously, and decided on coffee. It took a moment of rummaging in the kitchen before he located a half-pound cannister of Jamaican Blue Mountain, ground the beans, and set them to perking. The rich odor soothed his jagged nervousness, and by the time he took his first sip, the aura of wrongness about his condo had almost completely disappeared.

He carried his hand-painted Kirowara cup back to his desk and sat down, relishing the feel of the rich leather against his back and shoulders. He put his feet up and leaned back in the chair. He closed his eyes. . . .

The insistent chime of Berg's hotwatch alarm woke him. He sat up with a start, knocking his empty cup to the floor.

"God damn it," he muttered. The cup was part of a set, and there was only one set in the world. Kirowara had made it for him herself, by way of a thank you for past—and future—favors. Carefully he retrieved the delicate porcelain thing and set it on the desktop.

The alarm continued its monotonous chime. He reached over and switched off the sound, but something made him hesitate about punching up the insistent message.

He knew he wasn't involved in anything truly urgent, but the message was coming in on a very private line. That limited the number of potential callers considerably, since the line was routed through at least a dozen cutouts, including one very nasty switchboard located in the most corrosive part of the Denver Deep.

Toshi, maybe, or Glory. Which reminded him: he hadn't seen either one lately, and though he was careful to keep them apart, it was a rare day that one or the other wasn't in touch. . . .

Slowly he tapped in the release codes and keyed up the message. As he read the scrolling words, his pale features wrinkled in a puzzled frown.

The message was very simple, and utterly meaningless. DO NOT THINK ABOUT THE TANK, it read, and then repeated itself in an endless stream.

DO NOT THINK ABOUT THE TANK.

What the fuck?

But as the hypnotic flow of words continued to scroll, he found himself thinking about—of course— tanks. Armored military vehicles? Containers for pressurized liquids, gases? Something full of colorful fish? Something like a big, white coffin?

Coffin?

Suddenly he was overwhelmed by the strongest feeling of deja vu he had ever experienced. The emotion, the sure and certain knowledge that he had been here before, was so powerful that he found himself staring wildly around the room in near panic. Without thinking, he reached out and shut down the message line. After a moment, he forced himself to look at the screen.

Blank.

He shivered. Finally he got up and poured another cup of coffee. This time he laced it, half and half, with three ounces of XO cognac. A waste of good liquor— but something had walked across his grave.

When he woke the next morning, his head felt like a char-broiled marshmallow. He sensed the itchy patch on his neck that signaled a derm. Foggily, he wondered what he had mixed the night before. As he rolled over on the bed, he collided with a hard, round object.

Cognac bottle. Empty.

He peered at the label. Good stuff. The hangover shouldn't be a three-alarm mugging like this. Gingerly

he peeled the derm from his neck and held it up.
Endorphin analog.

The combination shouldn't have reduced him to utter ruin. But it had. And again he had the feeling that
something was very wrong in his carefully orchestrated
world.

Then he heard the soft clink of glass on glass coming
from his living room.

That somebody could enter his condo without his
knowledge was nearly impossible. That somebody had,
and that he was still alive, meant only one thing.

He yelled as loudly as he could, "Hey, Toshi, I like
my eggs poached."

The mellow, somber-voice reply came instantly.
"Yeah, massa, and cream in your coffee. I do walls
and windows, too."

Berg nodded once, then put his head over the side
of the bed and puked.


He caught a broken glimpse of his face in a shattered windshield. Pale, thin; he looked as if he belonged. His footsteps echoed sharply, like somebody
pounding steel spikes with a hammer. The locals had
strung surplus glowbulbs along the underside of the
roadway in this section, marking off a meeting ground.
They seemed to cast more shadow than light.

It was very cold.

Suddenly they were in front of him. He stopped.
They approached him with the wariness of animals,
sniffing.

She stayed well back, and let her two wolves check
him out. Sharp canines protruding from lumpy jaws,
and big clots of muscle implant in places the human
body was not designed to have muscle.

Her tattered lace moved like a windblown curtain.
Face turned in sunflower tropism. . . .

Saucers of blood, drowning—

"Berg," she said. "You need something done?"

He nodded.

Her wide mouth opened slowly, and there were

shiny points glittering there. She reached out and handed him the message.

DO NOT THINK ABOUT THE TANK.

His scream echoed down the shattered streets.

Panting softly, the wolves loped after.


He moved and the glass bounced off the wall behind him, showering him with very good scotch.

"You know what, Jack? You're an asshole."

"You knew that when you married me," he said.

"Not really, pal. Nobody likes to think the worst of the man they love."

She paused, her hands twitching slightly. He knew the signs. She was looking for something else to throw.

"Throw the frigging bottle," he told her. "I don't give a damn."

She threw the bottle.

Silence.

"I love you," she said.

"Sure you do," he told her.

She began to laugh. . . .


Toshi came across the room, his hand extended, and Berg reached for it, but the fingers exploded, one by one, and Toshi began to wave the bloody stump—


"Yeah?" Berg said.

He cleared his throat. "Mr. Jack Berg?" he asked.

"Maybe? Who are you?" Berg's monitor screen remained empty, but all his other telltales showed somebody on the ground floor, at the elevators.

"May I come up? I have a message for you. I can't talk in public."

"I'll bet," Berg snorted. "Who are you? General Electric Motors? RanData?"

"Please. Can I come in?"

The pickups said he was okay, so Berg decided to check further. "Sure. First elevator on the right." Then he punched the buzzer.

Berg let him stand in front of the door for a final minute.

"I think you're all right," he told him. "About the only thing I can't check for is some kind of bug you're immune to and I'm not. So understand. If I start to get sick, you won't leave this place breathing. Does that seem clear enough?"

"Perfectly clear, Mr. Berg."

Berg nodded. "Okay. Come in."

Berg had never seen him before in his life. The man was huge. His shoulders hulked as wide as the door which framed him. He paused for a moment, scanning the room with eyes the color of tarnished silver. His thick hair was streaked with the same color, and fell to his shoulders in heavy waves.

The visitor grinned suddenly and stepped across the threshold. "Not bad," he said approvingly. He moved closer to the desk. "Nice view," he said.

"Who are you?" Berg asked.

"Doesn't matter," the man said. His deep voice was a snarl of echoes. It seemed to fight its way from his barrel chest. He took one more step and halted, fists like stone-filled buckets planted on his massive hips.

"Listen, asshole," the man said. "Why don't you answer your fucking phone? I've been trying to call you for days."

## 17

THE GLAZED GLITTER of the metamatrix flicked on with the clarity of a heart attack, and then she saw the wall. Dizzily, she tried to orient herself. She saw the meatmatrix glowing just below—and from even higher, from the dark, empty places, the wall came down like a wash of black diamonds.

Huge.

It slashed down in a twisting, shimmering fall, and the matrix disappeared. Everything went, and the universe became a cloud of perfect hexagonal crystals, surrounding her.

"Hang on, babe," a familiar voice whispered.

She *twisted*—

Was gone.

Darkness.

"Hey, Calley, are you okay?"

"What?"

"You *okay?*"

"Uh—" Pause. "I dunno. Guess so. Who are you?"

"Ozzie."

"*Ozzie?*"

"Yeah. Hold tight, this'll take a sec—"

—*click*—

Light. She hung in the center of a glowing blue globe. Tiny red and blue lozenges chased themselves in endless shifting patterns across the surface of the interior. She laughed suddenly.

"Hey, what's going on? I feel like I'm on the inside of an eyeball."

"Yeah? From here it looks more like a plate of neon spaghetti."

"That's nice. Are you really Ozzie?"

"Sure I am."

"Prove it."

"If I put my finger one inch below your left nipple, your tit twitches twice. Every time."

She laughed again.

"Yeah, you laugh, too."

"Okay, Ozzie, you think you can tell me what the fuck's happening here?"

"Sure. We hijacked you."

"We? We who?"

"I'll explain later. We're still working on some shit. Hang on . . . oh."

" 'Oh, what?"

"They tell me you should watch the pretty dots."

"The dots. Right."

Now she noticed there seemed to be more of the small, colored shapes, and there seemed to be a definite, very attractive pattern developing to their movement. Yeah. Soothing. Something like—she couldn't remember just what—insect wings.

The faint smell of leaves burning.

Fall breeze.

—*click*—

She woke up.

Her back ached slightly. Ozzie's futon, worn thin from years of various acrobatics, was lumpy beneath her thin frame.

The big room was very quiet. That struck her as odd. Something, some bit of rotted metal or sagging fiber was always rubbing, tapping, groaning against some other bit of forgotten detritus in the crazed jumble of Ozzie's home.

Slowly she sat up. "Ozzie?"

As if her voice was a signal of some kind, she realized that sound had returned. Now the scattered junk sang to her in a thousand tiny voices. For some reason that made her feel better.

The air smelled of dust and rust.

"Ozzie!"

"Yeah, babe, just a minute. This is kinda complicated."

His voice seemed to come from the kitchen, but when she walked over, no one was there. She stood for a moment, touching the fridge, the greasy propane stove, the cracked porcelain sink.

The front door of the warehouse creaked open and Ozzie walked in, a grin splitting his folded face.

"Ozzie!"

"Calley, darlin'."

And then she was in his arms. "Oh, Jeezus, you motherfucker, oh, Jeezus, it's good to see you—"

"Hey, Calley, you're raving."

"Of course I'm raving, it's—"

She stopped. It all came back in a rush. "Ozzie?"

He squeezed her tight. "Uh-huh?"

"Are you real?"

"Sort of. Yeah. As far as you're concerned, I am."

Gently, she pushed him away. "I think, Ozzie dearest, you're gonna have to do some explaining."

It was raining outside. She thought that was a nice touch. They were in their usual tangled web on the futon, staring up at the skylight, watching fat drops spatter and explode on the glass in liquid patterns.

"So I'm not really alive, huh?" she said.

He squeezed her shoulder. "Sure you're alive. You're talking to me, aren't you?"

"But what about my body?"

"What about it?"

"It's in the tank, back in Double En's compound."

"Yeah. So . . . ?"

"So I'm not really here."

"Of course you are," he said.

She sighed. "I don't understand. I've gotta think for a while. You tell me everything, okay?"

"About what?"

"Everything—from when I saw you the last time," she said. "After I took off for my own place."

"Okay." He rolled over on his belly and propped his sagging, floppy face in his hands. "You were gone about a day, and this guy came knocking on my door. . . ."

She watched Ozzie pull off the heating strip from the pizza box, and then smelled the sudden sharp odor of pepperoni. "I'm starved," she said. "Give me."

Carefully, he opened the box, reached in, and pulled out a slice. "Here," he said. "Be careful—hot."

She took the limp, steamy wedge and gingerly bit off the tip of it. Chewed. "Mm. Good," she said. Quickly, she finished it. "More," she said.

Later, she said, "I think I'm gonna live. If that's the right way of looking at it." She licked her fingers. "Okay, so let me get it straight. This guy drops by, and he starts telling you all this wonderful shit about Double En, how they built their meatmatrix and now it's gone crazy, or something."

He nodded. "They said that Double En had used a flawed transfer process, or transferred flawed information—they weren't sure—but the end result was that the meat was dangerous to other databases. And they knew about you and Berg, sort of."

Her eyes narrowed. "What did they know about us?"

"That you were working for Double En, or would be, and that what you were doing was not safe for you."

"Seems to me that these people are awfully—wouldn't you say—*knowledgeable* about me and Berg and Double En and all. Like maybe they know too much, you understand? What's their hand in this game?"

He blinked. "I told you, didn't I?"

She slapped him lightly. "No, you didn't."

"Oh. Well, they're Lunies. I'm on the Moon right now."

The rain had stopped. Overhead, washed clean, the skylight showed a few weak stars trying to glimmer through the thin haze of dusk. Ozzie had turned on some lights; one, an ancient lamp in the shape of a nude, hugely endowed female, made her chuckle.

"So what do the Lunies want out of this?" she asked.

"They want to take out Double En's matrix," he told her.

She shook her head. "The Lunies move against Double En, they'll know they've been in a real street brawl. If they survive. That company isn't known for playing pattycake."

He nodded. "They understand. That's why they're doing it this way. They've got a matrix too, remember—only it's a lot different than Double En's—and they control it. They used their meat to grab you when you came through the metamatrix."

"So how come they didn't grab Berg, too?" she asked.

He shrugged. "Dunno . . . they didn't say. I think it's got something to do with their plan—what they've got in mind to do."

"Yeah. And that bothers me a lot. They know all this shit, but we don't. And it looks like I'm pretty much at their mercy."

"Well," he said doubtfully, "they *are* maintaining you in their own construct."

She looked around the big, cluttered room. "Some construct. Why couldn't they build the Imperial Suite from the Royal Beijing Marriott?"

He laughed. "Cause I've never been there."

Her expression sobered. "*I* have. So, what happens if they turn off the construct?"

Ozzie was silent for a moment. Then he said slowly, "Look, Calley, remember—you aren't really here. You're in that tank of Double En's, and no matter what happens, that's where you'll wake up. So don't worry about it. Besides, they tell me they're working on something. . . ."

"Right. But they don't quite say what it is. Ozzie, I don't *like* this at all." Carefully, she pinched her right forearm. "Ouch! I feel real enough."

He grinned. "What's reality?"

Calley grinned back. "You cogito your own sum, okay? Now be a good boy and go away. I want to think about this."

He stood up. "Okay. I'll be back."

"I'm sure you will."

She wandered around the drafty room, touching clumps of amorphous refuse, her forehead wrinkled in concentration. Finally she returned to the futon, lowered herself into a full lotus, inhaled, and said, "Okay, come out. Come out wherever you are."

The door buzzer sounded.

She smiled slowly. "Just walk in," she said. "I'm real sure the door's unlocked."

She had pulled two chairs out of the nearest junk pile, dusted them off, and sat on one. Her guest perched uncomfortably on the other. He was a young man, no more than thirty; high forehead, wide, pale gray eyes, the beginnings of a receding hairline, and a serious, small mouth. He said his name was Karl Wier.

"How come this?" she said, and waved her hand at the room in general. "And old Ozzie to do the welcome home number?"

"We weren't sure what condition you'd be in," he told her. "It seemed to make sense this way. Less mental strain for you. Remember, this is all new for us, too."

She nodded. "You know," she said slowly, "you got real big troubles."

He squinted in puzzlement at her. "Like what?" he said.

"Well, I've never met Bill Norton, but I've gotten pretty tight with Shag Nakamura. So: If Norton was able to keep old Shag in a number two position, and it seems like he was—and Norton has the full capabilities of a meatmatrix—I think the two of them are tough enough to wipe the floor with you guys. I mean, Nakamura is definitely no patsy. Norton must be one incredible sonofabitch—and while they definitely don't like each other, I think they'll be able to agree on one thing. And that's the necessity of stomping anybody who tries to fuck around with their company."

Karl Wier moved uncomfortably against the sprung seat of his ancient overstuffed armchair. "We'd been considering that, yes. We've tried to be very careful."

She laughed out loud. "Careful? The way you grabbed me, searchlights must have lit up all over that matrix of theirs. Not to mention Berg."

"Berg? What about him?"

"Jeezus—you guys really do need help."

"I don't understand."

"That's right. You don't. So you sit right there and be real quiet, and Mama Calley will explain it all for you."

Wier had left via the front door, and a short time later, while Calley was rummaging in the antique fridge, Ozzie reappeared. She wondered if he'd just popped out of thin air, or if he was observing their pretense of reality. It made her nervous to think about her position: not real at all, just a collection of electronic give and take, carefully maintained in an artificial construct created by a hunk of modified chicken brain on the Moon.

It sure felt real. She wondered what death would be like here.

"Oz," she said, "this is all very well, but why can't

they put some fucking food in your refrigerator? There's nothing here but beer and what looks like a doggie bag from maybe a year ago."

A hurt expression flickered at the corner of his eyes. "Calley, that's what I usually have in there."

She faced him. "Okay, then, what happens if I call out for Chinese?"

He spread his big hands. "Beats me. Give it a try."

She stared at him for a moment, then slowly grinned. "Why the fuck not?" she asked, and went to the phone.

"Give me a hand," she said. "I know you've got a table somewhere in this mess."

By the time she'd cleaned off the table and found two sets of silverware that matched, and enough plates and cups to make place settings, the food arrived.

Chateaubriand, salad nicoise, scallops en croute, a vegetable mousse, and two bottles of Lafitte Rothschild '06. "Pay the man," she told Ozzie.

Later, she said, "I could get used to this, you know."

He nodded seriously. "Me, too."

"There are some philosophical considerations," she told him.

"Uh-huh."

"Like why would anybody give a shit about anything if they could just jack into their friendly matrix and live like this."

He thought about it. "Those tanks cost money," he said.

"Are you in a tank right now?"

"Well, sort of. Not really."

"Technical problems," she replied. "Bullshit. In ten years they'll have it pocket-sized and costing the same as a pack of cigarettes, probably." A sudden thought struck her. "I wonder if somebody is working on that angle yet?"

"What?"

"The ghost of an idea. Forget it," she told him. She poured out the last of the wine. "So, you know this Wier guy?"

"Karl? Sure. He's one of their top guns. Did most of the systems work for their meat. Still doing it, I guess. Why? How'd you know about him?"

"He came to visit."

"Yeah? What happened?"

"We talked. We reached understandings. We reached agreements."

He sipped from his glass. "Sounds ominous."

"Could be," she told him. "But if it works out. . . ."

"If what works out?" he asked.

She put her wine down. "Ozzie," she said suddenly, "how'd you like to help me steal a world?"

He had found candles somewhere—she thought he could find anything in that room—and she had set them on saucers surrounding the futon, so that the thin mattress appeared, through narrowed eyelids, to be floating above a sea of tiny campfires.

His big, rough fingers traced patterns on her naked belly.

"You think about him much?" he asked.

"Who?" Her voice was rough and lazy and content.

"Berg?"

"The Iceman? Sure I think about him."

"What happened while you two were together?"

She touched the back of his hand. "Why? You jealous or something?"

"Maybe," he said.

"Look, Ozzie," she said gently. "I don't think I've given you permission to be jealous."

"Damn it, Calley, I don't need—"

"Oh, yes, you do," she interjected sharply. "You don't own me. I can't help what you feel, but I can sure as hell keep it from having anything to do with me. Listen, Ozzie, what I do with my life is my business—you understand? I can't have it any other way."

"Calley—"

"What I'm trying to tell you, Ozzie . . . I'm danger-

ous. I don't want you hurt. To hurt you. Whatever.
You're a big boy, you understand that. I don't make
promises. Not any more. What we're doing is as much
circumstance and hormones as anything else. And that's
how you're gonna have to deal with it."

"You still love the asshole."

"Never said I didn't," she replied.

She was silent for a moment. "Is there any law
that says you can't feel for two people at the same
time?"

After a while, his fingers resumed their movement
on her stomach.

When she woke the next morning, Ozzie was gone.
Karl Wier turned up soon enough, though, knocking
on the door.

"Yeah, come on in," she called from the bathroom,
where she was finishing the usual morning battle with
her hair.

Wier came equipped with croissants and coffee.

"You know the way to a girl's heart," she told him.

"I thought I remembered it the other way around,"
he said.

"Chauvinist swine," she replied, biting into one of
the flaky pastries.

Later, cradling a cup of the hot coffee in her hands,
she said, "Well? Can you do it?"

"I took it to my people and we worked on it," he
replied. "There's a lot of opposition. It's extremely
dangerous—we aren't strong enough to oppose Double En openly. Nobody is, by themselves."

She sighed. "I can't do you any good unless you
help me," she said.

He nodded. "I know," he said. "I told them."

"And—?"

He sipped. "And I convinced them. It's on for tonight. We . . . found an unexpected ally. A man."

"Don't fuck up, Karl," she said.

He exhaled slowly. "We'll try not to," he replied.

\*        \*        \*

Things chirped, tittered, clicked in the ragged darkness at the edges of the room. She sat alone at the table, staring at a single candle. It had started to rain again, and the rhythmic sound of it on the skylight soothed her jangled nerves.

She watched the flickering light, smelling hot wax, and remembered the look on Berg's face when he'd come to her door after gimmicking the interface mainframe at Double En.

"Damn," she said suddenly. "I need a *body*."

## 18

THE NECKLACE OF light bobbed around the inland sea, a shimmering chain separate from
the solid carpet of domes which covered the land from
the Pacific clear to the mountains. Where the jaws of
the land nearly came together burned the brightest of
the jewels: a solid fire of towers that once had been
San Francisco.

Nakamura's private jumpjet plummeted like an arrow into its burning heart.

Just outside San Francisco Orbital's main terminal,
Oranson paused and pointed at a spot across the street.
"Right there," he said.

Nakamura glanced in direction the security man was
pointing. "What?" he said.

"Where a guy named Collinsworth got himself blown
up," Oranson replied.

The four bodyguards tightened their formation around
the two men. Nakamura's face remained expressionless. "Collinsworth. Yes. One of the men Norton was
behind?"

"That's right, sir," Oranson said.

Nakamura stared at the spot, his dark eyes slitted.
"I want everybody connected with that removed from
any authority," he said at last.

"Is that wise, sir? As far as I understand it, it's
absolutely essential that we keep Mr. Norton's . . . ah
. . . condition a secret."

"Do it so there's no connection," Nakamura said

shortly. "I pay you to get things like that done, don't I?"

"Yes, sir," Oranson said quietly, his face thoughtful.

Nakamura looked at him one uncomfortable second too long, then turned. "Let's get on with it," he said.

First the bodyguards did their slow, menacing dance, checking each other with ominous precision, like a school of sharks slowly circling a piece of meat.

Oranson watched his opposite number with an amused expression on his face. The other man, a lean, impeccably clothed specimen, returned Oranson's amusement with a sardonic gaze of his own. Eventually the muscle boys reached a state of uneasy equilibrium, and seated themselves in various places around the nearly deserted restaurant.

It was a bright and sunny room, partially open to the sky. Red- and blue-checkered tablecloths covered spindly wooden tables. In various pots, planters, and beds, semitropical trees cast dappled shadows across the undressed concrete floor. Two regular guests watched this performance, motioned their waiter over, paid their bill, and left. Finally Oranson turned to the impeccable man with the crooked gaze and said, "It's clean."

The man, whose name was Eric Campbell, and whose reputation preceded him, nodded. "Our people checked it out, too."

"That's it, then," Oranson replied. He turned and went to the first of two long, armored BMW-Honda limos parked at the curb and rapped gently on the glass. He heard the magnetic locks snap open, and then a final bodyguard climbed out and held the door for Nakamura. Oranson scanned the street nervously as the short Oriental stepped across the sidewalk and into the safety of the restaurant.

Before following, Oranson spent one final instant trying to guess the location of the small army of Double En security people sealing off the entire neighborhood in an invisible web of watchful firepower. He shaded his eyes, but only spotted a single flash on a roof a half-block down, sunlight blazing momentarily from mirrored glass. His or Campbell's, he couldn't tell. He raised his right hand to his lips and whispered into the microphone bead imbedded in the first knuckle. "Keep it buttoned up," he said. Then he turned and followed Nakamura inside.

Oranson was never very sure about what forces shaped and motivated his boss, but, oddly enough, he understood well the delicate ballet about to be played out. As he entered the restaurant, he heard the magbolts of the second limo open with a heavy metallic clunk, and allowed a small grin to animate his features for a moment.

Arthur Kraus. He reviewed what he knew of the man, which, because of his position as security chief, was a very great deal. Fifteen years before, Kraus had married, in somewhat clouded circumstances, the daughter of Heinz Richter Solingen. Clouded because Kraus, although reasonably well educated, was of working class origin, while his bride, ten years older and ugly as a post, was a bonafide member of corporate royalty. Surprisingly, despite initial dubiousness on the part of old Solingen, the match had turned out well, and when the old man's elaborate life support systems finally gave out, he turned over to his son-in-law one thousand shares of Class B Preferred stock in his company—only half a percent of the total, but one hundred percent of the shares needed to elect members to Solingen's board of directors. Five years later Kraus forced the unwilling remnants of the ancient Krupp empire into a merger, and the resulting behemoth soon dominated the new technological wonderland of the rejuvenated Ruhr.

Now Kraus was the principal speaker for European business, and the unofficial head of a loose consortium of seven of the largest corporations on the continent.

Nakamura-Norton was immensely larger than Solin-

gen, Krupp—but not as large as the consortium. Therefore, in a convoluted display of corporate humility,
Nakamura entered the restaurant first, to await the
pleasure of Kraus' arrival. It would not have been
possible in any official setting—but this was as off the
record as it could get.

Oranson joined Nakamura at a large, round table
under a gnarled Ficus tree. "He's on his way," he
said.

Nakamura nodded. "Good," he said. "When he
arrives, leave us alone."

Campbell entered the restaurant, paused, then
stepped aside for a short, wide man wearing beautifully cut tweeds. The man's head was in perfect pro-
portion to his barrel chest and sloping shoulders, but
his entire upper body was shaped to fit a man well
over six feet tall. Kraus was no more than five feet
four inches.

His head, shiny bald except for a short fringe of iron
gray hair, rode his bull neck imperiously, and he walked
with the assured stride of a man with much longer
legs.

Nakamura stood to greet him, bowing slightly and
extending his right hand. Kraus smiled, and his surprising wide, soft brown eyes twinkled as he took the
handshake. "Shag," he said, his voice high and precise, "good to see you again."

Nakamura flashed his own smile and nodded, waving at the table. "Sometimes I think our meetings are
too ceremonious," he replied. "But sit—the pasta in
this place is heaven."

"Pasta?" Kraus said. "Is that in my dossier on you?"

"Probably," Nakamura said. "I'm Japanese, but it's
no secret I've been corrupted by your Western ways."

Kraus exploded in a sudden belly laugh. "Maybe I
should take up sashimi," he said finally, patting his
boulder of a gut.

Nakamura nodded politely. "Perhaps," he said.

Kraus put both his thick-fingered hands flat on the
tabletop. "Yes," he said. "Well—I suppose we'd bet-

ter get down to it, then. I don't know about yours, but my men get nervous whenever I venture out of the compounds."

Nakamura nodded. "Only natural," he said. "They're paid to protect us, and it's easier for them there. Arthur, what is this all about? Why couldn't we use our regular datanet? It's secure."

Kraus's face grew suddenly hard, all trace of the jolly Deutschelander suddenly wiped away. "Is it, Shigeinari? A lot of things no longer seem secure. Either to me, or to others."

Nakamura bowed his head. "To what, exactly, do you refer, Arthur?"

"There have been incidents. . . ."

"Yes?"

The German slapped the table suddenly, an explosive sound, but Nakamura moved not at all. "Hyundai-Europa was raided less than a week ago."

"Raided? How so?" Nakamura asked softly. His head began to bob in a gentle rhythm.

"Part of their R&D data core was gutted."

Nakamura continued his nodding.

"Damn it, Shag, those people have some of the best protected databases in the world today. Nobody should have been able to get in and out undetected, untraced." Kraus stared at Nakamura, tiny pinpoints of sweat beginning to dot his shiny skull.

"Why are you telling me this, Arthur?" Nakamura asked gently.

"You know damn—" The German bit the words off as a waiter approached, escorted by one of his men, and one of Nakamura's. The waiter was quite young, quite darkly handsome, and quite nervous at the unaccustomed chaperones.

Nakamura raised his head and smiled, his teeth like white lines down a highway. "Food, Arthur. Things like this always go more easily with nourishment."

"Yes," the German admitted smoothly, relaxing. "You say the pasta is good here?"

"Excellent," Nakamura replied. "And a decent selection of Moselles."

"The Germans," Kraus said slowly, "know absolutely nothing about wine."

For dessert they munched on flaky pastries that had been coated with honey and carmelized sugar. The waiter brewed the coffee at tableside, and added generous portions of cognac to the heavy mugs.

"That's better," Nakamura said.

Kraus motioned to the waiter for another pastry. "Just one more, Shag."

Finally he dusted off his fingers and removed the napkin from his lap. "All right, you inscrutable devil, the food was excellent. And I do feel better. But that doesn't change the situation, and we have to discuss it."

"Good coffee," Nakamura replied. "Then let us discuss it," he said. "Maybe I can save you some trouble." He raised his right hand and snapped his fingers. Oranson immediately rose from his own table and walked over, carrying a small leather briefcase secured by a heavy steel lock.

"Open it," Nakamura said. Oranson did, and Nakamura extracted a thick sheaf of hardcopy. He handed the papers to Kraus. "Here," Nakamura said. "We document six instances of major data intrusion within the last month. HyundaiEuropa was one, also General Electric Motors, RanData Worldwide, and three more. I have listed two others there, Arthur, and in so doing I place myself at considerable risk."

One meaty hand almost covering the pile, Kraus stared at him. "How so?" he asked.

"Nakamura Norton has been attacked twice in the same time. Our Los Angeles database was effectively destroyed, and in the same manner some of our payroll systems in the Chicago central operations area were wiped out."

The fingers of Kraus's hand began to dance on the stack of printouts. "So you are already aware."

Nakamura's face took on expression for the first time. "Arthur, those sonofabitches are stealing from you, but the assholes are fucking trying to ruin me!"

Kraus nodded shortly. "What are you doing about it?" he asked.

"The same thing you are. Watching my ass and trying to discover who's behind all this."

Kraus considered a moment. "What is Bill doing?"

"Norton? He's indisposed at the moment."

"Ah. His usual problem?"

"Do you mean, has he been drunk for a month? The answer is no. It's going on two months now."

"Mm. A pity he wastes such a mind that way," Kraus said.

"Don't pity him—pity me," Nakamura said. "I could use that alcoholic bastard. He understands this shit far better than I'll ever be able to. I've tried, but he prefers to remain incoherent." Nakamura shook his head in disgust. "At this rate he's going to have worse than just a hangover to cope with."

The waiter leaned in carefully and refilled their coffee mugs.

"No," Nakamura said, "no more cognac, thank you."

"An object lesson for us all," Kraus said. "None for me, either."

"Spare me the philosophy, Arthur," Nakamura told him. "Have your people come up with anything?"

Kraus shook his head. "It happens very quickly, and we've been unable to trace anything. But all our analyses indicate something very big, very powerful. On the order, perhaps, of one of your matrices." And he glanced slyly at the Japanese.

"Sure, Arthur. But we know all about the matrices. All of them are in trustworthy hands. Besides, all the matrices are rigidly monitored by the corporations involved."

"Yes?" said Kraus. "The Lunies, too?"

"The Lunies? What of them? Scientists," Nakamura said. Contempt dripped from the word.

"Like your partner, you mean?" Kraus said. "Don't let your emotions blind you, Shag. Norton may be a drunk, but he created the meatmatrix in the first place. And my espionage people believe that the Lunies are involved in some very far-out work."

Nakamura blinked. "Really? What kind of work?"

"We can't find out," Kraus said. "They have protected themselves extraordinarily well."

"Like whoever is doing this to us?" Nakamura said.

"Exactly."

The waiter brought the humidor with the air of an acolyte performing a hallowed ritual. Both men made their selections, performed the cutting and lighting in silence. A sudden chill breeze brought a wisp of fog over the back wall. As they smoked, their own companionable atmosphere seemed to undergo a comparable lowering of temperature.

Finally Kraus aimed the glowing tip of his cigar at Nakamura and said, "It could be the Lunies. But then, it could be any of us."

Nakamura nodded.

"You have my word, Shag, that when we find them, whoever it may be, we will destroy them."

Nakamura drew on his cigar, but remained silent.

"It's too important," Kraus said suddenly. "We operate, we do business, within certain agreements of necessity. Information is what we deal in. And data is our vulnerability. Anyone—and I do mean that—who threatens us there must be erased. Wiped out. Obliterated. Myself, you, the Lunies, whoever. And we will discover them, Shag. We have too much power for them to hide forever."

Carefully Nakamura laid down his cigar in the crystal ashtray which magically appeared just in time to catch the ash. "Of course we are in complete agreement," he said. "But you've not considered one final thing."

"Which is?"

"There is always the possibility," Nakamura said softly, "that they will destroy us first."

When they left, Nakamura was first to his limo. Humility did, after all, have its limits.

The heavily protected limo rode quiet as a ghost. Nakamura sat in the rear seat, facing Oranson, who crouched in front of him on a jumpseat. "Well," Nakamura said, "did you get everything?"

"Yes," Oranson said. "We had three men with laser-eyes reading his lips. Yours, too. Of course, his people got us, too. We spotted two of their copters loafing around upstairs."

"We were covered all the time?" Nakamura asked, a faint note of alarm tincturing his words.

"Absolutely," Oranson replied. "If those boys had gotten within three kilometers, we would have shot them down. We weren't taking chances, but they stayed out of range."

"Fred," Nakamura said, "it looks as if I'm going to have to trust you. Somewhat."

"Thank you, sir," Oranson replied.

Nakamura sighed. "We can't keep Norton a secret much longer. He's beginning to strike out at the other corporations. I've got no idea what he can do with that matrix. But Double En is now in a godawful crunch. I thought at first it was just a matter of getting rid of him. But it may be too late for that. You see my dilemma? If Kraus finds out that the Double En matrix is behind the attacks on the other data bases, his people won't look for any explanations. They'll just get together and squash us. They won't have any other choice."

Oranson's expression took on a somber cast. "But we don't know yet whether we can either control Norton, or stop him."

"Right. So maybe we quit trying to do either. There is another way out for us.

"There is?"

"Yes. I ally myself with Norton. Then we destroy the rest of them."

Oranson turned this over carefully. "But what about Norton?" he asked. "Is there any reason for him to trust us?"

Nakamura opaqued all the windows. "Not now," he said. "But after I take care of Berg and Calley for him. . . ."

He let the thought trail off. "By the way," he said, "did you get the name of that waiter?"

19

"**Now, who in** the fuck are you?" Berg said.

The big man stuck out a hand like a catcher's mitt. "Who do you think? You were expecting to find Santa Claus?" Berg's delicate fingers disappeared in the other's huge grip. "I'm Bill Norton. You must be Jack Berg. Pleased to meet you and all that shit."

Berg pulled his hand away. He stared at the big man, then abruptly sat down behind his desk. "Something is very wrong here," he said.

Norton lowered himself into a Breuer chair, causing the machined steel frame to creak audibly. "No, it's okay, Berg," he said. "Or it will be in a minute."

"What's that supposed to mean?"

It was very quiet. Norton leaned forward, his gaze widening on Berg's face. "Remember the tank now, Berg. That's all—just remember the tank. . . ."

"What?" But as Norton spoke the words, that incredible sense of deja vu washed over him again, picked him up, spun him around. Strobing pictures, freeze-frames—a coffin-like box, white—

His office disappeared, reappeared, did it again. Interspersed with visions of a galaxy of shining amorphous forms set on a floor of diamond dust in a maelstrom of light gone mad.

White . . .

—*click*—

\*     \*     \*

"Oh," Berg said. He blinked.

"You got it now?" Norton asked gently.

"You're Bill Norton," Berg said, his voice thick.

"That's right," the big man replied. "Anything else?"

"Nakamura . . . the tank. I remember now."

"That's good, then." Norton let his bulk relax against the chair, which groaned again. "You ought to get better furniture," Norton said. "This artsy-craftsy shit looks nice, but it doesn't last worth a damn."

Berg chuckled. It was an uneasy sound. "I don't think Breuer had people like you in mind when he designed it," he said.

"Well, he should have," Norton told him. "You feel okay? Want a drink or something?"

Berg nodded. "Some scotch. On that table back there. Laphroaig."

Norton heaved himself upright. Berg was reminded of a whale surfacing. "At least you drink good booze," Norton said. "Laphroaig. I've never tasted it, so I couldn't get any here before you arrived."

To Berg, the offhand remark seemed important, but he couldn't figure out why. He filed it to chew over later. "Don't bother with ice," he said.

Norton returned, set down a thick-walled glass of sculptured crystal full of amber liquid on the desk. "Happy days," he said.

"Days," Berg replied. "You know," he said, "you don't much look like the holos I've seen of Bill Norton."

Norton drained half his glass in one long swallow. "Ah. Good Scotch. You're only here a few days, and already there are benefits."

"And that's another thing," Berg said slowly. "A few days? I remember going in the tank—and I don't think a hell of a lot of time has gone by since then."

"Really? So what have you been doing?"

—*click*—

Berg stared at his drink. "I don't know," he said.

"Okay, then, do you know where you are?"

The scotch tasted cool and smoky at the same time. Berg let the malted warmth slide over his tongue, down his throat. "Yes," he said finally, "I'm in the Double En meatmatrix."

Norton put down his drink, then clapped his hands softly. "Good boy," he said. "You've got that much right, then." He retrieved the scotch, tasted again, and said, "So. You think you know everything about a transfer like that?"

Berg shrugged. Sunlight shivered from the grainy wood on the top of his desk. Patterns . . . "Evidently not," he replied. "Maybe you want to enlighten me?"

At this, Norton laughed out loud. "Enlightenment. Sure thing—I'm in the business. Okay, getting down to it, you have been out for several days. Well, not exactly out, but bonkers—crazy as a shithouse rat. It's part of the process. The matrix has to get used to you, more or less. All those weird dreams, nightmares— just a by-product. I went through it, too, and a lot longer. There was nobody here to help things along like I did for you."

Something about the explanation struck Berg as odd, something that didn't quite make sense. A little danger bell began to tinkle inside his skull. He didn't pursue it, however. "So you're the welcoming committee?"

Norton raised his glass. "You could say that," he agreed cheerfully.

"Well, good," Berg replied, lifting his own drink. "You wanna tell me then, why the fuck you've been doing your best to kill me?"

"How did you figure it out?" Norton asked.

Berg got up and walked from behind the desk to the tabletop bar. He devoted his attention to mixing the drink, wondering how much to say to this Norton who didn't look at all like Norton was supposed to look.

Finally he sighed. "I thought you had hired me, at first. But I found out that wasn't true. As I learned more about what the situation really was—you in the matrix and Nakamura running the company by himself

—I realized that only one party had any real interest in taking me out of the picture."

The big man nodded. "Go on," he said.

"My troubles didn't start until Nakamura hired me. Then the shit hit the fan—Collinsworth, Aldocci, Marie all taken out, my condo rocket-bombed, thugs of various description showing up out of the woodwork . . . It came to me that somebody didn't want me to take the job."

"A reasonable guess," Norton agreed.

"When I found out what the job was, it was simple. Nakamura hired me to wipe you out. Therefore—"

"Therefore, who had an interest in you not taking the job? Me, of course," Norton boomed.

"Right. And I figure you've got a lot more control of Double En's data base than Nakamura thinks you do. Maybe other bases, as well."

Norton's big, silver-streaked head bobbed as he swallowed the last of his drink. "You figure pretty good," he said. He regarded his empty glass, a brooding expression on his massive features. "You mind?" he said at last.

"Be my guest," Berg told him.

Norton shambled over to the bar and refilled his drink. This time, instead of sitting down again, he wandered over to the glass wall behind Berg's desk. Berg swiveled his chair to watch him.

"You know," Norton said, "I told you that you figured it good. I'd think the same way, if it happened to me. There's just one little problem."

"What's that?" Berg asked.

"I didn't have anything to do with any of the attacks on you." Norton said. "And I don't know who did."

"What do you see out there?" Norton asked.

Berg's shoulder's raised a bit. From somewhere came the sound of a cuckoo clock. Hesitantly, the rest joined in.

"Chicago," Berg said.

"Okay," Norton said. "And now . . . ?"

Berg's eyelids flickered. Outside his windows burned the serried waves of the metamatrix, a jeweled wave crashing on a sunlit sea, light and noise and chaos.

"Jeezus," Berg whispered softly.

"Yeah," Norton said. "It's the place where the machines dream. I don't know if the machines are aware of it, but this is what a human perceives. Pretty, huh?"

Berg nodded slowly.

Norton turned and faced him. "My world, Berg. The only world I have. I know all about that tub of cancer cells back in Chicago. I can't go back. For better or worse, this is it. So tell me, then—why did you take the job?"

Berg blinked. "Easy," he said. "I wanted to stomp your ass, and this was the only way to get it done."

The overpowering boom of Norton's laughter reverberated throughout the room. Berg found himself grinning in response, even against his will. "You think it's funny?" he said at last.

Norton gulped the rest of his drink. "Sure I do," he said. "Don't you? If there is anyplace you can't hurt me, it's here in the matrix. I own it, Berg. You think I'd let you come here if there was any possibility you could hurt me?" He chuckled then, a thick, grating sound. "No way. I wanted you here, man. You have something I need. That's all."

"Okay," Berg said at last. "Here I am. You want to tell me why?"

Norton's wild laughter roared out again. "Easy, you sonofabitch. You're gonna be my bodyguard."

Berg stared at the gargantuan figure. For the first time, he began to wonder if his habit of playing four moves ahead hadn't at last gotten him five moves behind.

Berg faced the window, watching the ceaseless interplay of information that was the existence of the machines. Behind him, Norton was opening a second bottle of scotch. The man seemed to have an unbelievable capacity for the stuff. The only effect Berg noticed was that, if anything, Norton became more talkative.

"That shithead partner of mine is going to do his convoluted best to take me out of here," Norton was saying. "I've got him by his yellow balls, and he knows it. His only chance is to snuff me, and that makes my strategy simple: convince him the price is too high."

Berg nodded to Norton's reflection in the glass. "I bet you already have me figured into that equation."

Norton joined him. "That's right, Berg. When I set this whole deal up, I made sure that our matrix was absolutely indispensable to the company. Our whole database is concentrated here. And I hold the trigger—hell, I'm the fucking gun—aimed right at the heart of it all. Nakamura isn't stupid. He knows the situation. But that won't stop him from trying to take me out anyway. He'll try anything, as long as he thinks there's a reasonable chance the matrix won't be destroyed. You were his first move, but I had that already figured."

"Why doesn't he just build another matrix?" Berg asked.

"Think about it. He has to use this matrix in order to build another one. All the programming is here. And he knows what I'll do if he tries."

"Interesting," Berg said. "You're the tool he needs to build any weapons against you."

Norton chuckled. "Yeah. Diabolical, isn't it?"

"I might have used another term," Berg told him.

"What's that?"

"Well, diabolical implies a fall from grace," Berg said.

"And?"

"I don't think you fell very far."

"Berg, you are not a nice man."

"Right," Berg said. "We'll get along, then."

They had gone out to dinner. Berg found the trip interesting. He was still trying to discover precisely what Norton's relationship—status, position, whatever—

was in regards to the matrix itself. Too many pieces of the puzzle were missing. He kept his mouth shut and watched and listened.

Things seemed completely normal. His lobby looked as it should look, right down to Amiar, the Hindu doorman, who waved an effusive farewell.

Outside, the sun burned a hole in a high-summer sky. Chicago thrust its spires into the afternoon, and Berg smelled a freshening breeze off the lake. The streets were crowded. Berg searched each face, but recognized no one. My world or his? he wondered.

The little bar tucked away just beyond the Michigan Avenue skyway was the same as it had been for years: Outside, a peeling concrete facade pierced by two thick-glassed windows about the size and shape of medieval arrow slits; inside, the warmth of polished wooden walls, soft, incandescent bulbs, and dark leather was as familiar to Berg as his own bedroom. Charles, the bartender, smiled a familiar greeting.

"Friend of yours?" Berg asked.

"I drink in here, too," Norton replied. "You just never noticed."

Berg glanced at him. "I think I'd have noticed you," he said.

"I didn't always look this way," Norton told him.

They stayed with Laphroaig. The big man ordered for both of them, a pair of New York strips, with hot German potato salad, snap beans, and a loaf of fresh whole wheat bread.

A waiter Berg didn't recognize served the meal. "I thought I knew everybody who worked here," he remarked.

"This guy worked at another place, and he was the only good thing about the joint. So he came here."

"Just like that?"

"What's the matter, Berg? It's a free country. Man can work where he wants to."

Berg broke a chunk of bread off the steaming loaf, and spread butter on it. "That so? Gee, Mr. Norton, in that case, I quit."

Norton shook his head. "You haven't heard my offer yet."

Berg chewed slowly. "I bet it's one I can't refuse," he said.

"Something like that."

"You think you can quit stuffing your face long enough to lay it out for me?"

Norton put down his fork. He looked down at the tablecloth, then up again. "In a hurry, are you? Well, I suppose you're entitled. You're gonna be my insurance, Berg. I designed this sucker, and I know it better than anybody else. But you have a talent. I know you brought some weird shit in with you—but I walled it off where it can't do any harm. The viruses aren't a problem. But the screens you built for them are genius stuff. I want you to do the same for the matrix. Nakamura knows what you can do. If he knows you're doing it for me, well. . . ."

Berg sighed. "You don't understand me very well, do you?"

"Maybe," Norton said. "You aren't much for lost causes, I don't think. So what do you figure my partner's gonna do with your body? Leave it in the tank? Reintegrate your personality when this is all over?"

Berg shrugged. "It's what he said."

Norton grunted. "And fork over the billion as well, I suppose."

"I'd taken some precautions. . . ."

"They didn't work," Norton told him. "Nakamura disconnected you from the matrix five minutes after you came over."

Berg froze. Something, just a pale shadow of the previous deja vu, began to tug gently but insistently at the edge of his awareness. Very carefully he said, "You're sure of that?"

Norton nodded, his eyes boring into Berg's own. "Yeah, Berg, I'm sure."

"It puts a new light on things," Berg told him. Again, that persistent itch, as if something were trying to get his attention.

"I thought it might. You are officially dead, pal."

"Then he knew," Berg said.

"He knew all along," Norton replied. "You're marooned. Need a job?"

The itch was growing into a full-blown irritation. Berg sighed. "One thing,'" he said. "What did you do with Calley? What happened to her?"

Berg saw the big man's expression change into something he hadn't seen yet. Blank puzzlement.

"Calley?" Norton said. "Who the fuck is Calley?"

There was no way he couldn't believe. In utter despair he said, "Oh, shit," and let the boojum in.

Immediately the itch disappeared and he felt relief. Then he sat spellbound as the man across the table began to melt. Change. Hair thinning. Smaller. Berg blinked. Norton's shoulders slumped, began to run like melting wax. Fingers curled, grew slender. Eyes of slow fire—

The man coughed. His face was etched with lines that reflected an agony Berg couldn't even begin to imagine. He looked across the table at Berg.

"I'm sorry," he said. "I didn't think you'd ever let me through." He paused. Then, "I'm Bill Norton," he said.

"It was the chip I got from the Lady," he said. "Wasn't it?"

The other man nodded. "I arranged for it to come into your possession," he said.

They shared two tall crystal mugs of dark coffee topped with generous puffs of whipped cream. Berg's cup steamed with the aroma of Old Bushmills, but Norton had refused any Irish whiskey for his own mug.

"I used to drink a lot," he said ruefully, "but in my present situation I prefer to keep a clear head. As much as I can."

"I'm having a great deal of trouble with all this, you know," Berg told him carefully. "It's hard for me to understand just what is real."

This man was much smaller than the other Norton: older, more sharply defined. Where the previous man had been rough, coarse, bursting with vitality, fleshing out the clichéd meaning of "larger than life," this Norton was more a part of life, and heavily used by it. His pallid skin was almost translucent. When he spoke, his voice sang with atonal memories that cut at Berg like insectile knives.

"It is all real, and none of it," Norton replied. "For me, I'm afraid it's all I have. For you. . . ." His voice trailed off and he shrugged lightly. "We will have to see."

Something warned Berg that he must treat this man gently. For all of the other Norton's blustering threat, Berg sensed that this man was far more dangerous.

"Did you call me here too, then?" he said.

Norton sipped his coffee. "In a way," he replied. "It would be more accurate to say I knew you would come, and prepared for it."

"Yes," Berg said. "Well, I'm feeling very fragile at the moment. Is there anything you can do about that?"

"Some," Norton told him gently. "You are the key to many things. I have to be careful."

Berg let the words form as precisely as he could. "Can you tell me why?"

"Yes," Norton said. "As I perceive all this, your role is to save my world. Certainly you are valuable to me. So I must be very concerned that you do not break."

OZZIE HAD ARRIVED with enough souvlaki to feed the Greeks at Marathon. Later, when nothing was left but a few wilted lettuce leaves, she poured the last of the retsina into two jelly jars.

"You think there's some decent plates and cups and shit in all this garbage?" Calley asked.

"Beats me. It was pretty much like this when I moved in," Ozzie told her.

"You've kidding—you bought it like this?"

He grinned sheepishly. "Well, I'd always wanted to have my own junkyard."

"Oh," she said weakly.

Ozzie took his glass and stood up. "There's a good show on tonight," he said, scratching the back of his head as he wandered to the wall by the front door. He reached up and unrolled an ancient liquid-crystal screen three meters square. "This sucker isn't holo, but the picture's still pretty good."

Calley regarded him carefully. "Good show? What the fuck are you talking about?"

He ignored her and fumbled for a moment with the controls. The screen suddenly came alive with a clear, sharp picture. It took her a moment to figure out what it was.

The point of view was from high above a large open space surrounded by miles of domes. It was night. Stars gleamed in the vast clear bowl of the sky. She stared at the screen. The open space resolved into a compound of some kind, an area crowded with large, boxy buildings. There was something familiar. . . .

"What is that shit?" she asked.

He shrugged. "Double En R&D," he replied. "You've been there. Still are, as far as it goes."

"What's going on?"

She was suddenly frightened. That was *her* body down there. That the Lunies were close enough to beam a picture of the locale into her data construct meant the operation was proceeding. Fine and good—she had done the planning, had in fact demanded that they carry out the strike. It had to be done. But her body, her flesh, was at risk there.

"Jeez, Ozzie—it's gonna come down now."

He nodded. "You bet," he said.

"What happens if I get hurt?"

"Don't worry," he said. "They hired the best for this deal."

She moved closer to Ozzie, needing his warmth. In the sky above a star grew suddenly, painting the night with light.

The viewpoint changed suddenly, and they found themselves watching the action unfold from a vantage point about the level of human eyes.

"Minicams?" she asked.

"Uh-huh," Ozzie said. "The first pics were from the mothership."

Now sound flooded the room. Heavy breathing, and the clank and chink of metal muffled by leather. A figure swam across the screen. It appeared to be male, its head enclosed in a rounded helmet and opaque faceshield. The man's heavy jacket shone dully. She recognized the garment: cutting edge amalgam of Kevlar III, with a tailored silicon fiber overlay and reflective coating. In theory, it was proof against both conventional slug weapons and portable lasers.

The flare overhead painted the blockhouse behind the chainlink fence in sharp-edged shadow. Three guards piled through the door, racing for the fence. In the distance, growing rapidly near, she heard dogs barking.

Somebody—a woman's voice—shouted, "Over here over here over here!"

A metallic, spidery, and preternaturally quick little machine scuttled in behind her, racing the first man for the gate.

Two explosions, fiery blooms with actinic hearts, grew suddenly at the fence. One of the guards pinwheeled out. His right arm was missing.

"Now now now!" the woman yelled.

"I heard you, sister," a masculine tenor panted. Their point of view surged forward, as the attacker who carried the camera which broadcast the scene suddenly moved to join the firefight.

Bursts of straightline light, green and orange, so short-lived they were seen only as a fading track on the retina, began to slice up the night. Overhead, the flare sputtered out. Another exploded, and Calley saw the gate was now off its hinges. Three figures in Double En whites lay crumpled at the edges of the blast area.

"Okay," the mellow tenor said, "straight in, now. Straight in and . . . on the mark. Go!"

The blacktop road showed the teeth of its hidden tank traps, but several of the metal spiders clambered quickly through and over them. She recognized the exotic machines: cybernetic heavy lasers, engineered for jungle work. Or lunar modifications of the original pattern. One of the deadly things paused, the cannon in its center swiveling like the head of a cobra.

Orange light bloomed. A corner of the blockhouse exploded.

Sirens. Off to her left, someone was screaming. White figures began to dot the ridge behind the guard station.

She heard the soft hiss of a ground car. As the spider-cannon finished reducing the tank barriers to rubble, the big machine eased up and over the wreckage, figures clinging to its armored sides.

Her soldier ran forward, grabbed hold and yelled, "Punch it!"

Confused gabble. ECMs were coming down now, fuzzing the radio messages with static.

"Team—ber three, hold and—guardhouse," the man said. "One and—with me!"

They roared over the hill, and roared straight through the platoon of guards positioned there.

"Somebody get that fucking blaster," the woman's voice shouted.

Two of the spider-cannons focused on the emplacement dug in beside the road, bracketing it with intersecting lances of incandescence. The defender's strongpoint blew in a sudden shower of sparks.

Darkness.

"Okay, now," the man's voice said calmly. "We're through. It's single track to the objective. Quick and hard. They can't bring up anything heavy in time."

Hidden by darkness, a dog suddenly howled, went silent.

"Two minutes and counting . . . ." the woman said. "Toshi, there's a couple of ground cars heading this way."

"Fuck—okay, Sadie, take a squad and slow them down."

"Balls—I'll stop them!"

"So stop them," Toshi replied.

Calley turned to Ozzie. "Toshi?" she said.

"I told you they hired somebody good," he replied.

On the screen, the raiding party ghosted past a group of low, white buildings. Shadow figures ran there. One of the buildings showed light from its windows. Calley recognized the cafeteria, and the small park in front of it. Suddenly the row of windows exploded. The lights went out.

The scene began to break up, as whoever was monitoring shifted viewpoints from one camera to another.

At last they were running down the hall toward the tank room. The camera had shifted to infrared, and the translation factors painted everything in flat, eerie shades of brown and orange and yellow.

The tank room door was locked. Toshi stepped up

and slapped a gob of plastic explosive to the jamb. The screen went black for a moment. When the picture returned, Calley saw the tanks themselves. A terrified technician stood nearby with his hands over his head.

Two of the invaders began to strip equipment from their packs. A third swiftly undogged the latches on two of the coffin-like containers.

Calley stared at her own form, unmoving, eyes closed, in the first tank.

"Be careful, you assholes," she breathed softly.

She noticed that the holotransfer band was no longer around her head. The two raiders gently lifted her from the tank and swiftly placed a respirator over her face. Then they strapped on a field heart pump and carefully lifted her to a stretcher. They repeated the process with Berg's body.

The viewpoint shifted back to Toshi. His breathing was heavy, and had a ragged edge to it, but, amazingly, he was humming a snatch of a tune, over and over.

"When the saints. . . ."

He stopped. "Okay, children, let's get them home."

Again a shifting kaleidoscope of scenes. Something huge settled on a pillar of fire next to the tank complex. Quickly the raiders handed the unconscious bodies of Berg and Calley into waiting hands, then climbed aboard.

Closing swiftly, Calley heard the beat of helicopters.

"Get the fuck *out* of here!" somebody shouted.

They did.

Finally, his face distorted by G forces, Toshi held a hand mirror up in front of his face. Calley stared into his black, dancing eyes.

"Hiya, kiddo," he said. "Bet you didn't expect to see me. . . ."


"Motherfucker," Ozzie said.

She found that her hands were aching claws. She had gouged deep cuts in her palms with her fingernails. "They made it," she said. Her voice was dull and flat.

"Yeah," he agreed. He sounded shaky with the aftereffects of an adrenaline rush.

Slowly she unkinked her body, stood up, and stretched. "Ow. That hurts." Her vertebrae cracked audibly, one by one. A momentary wave of dizziness made the room swim around her. She waited till it had passed, then took a deep breath. She let it out.

"Well, what happens next?" she asked.

He stared up at her. "If they make it back, and if everything is okay with your body, then they'll try a transfer."

"That sounds pretty dubious," she told him.

"It was your idea," he reminded her.

She nodded. "Let's hope it's one of my better ones," she replied.

Dim red circle of light, like the crater of a volcano seen beyond the horizon. . . .

Slow pain.

Brightening now, sunrise, needles of flame piercing her eyes.

"No," she said.

They pushed the lid back, and she breathed.

Freeze-frame.

*One:*

White walls. Banked racks of exotic equipment. Mainframes. Data outlets, monitor screens. Overhead, a convex mirror, cloudy, out of focus. She heard the faint hum of air conditioning, gradually began to smell the flat, antiseptic odor of air filtered many times, so that the undertang of human sweat, and breath, was almost disguised.

*Two:*

Faces. A round, yellow face. Serious black eyes. Familiar. Another face, male, high-browed and unsmiling. Gray, worried eyes. A woman, her hair a red cloud. Deeply lined face, wide, competent lips. A scar.

Faint buzzing in her ears, growing louder, whining up the scale from deep subsonics into a piercing scream—

Cut off.

She blinked.

"Hi, guys," she said.

Her first surprise was that it was so *big*. For some reason she had expected Kennedy Crater to be a claustrophobic warren of endless, twisting tunnels and small, closetlike rooms, but the vast and airy caverns were welcomingly opposed to her expectations.

"Why not?" Doctor Wier said. "Tunneling is easy. The machines are cheap to operate, and this far down there aren't any sealing or shielding problems. We just let them keep chewing away. It's as simple to chew big holes as it is small ones. Makes for a psychologically better environment, too."

"That's for sure," she agreed.

They were standing on a small viewing area at the end of a wide, high-ceilinged tunnel which opened about halfway up the side of a huge cave. On their right a bank of elevators—a continuous series of steps attached to a constantly moving belt chain—whirred up and down. Lunies of every description clung to the small platforms, stepping off or on them with the ease of long practice. The elevators looked flimsy to Calley, but Ozzie said, "Don't worry. You get used to it real quick."

Down below was a large warren of unroofed construction. "No rain to worry about," Wier had told her cheerfully. It was mostly workspace; private housing tended to burrow into the walls of the caverns or be roofed over for seclusion.

"Come on," Ozzie said. "Let's go down."

She gritted her teeth, smiled faintly, and copied the way he leaned over and took a handhold on the moving chain, stepping onto the platform with an economical movement.

"Okay?" he asked as they swept downward to the floor of the cave.

"I'm fine," she told him. "It's almost fun. Makes me feel like I'm flying. A little bit."

"Low grav," he reminded her with a grin.

She stumbled at the bottom, and Doctor Wier caught her under her elbow as he stepped off the elevator. "You'll get used to it. Everybody does," he said.

"I'm gonna have to," she replied. "Looks like I'll be here for a while."

He smiled a short agreement and pointed toward a cluster of buildings not far from the wall of the cavern. "Over here," he said. "We can walk it."

The three of them set off tramping across the floor of the huge cave, Ozzie and Wier moving with long-strided elegance, Calley more awkwardly as they both held onto her.

The room was sparsely furnished: one large round table, chairs, a couple of data remote stations on either side of the open doorway.

There were five techs seated around the table when they arrived. As Calley entered the room, they all stood and applauded. She grinned at the reception. "Am I a hero, then?"

"Heroine," Wier corrected.

As soon as they were settled, Wier started talking. He seemed the designated spokesman for the group, which was content to let him carry the burden of the conversation.

"It was Ozzie's new designs which let us pull this off," he said. "A real breakthrough."

She nodded. "How so?" she asked.

He glanced at the dog-like face of the man next to her and smiled. "We were able to modify his hardware, and more important, his programming, so that we could insert an awareness into the machine space much more efficiently than the Double En process." He paused. "In fact, we really didn't know that machine space—the metamatrix—itself existed. Our matrix had given us a lot of anamolous data—but we weren't able to understand it until Ozzie gave us a whole new paradigm."

"You get a patent on this shit, Oz?" Calley asked.

He grinned. "Filed nationally, internationally, and here on the Moon," he told her.

"Good," she replied.

"Our matrix picked up your and Ozzie's activities there," Wier told her. "That was how we made the connection with him. Unfortunately, that was after you'd already accepted Double En's commission and gone to their research compound."

She stared at him. "Why 'unfortunately'?"

"Because what has happened has complicated matters immensely," Wier told her. "We've got Berg's body, but his awareness is in their matrix."

She looked at her fingers. Been biting my nails too much, she thought sadly. "We're gonna get him out, though," she said.

Wier's expression turned grave. "Maybe," he said. "We'd better. If we don't, Double En's matrix is going to achieve absolute control of the metamatrix. And it's crazy as a bedbug."

Calley regarded him calmly. "Not to worry," she replied. "Berg is data in that matrix, right?"

"Essentially true, yes," Wier said.

"Well, that's what I'm good at," she told him. She felt Ozzie stir slightly.

"What's that?" asked Wier.

"Armed robbery," she replied. "At that, I'm the very best."


"Toshi, you old sonofabitch," she said. "I never got a chance to thank you."

They were in a Lunie bar. She noted that the imperatives of function seemed to impel design even on the Moon: battered tables, a flashing Michelob holo, and a bartender with the personality of an exhausted used car salesman who dispensed booze and stale jokes in monotonous rhythms without ever looking at a customer.

"No problem, kid," Toshi said. "Happy to help."

"Nakamura told me they brain-scrubbed you."

Toshi grinned. "They tried. There was some stuff in

my skull they didn't understand, though. They ignored it and the scrub wasn't entirely effective."

"Yeah? So what happened?"

He shrugged. "A team of Lunie rowdyboys busted me loose. Double En didn't have me in a high-security area. I guess they figured I was harmless."

She glanced at his right hand. It appeared as normal as his left.

"What about the old mitt?" she asked.

"Nice stuff," he replied. "State of the art. I might have done it on my own, if I'd known."

She looked at the two of them. "You know that Berg is gonna be a problem, right?"

Ozzie said, "You think so? Data is data, Calley. We crack their matrix and just suck him out. Is that gonna be real major?"

"You still don't understand," Calley told him. "We're not going to be just fighting their matrix."

"How come?" Ozzie asked.

"Berg's part of it now," she replied. "We'll be fighting him, too."

"How do you figure that?" Toshi asked.

"Their matrix monitored the tanks," Calley said. "If Berg's in there and functioning like he was supposed to be, he's gotta know by now."

"Know what?" asked Ozzie.

"That he's missing a body. And that, guys, is gonna make him nervous, don't you think?"

They stared at each other.

"I know it sure as fuck did me," she said.

## 21

**H**E CAME AWAKE, uncertain whether the distant wailing was part of a forgotten dream, or reality intruding on his carefully structured plans once again. He sat up slowly, blinking sleep from his eyes.

Yes.

The thin, distant keening was still there, a ghostly sound diluted by night.

"Shit," Shigeinari Nakamura said, groping for his bedside lamp switch. Batted it, blinked again as light burned his eyes shut again. He waited until the reddish-yellow afterimage subsided, his teeth set in frustration. Somebody had undoubtedly fucked up again. It offended him, grated on his innate sense of order, mocked him with the necessity of reliance on fallible humans and crotchety machinery—not to mention a schizophrenic, alcoholic computer—to achieve the simple, clear goals he had first envisioned as a child: wealth, order, serenity.

Except for the first, all foreign to the world of the round-eyes. Or so it seemed.

The crimson alarm light on his comm monitor began to flash, bathing his angular features in harsh, bloody shadows.

"Shit," he said again, and heaved himself out of bed. He put on a raw silk robe, relishing the smooth, slick feel of it against his skin. Pushed his fingers through his hair and padded out into his office.

Here at least three silent alarms pulsed stridently, their red and orange beacons transforming the room into a maze of hunched, strobing shapes. As he entered the room, overhead lights began to glow brightly and the warning lights shrank to pinpoints flashing from various telltales on his desk. He moved quickly to roll back the desktop and pop up his screens.

"Report," he said.

The pictures were sharp and hard. Frederick Oranson's face, stiff with strain, filled the left-hand monitor. "What the fuck's going on, Oranson?" Nakamura said. His voice was absolutely steady. Whatever his inner fears, centuries of samurai breeding assured that nothing in his tone or demeanor would betray him.

The security man's voice was thick with lack of sleep, but his language was precise. "Three minutes ago, a raiding party of unknown size and origin began an attack on this compound," Oranson said. He glanced off-screen. "Pictures coming in now, sir. Please wait for resolution."

Nakamura turned to the middle screen, which crackled with random light, then cleared into a dim, fuzzy picture. As he watched, a horizontal line scrolled rapidly down the monitor. Above it, as the computers cleaned up the information, the picture settled into easy recognition, although the illumination of the scene had an eerie blue overtint.

The videocam was focused on the main road leading into the facility. Nakamura watched as the distant, shaded figures, their ranks crisscrossed by the hard, colored light of defensive lasers, followed their squad of mechanical spiders and the huge ground-effect armored car deeper into the complex.

The picture shuddered suddenly, shaken by a distant explosion. Nakamura felt it as the familiar, faint rumblings of earthquake, and throttled down his atavistic fear.

"Who are they?" he asked Oranson.

"We don't know. Later," Oranson replied harshly. "We stop them first." His lips were drawn back from his teeth in the beginnings of a snarl. "I'll post you as I'm able."

"Yes," Nakamura replied. Whatever he thought of Oranson personally, the man had been hired because he knew his job. Nakamura decided to let him get on with it.

He sat in his office and watched as the invaders breached the inner defenses and came roaring up the main road toward the middle compound—the tank room, his apartments. Explosions shook the room, caused the scenes on his monitors to jump and shift. Nakamura watched silently. When it became evident that the raiders would not be stopped before reaching their objective, he stood up, turned, pushed a hidden latch in one of the bookcases behind his desk, and waited as it slid smoothly back to reveal a small elevator. He entered and dropped two hundred meters into bedrock. As he descended, he was aware of blast shielding thudding home in the shaft above him. The small room at the bottom of the shaft had its own power and air, and rode on pneumatic bags inside a shell of hardened concrete. He'd had it designed to be proof against nuclear threats; it would suffice to protect him from this.

As the thick airlock door clunked shut behind him and the maglock bolts slid into their deep receptacles, he settled himself into a beautifully carved primitive American rocker and began to wait. He could access information from this nerve center, but he made no move to switch on any monitors.

The invaders would, or would not accomplish their objective, but he would survive this raid.

Vengeance could come later.

The security control room reverberated to a bedlam of incoming messages. Frederick Oranson sat in a padded chair in the center of it, an island of tight-lipped calm, speaking softly into the vocal pickups on the half-circle of screens where he followed the action, marshaling his troops, directing his fire.

"Tango Zulu three," he said softly, "approach fire zone Baker, on the mark. Go."

He turned, and motioned to a tech who stood behind him. "Anything on computer ident?" he asked.

The technician immediately turned and went to a monitor against the back wall. Oranson listened to the sudden whir of a printer with half his mind; the main focus of his attention remained on his screens, and the ever-advancing raiding party.

It was almost humorous. Nakamura-Norton was one of the most powerful conglomerates on the face of the earth, vastly stronger than all but a few countries. He had at his command armies of mercenaries, the most modern weaponry, unlimited funds. But against a strike like this, the giant corporation was peculiarly helpless.

The research facility, situated near the fringe of a major American city, was somewhat limited in the kind and effectiveness of its weaponry. Certainly no city council would allow him the type of armament he could bring to bear on an emerging African nation. Nor was it considered necessary to have that sort of firepower. When the corporations waged war, it was by unspoken agreement never carried out so crassly, or so near their vulnerable hearts. Armies might clash, but they would be proxie armies in faraway places, warring for control of natural resources or puppet governments. In places like Chicago, Tokyo, and San Francisco, the battle was of a different kind: shadowy, silent, played out in darkness, with information as the prize. Soldiers fought with esoteric electronics, money, and the occasional hidden knife.

Against terrorists, the facility was deemed secure. The ragtag bands of fanatics which still bombed for their eccentric, passionate causes were a problem, but one that could be controlled in the course of normal operations. Yet against a large party armed with articulated laser cannons and armored tanks, protected overhead by a shadowy mothership which had already fried three of his helicopters on the ground, Oranson could do little more than marshal his ground forces and try to slow down the invaders until reinforcements could be brought up from other, more secret facilities scattered outside the great city.

Four minutes into this episode, he was growing afraid that he wouldn't be allowed the time.

"Not much, sir," the tech said, returning with a sheaf of hardcopy in his hand. He extended the pictures to Oranson, who began to scan them. "As you can see, they're wearing body armor and face shields. We can't get anything much except general shapes. Though—" He reached forward and placed one finger on the print Oranson himself was regarding carefully. "—as you can see, this one doesn't fit a human template."

Oranson squinted his eyes. The picture wasn't very good, even rectified by computer processing, but he could make out the large bunches of muscle on the lower arms and high up on the back of the attacker's legs. Finally, he had it.

"A wolf," he said. "It's a goddamned wolf."

He returned the printouts to the technician. It didn't make a whole lot of difference at the moment, but afterward he would have a place to begin.

"Well," Nakamura said, "I suppose we'd better get started." He and Oranson were in his office. He sat behind his desk, again wearing a perfectly tailored black suit, his face smooth and unwrinkled. Oranson was slouched in one of the chairs in front of the desk. On the right side of his face a livid wound, covered with a gel bandage, snaked down from his ear and across his chin. A large patch of his blond brushcut was singed away, revealing raw, red flesh beneath. His left hand was encased in a lightweight cast.

The lights in the room were bright and harsh. The air smelled charred—hot and dry and laden with another, more fleshy scent: Burnt meat.

"How are you, Fred?" Nakamura asked. "Is any of that serious?"

Oranson shrugged. "Scratches and burns, mostly.

The hand will be okay within a week, the medics said."

"Good," Nakamura said. He glanced at the security man, and Oranson almost believed he recognized a species of grudging admiration in his boss's eyes. "You really shouldn't have joined in the defense of the tank room," he continued slowly. "That's what we have guards for."

"It seemed reasonable . . . at the time," Oranson said slowly.

Nakamura smiled suddenly. "I know. I wanted to kill a few of those fucks myself," he said.

Oranson nodded.

"Yes," Nakamura said. "You'd better give me the report, then."

The security chief said, "Well, you saw most of it. We get a final count of twenty-eight in the raiding party. They were very heavily armed—those laser cannon were state of the art. The mothership was a VTOL. General OmniDyne job, made for the Israelis."

Nakamura glanced up. "Do we have a track?"

"Over the pole," Oranson replied. "I doubt if it'll be much help. Our people are checking, but if we find anything more than a crater in the ground, I'll be surprised. These raiders, whoever they are, knew what they were doing. I don't see them slipping up on something like that."

Nakamura clicked his tongue against his teeth. "I was afraid of that," he said. He began leafing through a stack of printouts: final, computer-enhanced views of the engagement. He paused. "This one?" he asked.

"A wolf," Oranson replied.

"Which is?"

"Kids," Oranson told him. "They go in for weird muscle implants. A cult, more or less. Street people. Strong in Chicago."

Nakamura's eyebrows lifted. "Local? That's a lead, isn't it?"

Oranson nodded. "It will be. I'll follow up personally."

The Oriental came to the end of the pile, and paused again. This time, he hissed softly. "And this . . . ?"

"Yeah," Oranson said. "Berg's bodyguard. Toshi something or other. We snapped that in the tank room when he raised his shield."

Nakamura stared at the picture, his eyes dilated. "He escaped? Why wasn't I informed?"

"No priority," Oranson said. "Happened a while back, and the message was forwarded here. But since he was just hired muscle, nobody thought to rate it for my attention."

"Your department fucked up, is that it?"

Oranson exhaled slowly. "Yes, sir, if you want to look at it that way. I'm following up on that, too."

"Any chance of . . . inside involvement?"

"You mean Norton? Who the hell knows?" Oranson said, his voice thick with exhaustion. "We'll find out, unless he's gotten better at covering his tracks."

"Assume that he has," Nakamura said slowly. "All this," he said, contemplating pictures of broken bodies, tortured, strained metal, collapsed walls. "All this, and for what? What the hell does somebody want with Berg and Calley?"

"I don't know," Oranson replied. "Maybe the same thing we do."

Nakamura stared at him. He placed the printouts carefully on his desktop. "Or maybe not," he said. "Just . . . maybe not."

He flew back into a city shrouded in silver mists, his bodyguards flocked around him like bulky, watchful birds. A sharp wind bit at him as he strode quickly across the helipad atop the Double En tower. Down below, great walls of white fog bellied in off the lake, catching what light there was and reflecting it back to the low hanging clouds overhead. He felt trapped in some high, ethereal world, moving in a fantasy plane between earth and heaven.

A day the gods weep, he thought as he entered the

express elevator to his office, shedding anonymous musclemen like drops of rain.

The great room was quiet. He paused, staring at the rock garden—in this light, slow and tinted like an ancient, tarnished photograph. He saw perspectives of distance and mystery in the raked sand, the rocky islands, that he'd never before perceived.

He stood a moment longer, frozen in a tableau of reflected memory, savoring and mastering the fear locked in that instant of time, then shook himself.

The kickstarted seconds slowly ground into the present. He moved to the special bank of monitors and keyed in the codes only he knew. Then he waited.

"You look different," he said.

The great, florid face regarded him calmly, its sweep of streaked and silver hair framing eyes the color of the day.

"I wondered if you'd get around to calling," Norton told him. "Have you figured it out yet?"

Nakamura nodded his head slowly. "I think so," he said. "You've got them now, Berg and Calley?" As he said this, he thought he detected a momentary flicker of uncertainty in the sudden movement of Norton's eyes.

"Yes," Norton said. "You can't use them against me any more."

"Was it you? Did you set up the raid?"

Norton shook his head. "You give me too much credit," he said. "I'm not as dangerous as you think I am."

For the first time in many hours, the small Oriental laughed. "Bill," he said, when the harsh sound had lost itself in the silence of the room, "you can't shit a shitter. What would you do if it was me inside the matrix, and you here?"

Norton grinned at that, his large teeth flashing whitely. "Blow the damned thing up," he said.

"Well, you've fixed it so I don't have that option,"

Nakamura replied. "Maybe you fixed it that way from the beginning. I think you probably did, didn't you?"

Norton stared from the screen at his partner. "Did you call just to chat, Shag? On the unfairness of things?"

Nakamura shook his head. "No, partner of mine. I called to make a deal. You remember Arthur Kraus?"

"Sure. Little German bowling ball? Mean?"

"That's the one," Nakamura agreed. "I think it's time to put down the guns, Bill, and talk a little trade."

"So, talk," Norton said.

Carefully, his life and company riding on the outcome, Nakamura did.

Frederick Oranson glanced sharply around as he approached the small apartment building on Ogden Street, in Denver's Capitol Hill area. The neighborhood had once been elegant. Now unpainted houses rubbed their peeling walls against buildings that had been condoed, sold, remodeled, sold again, until, like their tenants, they drooped beneath the weight of years and a long, bad trip down.

The night air was crisp and cold, with the breath of mountain winter on the slow breeze. A few streetlamps burned with halide harshness; one thin, hunched figure hurried past on the sidewalk below, a plastic bag of indeterminate contents slung carefully over a shoulder. He couldn't make out gender. The traveler's steps echoed sharply on the concrete.

He smelled garlic and heard the rustle of dry leaves. There was a rusty spot—dried blood, he decided—on the small stoop in front of the building's door. He scraped at it with the toe of his shoe, then tried the door.

The lock was a shattered memory; the door opened easily. He stepped inside, shutting out the wind and smelling garlic more strongly. Somewhere music whined. A baby began to cry. He pushed open the inner door, ignoring the savaged brass fronts of what once had been a rack of private mailboxes. In this neighborhood, he knew, there was little real privacy.

Unless, of course, you knew what you were doing. Money always purchased safety, provided you spent enough of it.

The apartment on the third floor opened easily to the magnetic key he took from his pocket. The front door looked as scarred and ragged as any other on the dim hallway, but it swung wide smoothly, and with a slow, graceful arc that betrayed its hidden steel core.

The interior of the room was sparsely furnished, neat and clean, and filled with stale air. He shut the door, crossed the room, and opened one window a crack. Pulled the drapes tightly shut, lit a cigarette, flipped on the single overhead lamp.

A brand new Double En comm center dominated the wall next to the window. He stood for a moment, puffing silently, then flicked ashes onto the floor. Found an ashtray in one of the kitchen cabinets, brought it to the sleekly modern screen.

Slowly began to key in codes purchased at great price.

The monitor flashed once, then steadied into a face: bald, white fringed head, thick neck, hard eyes.

"Talk to me," Arthur Kraus said. "It had better be good. We are tracing this now."

Frederick Oranson nodded. "I understand," he said. "I have information you need," he said. "And I need something from you."

## 22

"**W**HAT HAPPENED?" BERG asked finally. "Why are there two of you?"

The man Berg already privately thought of as the real Norton leaned back in his chair. The small restaurant was dim and silent, a place of shadows. Even the waiter seemed to have disappeared. With a start, Berg reached for his coffee. For a moment he had the uneasy feeling that time itself had stopped.

"You have to understand a bit of what I was trying to do," Norton Two said softly. His smoky eyes were opaque. He picked his words carefully, pausing after each sentence. "The techniques I used to build the first matrix were extremely experimental, but from the very beginning I anticipated the linkage I would eventually make. You see, the cancer came first, not the discoveries."

Berg nodded. "You knew you were dying, and this was a way out?"

Norton's lips tightened. "Not everybody had my resources," he replied. "Some of the techniques already existed, some were new. I worked toward a specific goal, and used what I needed. I didn't want to die, Berg—do you understand?"

Again Berg experienced an undefinable feeling of menace, of cold, concentrated will emanating from the man. "So you built the matrix with the idea of storing your personality in it?"

"That's right," Norton agreed. "Cryogenic storage

has never worked, and I didn't want to go to sleep, anyway. Mechanical methods simply didn't offer an alternative. For all our advances, Berg, no chip or combination of them suffices to contain all the data encased in a human brain. I was faced with a dilemma, then: flesh or sand." The older man glanced up at Berg, his eyebrows raised slightly.

"I don't understand," Berg told him.

"A rather poetic way of putting it," Norton said. "Chips are made of silicon—nothing more, really, than sand. I could either try to develop more efficient chips, or combinations with greater capacity—the thinking-box concept—or I could go the way of flesh. Brain tissue, to be precise. I didn't think I had enough time to take the first way. And much of my previous research had been directed at the second. All I needed was a breakthrough."

Berg watched Norton's eyes, saw the film of memory rise to cloud them in the dusky light, and his mind's eye pictured the man struggling, planning, working to evade the inevitability of his own death. He saw again the awful remains of Norton's physical body, and wondered if Norton had, even then, been driven by some kind of premonitory vision.

"Henrietta Lacks," Norton said.

"What?"

"HeLa cells," Norton said. "Back in 1961, a black woman in Baltimore checked into a hospital complaining of vaginal bleeding. She had a tumor, which was removed, although she later died. The cancer had metastasized too quickly. Later, some of those cancer cells were cultured. They turned out to be immortal—at least, the cells are still growing today. In fact, they had quite a problem in cell research during the eighties and nineties, because cultures all over the world became contaminated with HeLa cells in odd, sometimes unexplained ways. Those cells live forever, grow anywhere, and reproduce with unexpected rapidity. They were my breakthrough. I used a method of DNA transfer to get the kind of fast, uniform growth I needed in nerve cells. The matrix was the result."

At last Berg began to understand the monumental undertaking, the fantastic weave of fear and technology and greed into which he'd unwittingly been sucked. He could almost picture the entire resources of a great corporation being warped to the effort of preserving one man's mind. "What did Nakamura think about all this?"

Norton shrugged, grinning faintly. "Shag is a businessman, Berg. And a fighter. I went to him with my first neurotechnologies because I knew he would appreciate their value and put together the kind of corporate structure that would not only protect them, but make us both wealthy. He did that, and, without those efforts, I couldn't have done what I did later. So I suppose I owe him—no, I *do* owe him, more than I can repay. But I never trusted him, and I don't trust him now. Rather, let us say I understand him, and therefore I fear him."

"In other words, you didn't tell him."

At this, Norton laughed aloud. "Of course not. The matrix is the most powerful data processing construct in the world today, and it will make Double En incalculably wealthy. It was, shall we say, an easy sell. Shag moved heaven and earth to see I completed the project successfully. And why not? We've made a ton of money on it."

"But it was all for you, really," Berg said. "I still don't understand. Why are there two of you here, in this world of yours?"

"Three, now, Berg," Norton reminded him. "You're here, too."

The light in the room had grown dimmer still, until Berg felt very much like a disembodied viewpoint hanging in the dark, his attention focused on the other man's words.

"Why two?" he repeated.

Norton sighed. "I wasn't as smart as I thought I was. The transfer process—no sane man would have tried it, as experimental as it was. But I did, because I had no choice. The cancer was advancing rapidly. I had to bail out, as it were. But I didn't fully understand the mechanics of memory transfer—it didn't happen all at once. My unconscious went across first. The matrix was a blank. A tabula rasa. I—me—the man you are talking with—I am my ego. I came over last. My unconscious was already established here, and was hence in the more powerful position. A reversal of the normal order of things. My unconscious became conscious, in other words."

Berg raised the last of his whisky-laced coffee and swallowed it. The room was pitch dark, yet still he could see Norton's face shining in front of him. "You want to turn up the lights?" he said dryly. "It's easier for me."

"Oh. Sorry," Norton said. The room suddenly brightened. The waiter, Charles, returned, bearing a heavy silver coffeepot.

"More, gentlemen?" he asked.

Berg nodded, and pushed his mug to the edge of the table. "And some Bushmills, if you don't mind," he added.

"On the way, sir," Charles said, and marched off into the polished recesses of the room. He was back in a moment, carrying the familiar square, tan bottle on an intricately chased tray. "Will there be anything else?"

Berg smiled happily. "I don't know," he said, "whether I'm a ghost, or a dream, or the dream of a ghost, but the whiskey is wonderful."

Norton sipped at his newly refilled mug. "Be careful what you dream here," he said. "They have a nasty way of turning real on you."

Berg poured a large dollop of the Irish whiskey into his coffee, then glanced around the room to make sure it was showing no signs of fadeout again.

"Do you have to work at keeping this illusion going?" he asked.

"It's no illusion," Norton said. "The thing is, you interfere. It's all analogs, Berg. Remember, we are nothing more than complicated arrangements of data —all the information that makes up a human personality. What we do here is a kind of game: we create our world, and since we are its only judges, it is a real world as far as we are concerned. At the moment, you and I agree on what's real. Call it a consensual hallucination—we both inhabit the same brain, after all. But when our concepts clash, something has to give. Tonight, for instance, things just faded away until you pointed it out."

"So what you're telling me is I have an existence here independent of yours."

"It's a very big brain, Berg. Room for a lot of things."

In the background, the strains of Beethoven began to gently fill the room. The black coffee, the rich, aromatic taste of the whisky, the music, all combined to make Berg feel drowsy and comfortable. "I still don't understand why I'm here," he said. "Your alter ego, your unconscious—he told me he wanted me for a bodyguard. You tell me you arranged for me to get the chip. A lot of things have happened to me recently, none of them pleasant. My friends have been murdered, my apartment bombed, attempts made on me, as well. Did you have anything to do with all that?"

Norton shook his head. "No—no reason. Berg, that chip does more than let you talk to me. That's why it had to be programmed from the outside. I couldn't do it myself. Between the information it carries, and certain of your own talents, we can unify this brain— submerge my other Norton personality into a true subconscious again. For all intents and purposes, this brain is insane, as crazy as if a real human being was ruled completely by its unconscious. Childlike, operating on the emotions only, no real conscience or understanding of consequences. That is the Norton you first met—a willful, dangerous child. What do you think is locked up in *your* unconscious?"

Berg nodded, considering: scenes from lesser hell. "Not much I'd like out in the light of day," he said.

Norton raised his coffee mug in silent toast.

"So what," Berg said, "are these certain talents I have that are so valuable?"

"Bodyguard," Norton said. "Same thing the other Norton was talking about. You see, when we trigger off the programs in that chip you brought, he will fight me. The process takes a while to run. I will have to be defended during that time."

Berg toyed with his mug. "Then you really need me."

"I do," Norton said flatly.

"So you will have to pay."

Again that vibration of danger crossed the table in an almost palpable wave. "I am the only one who can ever get you back to your body," Norton said.

"Calley, too?"

He looked mildly startled. "Calley? What about her?"

But this time Berg didn't believe him at all.

Slowly the lights in the room began to brighten. Berg blinked. "What—?"

Charles came over. "I'm sorry, gentlemen, but we are closing."

Berg looked at Norton. The other man raised his shoulders. "I think we've talked enough for now. Maybe you should sleep on it."

The weave of the linen tablecloth made an interesting pattern beneath Berg's fingertips. "Yes," he said. "That's a good idea. For now." Slowly he stood up, suddenly aware that his right foot had gone to sleep, and his ass was sore. He winced. "Good night, then," he said.

"If you need me, just think hard. I'll be there," Norton told him. His demeanor had changed somewhat. That aspect of kaleidoscopic danger was no longer present. Berg stared at him for a moment, then turned away.

The street outside was dark and empty. Overhead, the pink haze of the city masked all but a few bright stars. He put his hands in his pockets and began to walk.

Behind him, the door to the restaurant creaked open, and a booming voice shouted, "Hey! You forgot to pay the fucking bill!"

Berg knew who that voice belonged to, so he didn't turn. "You're rich," he said bitterly. "You pay it."

When he got back to his condo, Berg flicked on all the lights. He'd had enough of darkness. He didn't bother resetting all the security devices. Who could hurt him here? It was his world. Then he paused. Perhaps Norton could not exert control, but he might be able to invade. He had no idea what rules governed the interactions of the personalities inside the matrix.

"Shit," he said softly, and went through the ritual of activating the various alarms and defenses. Then he padded into his bedroom and flopped down on the bed. The miniature clock-holo belched cheerful smoke rings at him. The little engine that could, he thought wryly. Not like me.

Dreams. Flesh and sand, he thought. Who is lying to me?

The answer was a ghost. Everybody. Where is Calley? Where is my body? How do I find out? What do each of the Nortons really want? Why is it so important the two of them are reunited? What is Shag Nakamura doing about all this?

Am I even alive?

He shook his head. It was too much. The remark Norton had made, that everything was an analog, gave him the shred of an idea. He sat on the edge of the bed and took off his clothes, then lay back down.

"Lights off," he said, and obediently the room was

suddenly filmy with reflected light from the undraped windows.

He put his hands under his head. The idea grew the beginning of gossamer wings.

All right, he thought, okay. But first, sleep.

No:

Oblivion.

He climbed out of the shower and combed his hair and put on a faded pair of jeans and a thick sweater with a hole in one elbow. When he went out into the living room, he found Shag Nakamura sitting on the sofa, cradling a mug of steaming coffee in his hands.

"You sleep late," Nakamura told him.

Berg stared at him. "What are you doing here?"

Nakamura shrugged. "Later. Coffee first." He filled another mug from the Melitta pot sitting on a warming pad on the Lauren table.

"You're not real," Berg told him.

Again, that fatalistic shrug. "It's your game, Berg," he said. "So I guess you wanted me here. Norton told you there was leakage among the personalities, didn't he? From the consensual hallucination?"

Berg took his mug and tasted the coffee. The dark, hot liquid soothed his throat. "I don't really know you," he said.

"Norton does," Nakamura replied.

"Oh."

"Call it an indirect way of picking brains, if you like," Nakamura said. "By the way, why do you drink Blue Mountain? It's terrible coffee. Snob coffee."

"I'm a snob," Berg told him.

"Right," Nakamura replied. "So, what do you need to know?"

"Shit," Berg replied. "I haven't got the foggiest. No—wait a minute. Can you think why Norton needs me? He said it was because I had to help him unify the personalities. Why would that be important?"

Nakamura stared at his mug. The morning sunlight

made the thin tracery of veins on the back of his hands stand out like a roadmap. His eyes were hooded. Berg wasn't at all sure he really wanted to see Nakamura's eyes. What if they were empty?

Be careful. Dreams have a nasty way of turning real. . . .

"Norton likes to pretend he's nothing but a scientist, but he knows the company as well as I do. He understands the business world. With two personalities warring for control, the matrix is crazy, right?"

"Uh-huh."

"Well, a crazy computer as powerful as the Double En matrix is a threat to the existing order of things, businesswise. There's too much the matrix can do—too much other companies couldn't allow. So maybe Norton's worried that somebody else finds out. I can think of several guys who'd only see one option."

Berg nodded. "Makes a weird kind of sense, I guess. What option?"

"Destroy the matrix," Nakamura told him.

"But you said it was too powerful—"

"Not against somebody chopping up the brain itself with an ax," Nakamura said. "That would pretty much finish the whole thing. Norton, too."

Berg felt his heartbeat accelerate. He hadn't exactly thought of that. Somehow, he'd always assumed that he would get out of this—but if the matrix itself were destroyed, then not much else remained.

"I think I'd be inclined to help prevent that," he said.

"Thought you would," Nakamura replied.

"Are you real?" Berg asked again.

Nakamura grinned. "Call me an interoffice memo," he said. "Sort of electronic mail."

When the little executive left, he didn't do anything fancy, like vanish into thin air. He simply finished his coffee, advised Berg to switch to a different brand, and marched out the front door.

Berg watched him go, noting that his automatic

defenses appeared to have little effect on the man. Well, maybe it was because Nakamura had been his dream.

Analogs.

The idea had followed him into sleep. There were so many questions, so much he didn't know. He needed information. There was only one place to go for that. He turned and walked to his desk.

The matrix was supposed to be the most powerful computer in existence. Berg stared at his touchpad, and then slowly began to type in the instructions that he hoped would put him in touch with the tank room at the Double En research facility.

He hoped somebody was on the other end of the line.

It was a beautiful night. Outside Berg's wall of windows, Lake Michigan glittered like a plate of spilled coins, a vast silent space filling the world to its horizon. A thick moon rode high above, illuminating thin tendrils of fog, like fox tails, across the face of the inland sea.

Berg checked to make sure that everything was ready. He had enough booze set out to incapacitate all of Napoleon's immortals. He'd called the order into the caterers early in the day, just after finishing with the computer.

He checked his chrono. They should begin to arrive soon. One more time around the room. . . .

The elevator alarm in the lobby sent a soft buzz into the room. He switched on some classical rock and went to open the door.

"Hi, Toshi," he said.

The party was fairly loud. Berg circulated, filling glasses, smiling, trying very hard not to betray the unreality of it all.

He stared at the familiar faces.

Toshi.

Calley.

Collinsworth, lanky and perfectly tailored, lounged on the sofa next to Marie, who was pushing his hand away. Aldocci, dark and taciturn, looked uncomfortable and out of place. Two wolves, relaxed and happy, resembled, despite their odd shapes, nothing more than kids out for a good time.

Finally he waded into the middle of room and held up his hands for silence. Gradually, the noise faded. When everybody was quiet, he grinned and said, "You're probably wondering why I called you here today. . . ."

**23**

THERE WERE THREE main caverns in Kennedy Crater and kilometers of tunnels radiating from them. Calley didn't mind the central caves that much, although for some odd reason the vast enclosed spaces made her nervous. But the low gravity made her feel, in the tunnels, as if she were in one long continuous stumble down Alice's rabbit hole. Perspectives changed as her body stubbornly refused to admit it was no longer where it had been designed to be.

"Damn," she muttered, reaching out for Ozzie. He loped beside her, grinning. The gravity change and the peculiar, half-fall, half-glide style of movement didn't appear to bother him at all.

"Really, darlin', you'll get used to it. Honest."

She gritted her teeth and tried not to think about her rebellious lower extremities. "When?"

"Any day," he said soothingly.

Finally they came to the smooth, blank door which marked her apartment. She pressed her palm to the lock and the door slid back. As they entered, the lights came up bright. The large room was sparsely furnished: a remote against the left wall, a rickety steel table and two chairs next to it, and a pair of wire-framed easy chairs opposite a narrow bed on the opposite wall. Calley sank gratefully into one of the basket-chairs and grabbed hold of its cushion with both hands.

"Gravity," she said with relief.

"No, just stability," Ozzie grinned, flopping into the other chair. He cocked his big, wrinkled face to one side and regarded her quizzically. "You want to talk about it?" he asked.

"Talk about what?"

"What you're really gonna do," he replied. His eyes were like polished marbles in the folds of flesh surrounding them. Calley was reminded for a moment of an old nursery rhyme. Gingerbread man. She blinked, and the thought went away.

"Who says I'm gonna do something?" she asked.

Ozzie spread his big hands, palms up. "Calley, darlin', I know you. You've been awfully meek and mild through all this—getting jacked around by Nakamura, jerked up here, everybody telling you what they want you to do, and you just nodding and smiling and going along. Not like you at all, is it?"

She stared at him. The rough-finished walls of the room, coated with a polymer sealer, glittered dully. The temperature was slightly cool, and she became aware of the ever-present breathing of the air conditioning system. Somehow it was like being trapped in the bowels of a giant stone beast.

"Ozzie, can you think of any reason why I should trust you?" she said slowly.

He looked hurt, but he thought about it. Finally he shook his head. "From your point of view, I guess not," he said.

She kept her green eyes on his face. "How about these Lunie bozos? What do you know about them, really? Would you turn over your bank account to this Wier guy? Give him the key to your house?"

He shook his head again, this time more emphatically. "Then why the fuck did you give him your box?"

The answer came quickly. "They told me it was the only way to get you out of there," he replied.

Her expression softened. "Ozzie," she said. "Oh,

Ozzie, I like your reasoning there, but . . . it wasn't the brightest thing you ever did."

He looked down at his feet, and she was reminded of a small boy caught with his hand in the cookie jar. "Sorry," he said at last.

She stood up, crossed over to him, bent down and kissed him. "Ozzie," she said, "maybe you just gave me the reason."

"Huh?"

"To trust you," she told him. She returned to her seat, brow wrinkled above the bridge of her nose. "What about this room?" she said. "How many ways do they have it kinked, you suppose?"

He shrugged. "Dunno. Do they have a reason?"

"Probably," she replied. "What this all looks like to me, *everybody* is scheming on everybody else. So let's go take a walk."

He unfolded his lanky frame from the chair. "Sure. Where to?"

She smiled. "I think it's time I really learned how to ride those elevators," she told him.

They shared the same small platform. She held onto the curved safety handle with both hands, and Ozzie held onto her. After a while, the dizzying strangeness began to pass and she felt as if she were riding some sort of gigantic amusement park attraction. "See the caverns of the Moon," she said. "Thrill to the exciting elevator ride."

He laughed. "Why this?" he asked.

"You think of any way to bug this thing?" she asked. "I figure even a big directional mike wouldn't be able to track us, especially if we face the wall. Lip readers, either."

He nodded. "A mike bead would be tough to spot."

"Right," she agreed. "If they knew which platform to gimmick. We've got, what—maybe two hundred here?"

He grinned slowly. "I think we're okay," he said.

"Good. Keep hold of me. I still don't like this crazy thing." She looked down at the floor of the cavern, watched the figures disembarking from the elevator and spreading away like insects scattering from a hill. Ozzie tightened his grip reassuringly.

She exhaled. "Remember when we first saw the metamatrix together?"

"Uh-huh."

"Well, you think about it, what was the weirdest looking thing in there?"

He was silent a moment. "I dunno. The meats, I guess."

"Yeah. And which matrix was the most screwy looking?"

"The Lunie's. All that bizarro stuff sticking out from it."

Calley nodded. "So what the fuck you think they're doing? They tell us Double En's matrix is dangerous. To who? Them? They come on dripping with altruism—save the world, all that crap. You believe it?"

She answered her own question. "Not much. Everybody has their own pot in this game, and what pisses me off, they're using me like another chip. Someplace, every once in a while, somebody says, 'Play the Calley chip,' and off I go again. You think I like it?"

Ozzie looked over her shoulder. Above them, two Lunie kids climbed about their own platform like a pair of monkeys, oblivious to the hundred-meter drop. "Not much, I guess," he said. "That's what I asked in the first place. How come you go along with it?"

"First, because after I took the Double En job, I didn't have much choice. When things got rolling, all I wanted to do was keep myself in one piece, survive until I got my own chance. The second thing, I didn't know what I needed to know."

"Which was what?"

"Where everybody keeps their pots stashed." She let go of the safety bar with one hand to brush hair from her eyes. "Ozzie, think about it. The players.

Double En, the Lunies, God knows who else. Somewhere in this mess there has to be a pot of gold. All I have to do is follow the rainbow."

His big hand massaged the small of her back. "So where's the rainbow?"

"It starts right here," she said. "That's one thing I'm sure of. The fucking rainbow starts here."

They paused for a few minutes at the top of the elevator run, on the wide staging area at the mouth of the tunnel, where they'd first entered the cavern. She pulled a ragged strand of hair down and began to gnaw it thoughtfully. "Get back from the edge," she told him. "We're stationary here."

"Right," he agreed, and obediently followed her away from the precipice.

They found a quiet spot just inside the tunnel. Lunies of various descriptions loped past, ignoring them.

"Sorry," she said. "I need a break from that overgrown stepladder."

He stepped in front of her, so that his body shielded her from the hurrying crowds of people. She was astonished that there were so many of them. Somehow she had always regarded Kennedy Crater as a primitive place, filled with a few lonely refugees from civilization: a hangover from the days when Kennedy was nothing more than a few holes in the ground, inhabited by the techs and engineers who supervised the tunnellers, the automated factories, and the magnetic rail launcher which hurled raw materials into near space for the construction of the great orbiting stations.

She paused for a moment, thinking. Yes. Almost twenty years since the Lunar incorporation. The consortium of governments and corporations that had built the beginnings of Kennedy had financed the project through immense stock issues. From the very first, the Lunie adventure had been a public company. What the Lunies had done was simplicity itself. As the profits began to flow in, first a trickle, then a flood—the drug returns had been enormous, by themselves—they began to buy back their own stock. Nobody had really noticed until, with the help of a genius-level stock manipulator, they engineered the biggest leveraged buyout in the history of stock trading. What was the guy's name? Schollander, something like that. He became the first chairman of the board, and before he stepped down the Lunies had paid off the entire mountain of junk bonds that financed the takeover. They took themselves private, and in the corporate scheme of things, they were called Big White, just as in forgotten decades IBM had ruled as Big Blue.

Luna Industries, Inc., was the largest corporation in the solar system, and Kennedy was home to thirty thousands citizens, each one a stockholder, each one a millionaire many times over.

"So *much* money," she mumbled softly.

"What?"

"Nothing. Just thinking out loud."

"You've got a plan, don't you?" he asked her.

She grinned. "Honeybun, I've always had a plan, just as soon as I figured out what kind of shit I'd stepped into. But you're gonna have to help."

"Uh-huh. I figured that much. You want to rip somebody off, right?"

She glanced at the figures rushing toward the elevator, searching for dawdlers, anybody paying more than ordinary attention to them. "You know what the Lunies say they want to do, right?"

"Sure. Go in, get Berg out of there, and fuck up the Double En matrix."

"Yeah. Suck Berg out of there like soup through a straw. And for that, they've got me designing the biggest straw I ever heard of. But you know what?"

"What?"

"You build that big a straw, maybe you suck more than soup."

"Oh," Ozzie said.

"That's right. If everything goes okay, I'm gonna punch a hole in that matrix big enough to drive the Moon through. And you know what else?"

He shook his head. "Ain't nobody gonna even try to come after me."

He stared at her.

She grinned. "Come on. Let's take another elevator ride."

Wier found them at the bottom of the elevator. "Hey, you guys," he called. "Where you been? I've been looking all over. Did you turn off your beepers?"

"I personally hate the damn things," Calley told him. "I've been learning to ride your elevator, and the last thing I needed was that nasty little alarm going off."

"Well," he said, "you really shouldn't, you know. What if I wanted to get in touch?"

That's the idea, Calley thought, remembering how she'd carefully placed the dime-sized silver instruments on the table in her room. They probably bristled with monitors.

"Sorry," she said. "I'll try to keep that in mind for the future. *Is* something going on, by the way? You look out of breath."

He shook his head. "I jogged over. I usually do. I don't get much exercise in my job, and even with the supplements, Lunies always chance some bone deterioration."

"So what's up?"

"Not much. I wanted to see if I could interest you in lunch."

Suddenly she was aware that her stomach had contracted into a tight little ball of starvation. "Could you ever," she told him. "Where to?"

He grinned, and it made him look like a sixteen-year-old kid for a moment. "Follow me," he replied.

The cafe was near the edge of the vast work area, an "open-air" place that featured several large, round tables shaded by Cinzano umbrellas. The last was an odd touch, for the cavern was mostly lit by the illumination of the workspaces. Its distant ceiling was shrouded in darkness. Nevertheless, she liked the bright brave colors of the big shades, and the whimsical red and blue stripes on the waiter's apron when he came to their table.

"Afternoon," the waiter said affably. "You folks want a cocktail to start?"

"Sure," Calley said, thinking of the umbrellas. "A *pastis* for me." Wier ordered Absolut on the rocks, and Ozzie asked for Kirin beer.

"You don't go in for a lot of automation, do you?" Calley observed, watching the waiter walk away.

"Sure we do," Wier replied. "You just don't see it everywhere, the way you do on Terra. Take Bobby, there, for instance."

"Bobby?"

"The waiter," Wier said. "You think he does this because he's a poverty case or something?"

She considered for a second. "You aren't structured that way, are you?"

Wier nodded, his face taking on a serious expression. "All Man needs is power and raw materials, and wealth becomes a given. We have lots of both: Bobby's last name is Schollander."

It took her a minute. "Wait a sec—like the guy that—?"

"Uh-huh. Bobby is his grandson. He dabbled in particle physics for a while, but got tired of it. He waits tables because he likes it, Oh—and he owns this place, too. Well, leases it from the company."

Bobby returned with their drinks, grinned cheerfully, and took their orders for lunch. After he had gone, Ozzie said, "Wait a minute. A guy that rich, he could do anything he likes. Have palaces on Terra. Whatever."

Wier shook his head. "He's a Lunie," he said.

"What's that mean?"

Calley broke in, "I think what the man's trying to tell us, Ozzie, is that no self-respecting Lunie would even think about living on earth. I'm not sure, but I think we are kinda regarded as poor, benighted barbarians by the folks up here. That right, Wier?"

The scientist smiled faintly. "Well, I wouldn't have put it quite that way. Let's just say that Bobby *is* doing whatever he wants, and leave it at that."

"Very discrete of you," Calley replied, but her grin took the sting from the words. "So, is this a working lunch, or you just want to slum with the savages for a while?"

Wier diplomatically ignored Calley's final shot and said, "A few things have come up. . . ."

"Like what?"

"Well, the raid caused a situation to come about that we'd hoped wouldn't occur. The possibility was always there, but our people rated it low-probability. It's high-prob now. Close enough to certainty that it doesn't matter."

"You like suspense or something? Spit it out," Calley said.

"Nakamura appears to be arranging an accommodation of some kind with Norton and the Double En matrix."

She knew, but she asked anyway. "Is that bad?"

Wier began to tap the fingers of his right hand on the tabletop. "As long as they were fighting each other, and trying to keep the whole thing secret, they were too busy to bother with the real potentials of their matrix," he said. "If that is no longer the case, then we have much less time than we thought."

Calley stared at his nervous, jumping fingertips. "How much time?" she asked.

He sighed. "Our wargamers have been working on the problem all day. They say two weeks, max."

"Yeah, and . . . ?"

"Before Norton is ready to use that chip Berg brought in with him, to attack our matrix here on the Moon."

Bobby returned with their sandwiches. Calley bit into hers, chewed, and swallowed slowly. "You're saying we'd better hurry, then."

Wier lifted his eyes to her face. "Unless you want to meet some of Nakamura's assassins personally," he told her.

"Not really," she replied. And took another bite of the sandwich to hide her sudden smile.

Later that day they practiced on the elevator again. Calley's face was close to Ozzie's right ear as he hunched over her protectively.

"I was hoping something like this would happen," she said.

"Like what?"

"An emergency situation. Maybe they don't think quite so well when the hammer's coming down."

"So?"

" 'Cause we're gonna have to do some off-brand stuff, and we'll have to convince them that it's the only thing to do."

A sudden, warm updraft caught at their loose coveralls. Calley pulled herself closer, clinging to Ozzie. "First thing is, we have to get back to Earth for a while."

She felt him stiffen. "Are you crazy?" he said. "Nakamura's people will latch onto us like cats on rats."

"Maybe not," she whispered. "That's another thing, by the way."

"What is?"

She squeezed his ribs tightly. "I know you've grown attached to that beautiful face of yours, but I think the time's come when you're gonna have to give it up."

He didn't say anything.

"You think you can build another metamatrix access box in less than a week?" she asked.

He moved slightly. "Maybe," he said.

Her voice tensed up a bit. "You better," she said. "When I come blowing into the Double En matrix with all the power of the Lunie meat behind me, you gotta believe a lot of goodies are gonna fall out, just like a piñata at a Spanish christmas party. And when that happens," she continued, "somebody'd better be there with a net."

Slowly the elevator approached the floor of the cavern. She glanced out, and saw two hang-gliders, like great, jeweled butterflies, drifting in and out of the updrafts.

"How come *my* face?" Ozzie asked slowly. His voice was thick and soft.

" 'Cause, buddy, *you* are the net, and at the moment, you are a little too conspicuous to get the job done. So. Are you in, or out?"

Again Ozzie was silent for a long time. Finally he said, "In. I'm in, Calley."

"Good," she told him. The elevator grounded and they stepped off. She patted his bony shoulder gently. "It'll be okay," she said. "Really. It will."

**24**

**I** T RAPIDLY BECAME one of the most difficult
conversations Nakamura had ever forced himself to endure, and that he did so testified more to the
strength of his will than the danger of his situation.

"First," Norton said, "before anything else, you
will have to stop trying to kill me."

"I've already indicated that is acceptable," Nakamura
said calmly.

"Right," Norton replied, "which doesn't mean a
goddam thing, you treacherous bastard. You've despised me since the beginning." He bit off the words,
a thick vein throbbing in his wide forehead.

Nakamura stared at him in puzzlement. Something
was very wrong here. It was like dealing with a five-
year-old child. Although he'd never particularly liked
Norton, over the years he'd developed a certain grudging respect for him, and honor alone had demanded a
peculiar but real honesty in their relationship. Now
Norton sounded as if he were recalling a time that had
existed only in his own mind.

The man really *is* crazy, Nakamura warned himself.

"Bill, that's not true, and you know it. But even so,
it's in the past. We've got to talk about today. Arthur
Kraus and the consortium represent a threat to both of
us. Even when we disagreed, we were able to put it
aside in the face of an attack on Double En. Well—for

me, the company is now at risk. For you, I think the stakes are even greater."

Norton shrugged. "The consortium has a matrix," he said. "That means they're vulnerable."

Nakamura raised his eyebrows. "Can you explain that?"

"I haven't been just dicking around in here," Norton replied. "Aside from dealing with all your sneak attacks, I've discovered several capabilities nobody realized a matrix in this situation would have." He shook his head. "No, I'm not going to hand out details, but I can say this: Kraus's matrix will not be a problem if we decided to take him out. I can burn the consortium to a cinder in nanoseconds. Their data processing capability, at least." Norton rubbed one side of his face. "I assume," he said dryly, "you could handle the more physical aspects of such an encounter?"

Nakamura nodded. "If the consortium doesn't have rapid data analysis, Oranson would make hamburger of their mercenary forces."

"Oranson? That blond thug who runs security?"

"Thugs make excellent security people," Nakamura said equably.

Norton grunted. He glanced offscreen for a moment, then turned his eyes back. "Well, I'm glad you trust him. Maybe you can tell me why he's making private, shielded calls to Arthur Kraus from some place in Denver, then."

Nakamura blinked.

"What?" he said.

"Your bully boy looks like he's selling you out, Shag," Norton said with relish. "Hope he's cutting a real good deal."

Nakamura's button eyes glittered suddenly. "Can you intercept the conversations?"

"Already have," Norton replied. "You want hardcopy?"

"If you please," Nakamura said.

The printer slot next to the screen hiccupped once,

then began to spool out sheets of paper. "Do you mind?" Nakamura asked.

"By my guest," Norton told him, grinning. Nakamura looked away from that grin.

"That sonofa*bitch*," he said softly, after he finished reading.

"Thugs make good security," Norton reminded him.

"Bill, you don't have to enjoy this quite so obviously," Nakamura said. "You have occasionally made mistakes, as I recall. And this isn't entirely unexpected. I've had somebody keeping an eye on Oranson for several days now. Half an hour from now, young Fred's indiscretion will be nothing more than a memory."

"You going to scrag him?"

"Of course," Nakamura said.

Norton shook his big head. Strands of full, silver-streaked hair flew up in a halo. He looked like a successful data net evangelist. "Shag," he said, "I thought you were the corporate snake. You're not thinking."

"What do you mean?"

"Why kill him? When we can use him instead?"

Nakamura's forehead wrinkled as his eyes slowly widened. "Yes . . ." he said finally. "Now that you mention it, I can see some possibilities with that."

"Thought you would," Norton replied.

Nakamura bowed slightly to the screen. "If you'll excuse me for a moment, I'll go and take care of that bit of business."

Norton smiled. "Get him back in one piece, would you?"

"Of course." Nakamura smiled in return. "In the beginning, at least."

Frederick Oranson stepped out of the Fox Tower at the corner of Market and Polk in San Francisco. Immediately, sharp gusts of wind from a cloudless blue sky whipped at his pant legs. San Francisco weather always disconcerted him; each little neighborhood, lovingly preserved, seemed to have its own weather. He paused on the broad sidewalk and adjusted his light overcoat, glancing toward the intersection with its jam of pedicabs and electric scooters, and saw him.

He knew the thick face, recognized the disfiguring scar that the man kept only because he enjoyed the permanently threatening look it gave him. The short, viciously chopped thatch of white hair. The eyes, small, red-rimmed, hungry in a vacant, uncaring way.

A dozen times in as many years, Oranson had seen that face: partially hidden behind the sights of a Signal Device portable tank smasher; moving briskly away from a man who lay on the ground, a pool of blood thick and gluey beneath the spot where the umbrella knife had cut his spinal cord; watching with bland impassivity the scene of an explosion which gutted an entire legislative building. The face was death.

Oranson let his gaze slide on past, turned, and began to walk up Polk. He knew the man was following. Oranson had no illusions: for him to meet Hanagan on a San Francisco street was not coincidence. His kind of death was never casual.

As he walked along, holding his coat closed against the wind, Oranson wondered who had hired the legendary killer. He remembered the secret calls he'd made. Had Kraus betrayed him? Or had Nakamura simply discovered his treachery in some arcane way? He shrugged mentally. It made no difference. The watchers were always watched.

He lengthened his stride slightly, turned at California and crossed Polk, walking up the hill toward the Van Ness Mall. Hanagan kept pace, making no effort at concealment, his short, muscled body reminding Oranson of a crocodile without armor. There was something heavily reptilian in the way the man moved.

Oranson realized that, rather than the terror he should be feeling, he was infused with a hard, manic kind of relief. Nakamura had caught him. That understanding was a sharp, brittle bit of certainty around which his tiny universe now revolved. Somehow Nakamura knew of his calls to Kraus, and his reaction was Hanagan, the inevitable killer. The only thing that puzzled Oranson was that he'd been allowed to see the means of his own death. Had Nakamura ordered that, a final, disdainful slap? Or was Hanagan so confident of his own skills that he preferred this final play, this brazen charade of cat and mouse?

That made Oranson angry. His chin rose slightly as he stepped down into the mall, turned right, and began to follow the endless chain of shops, boutiques, coffeehouses, ice cream parlors and vegetarian restaurants north toward the bay.

Oranson had spent six years in Special Forces, had resigned as much from boredom as anything else, and joined a crack merc brigade which did a lot of very wet work for Double En. As he threaded his way through the maze of gabbling salespeople, he decided that maybe, at last, the fabulous Hanagan might have made a mistake. Never underestimate the opposition.

He wondered if Hanagan had a team with him, or was working solo. By himself, Oranson decided finally. Taking out his own head of security wasn't something Nakamura would want to advertise. It compromised the whole organization, made it vulnerable in complicated, unpredictable ways. No, Hanagan would most likely be working alone. It was stupid, but the crazed Irishman's ego was supposed to match his rep.

Oranson reached into his coat pocket and took out a slap bomb, a thin, monomole reinforced glove with a sealed chunk of plastique embedded in the palm. The charge was shaped; its force would be directed away from his hand.

Smack that against the side of Hanagan's head and there wouldn't be any further problem. No more head, either.

He glanced at the dark face of a very slender, pretty Indian girl, and as he watched her eyes widen, he marveled at the eerie calm he felt.

He knew why she'd opened her eyes, and he turned, the slap bomb coming up in a slow, calculated arc that should barely sidestep the head blow Hanagan would most likely attempt.

Which it did, but the burly Irishman's head wasn't where it should be, either, and in one crystal moment of clarity Oranson realized several things: the oddly shifting lumps of muscle in Hanagan's broad shoulders weren't natural; the Indian girl was a marvel of attenuated motion as she raised her small, silver dart pistol.

Yes, Hanagan had brought a team.

Norton decided that today was going to be one of his better days. Breakfast had gone well. There had been no odd visitations, no fragmentary ghosts from his past. As his time in the matrix had lengthened like some chronic worm, he had begun to judge conditions by things that had not happened. Sometimes his world seemed thronged with unwanted memories. Dreams became real. Friends and enemies alike made strange appearances, threatening gestures, bizarre intrusions. His life had become an allegory.

Reality is what you make it, he told himself. Especially in the matrix. Yet he was always conscious of some essential lack of control, so that more and more often it seemed that reality was remaking him. It took increasingly stronger efforts to banish some of the disturbing apparitions which now plagued him, so that the phrase "It's only an analog" became an oft-repeated mantra, muttered under his breath while some outrageous synthesis of person and place flickered madly just at the edge of his vision.

Things were definitely getting out of hand.

Today Chicago looked pretty much as he remembered it, its towers thrusting into the sky like neon swordblades raised in perpetual salute. The morning fog had blown away early, and waves of anonymous faces surged past his alfresco table in front of the tiny sidewalk cafe. As he sipped his coffee and watched the hurrying figures, he was struck by a nagging feeling of familiarity, as if he should know these people, as if their names were on the tip of his tongue.

Suddenly, as it now seemed to do more often, a wave of anger crashed over him, leaving breakers of cold rage in its wake. He squeezed his coffee mug tightly, then blinked, as for one disconcerting moment he felt the hard shape of it shift and melt, as if the thick porcelain had become plastic and alive—but when he looked, it was just a coffee mug.

Nakamura wanted to kill him. Berg, his emissary, was the tool, the weapon selected for the job. But nobody understood his power here, realized that the matrix was his tool, his weapon, and with it he could defeat them all. Already he'd infiltrated the other matrices—that, at least, had been no lie. If Arthur Kraus and his consortium moved to destroy him, he would destroy them first. No modern company could survive without its data base, and he was fully prepared to lob the electronic equivalent of nuclear devices into their soft, unprotected brains.

He sighed, drained the last of his coffee, and looked around for his waitress. The pretty young girl, who vaguely reminded him of somebody else—he couldn't quite remember who—was nowhere to be seen, so he put a few coins on the table and stood up. Somehow the idea of coins seemed wrong. Was it a hangover from childhood, before credit chips? Did people still use money?

He shook his head and stepped out on the sidewalk, his face turned toward the Double En tower glittering in the distance.

He changed his mind at the last moment. He couldn't really say why. As he approached the bustling figures who popped in and out of the great building, a small boy caught his glance. The child was as strange, and as familiar, as an old friend seen after an absence of many years.

He stared at the boy. Four, maybe five years old. Filmy, blond-white hair, a baby color. Thin, sharp facial lines on an oddly shaped skull—something wrong there, lumpy and alien. But it wasn't those mundane aspects that imprinted the child on his attention like a sudden punch in the mouth.

As he picked up his pace, eyes still on the tiny figure, the boy raised his head and stared at him. Surprised, Norton let their eyes lock for an instant that was like touching a naked electric cable.

The boy smiled. His whole face broke into a leering, expectant, adult grin. With tangible effort, Norton tore his gaze from those eyes. Eyes the color of cracked rubies, dirty and knowing. . . .

He glanced away. When he looked again, the boy was gone. Was it only his imagination, or did he hear the sound of childish laughter, high and silvered, drifting in the air?

He shuddered. Once again he felt a definite emptiness at the very core of his being, as if some basic piece of foundation work was lacking there.

It was all tied up in his purpose, and for the first time he began to realize it might be something other than mere survival.

The thin gray man with the face of weathered stone watched this scene from a nameless place crowded with the tangible aspects of data manipulation. Half a hundred screens constantly fed him information from as many scenes. When Norton—he found it disconcerting to watch his other self—stopped, frozen solid by the childish apparition, he stared at that particular screen with gelid intensity. As Norton turned away, his florid features contorted, the man chuckled.

"Deal with it, monkey brain," he said. He tapped his bitten fingernails on the smooth, laminated top of his desk. Things were progressing. He turned away, a fan of lines like scars growing at the edge of his mouth. And what, he wondered, was Berg doing?

\*      \*      \*

Berg raised a thick-walled chunk of lead crystal and watched the rich, amber fluid within catch and refract the light. It was a pretty question.

Did these people, these happy, chattering ghosts, have any validity? Of course he could talk with them, laugh with them, turn his back and listen to their voices, but were they anything but himself in different clothes, his memories of them, his ideas of what they were?

It struck him as ghoulishly absurd that three of them were truly ghosts. He wished he could simply ask Collinsworth who had killed him, or Marie—her death had been violent and personal, not the work of some remote and mechanical hand. Could she describe the faces of those who'd forced her on that last long, screaming trip down?

Perhaps. Perhaps she would answer. But it would be a lie, he told himself. The absurdity: no one will tell the king about his new clothes, because the king was everybody, and everybody was naked.

They would serve, though. All analogs, he reminded himself. The dream of flesh and sand. Something in his heart pulsed coldly, implacably. He was tired of being pushed around. Here were his troops. The chill center demanded an end—here and no more.

Time to draw the line.

The mad Norton stared at the high, baronial doors of his office, wondering if anything existed on the other side but chaos. He set his machines to search for Berg. It was a terrifying feeling, as if there were a hole in his brain. Everything in the matrix was his—had been, until Nakamura squirted in Berg's persona like an injection of acid. Now part of the matrix was no longer under his control as the molecules which constrained Berg settled into the structure of the brain itself.

After a while he found the party, and watched with interest as Berg circulated through his guests. Automatically, his programs identified them.

Collinsworth.

He stared at the lanky, competent-looking man, and once again what he'd come to regard as a central puzzle rose to confront him.

Who had killed Collinsworth?

As Berg talked to her, he was again impressed by the inventiveness of his own imagination. She seemed unchanged, bright and sparkling and utterly feminine, yet he knew she'd killed at least eight men with her own hands.

"Good party?" he asked.

"You bet," Marie replied. Her dark, curly hair, cut in a short, intricate style that accentuated her wide, innocent blue eyes, bobbed with the force of her reply. "You know me, Berg. Pour the booze and bring on the men. I'm a simple soul—it doesn't take much."

Behind his grin, memories of happier times crowded against each other. He and Marie had met under novel circumstances—she'd been trying to kill him—and, surviving that meeting, had gradually evolved the kind of friendship professionals often develop, based on mutual respect and paired understanding of the peculiar necessities of their trade.

"Well, I got plenty of booze," he told her. "The men—that's up to you."

"Wouldn't have it any other way, Iceman," she said, chuckling.

He nodded, poignantly twisted by the personal spin she put on his code name. Ice? Was that how she regarded him? Or how he regarded himself?

He glanced over at Calley, saw her chatting happily with Toshi in a corner, then looked down at the woman in front of him. He was beginning to put together final answers, but a central piece remained a mystery.

Who had killed Marie?

Nakamura ran over the assembled data one more time. Next to his right hand a tea service waited, and he longed for a soothing cup, but he wouldn't allow himself the pleasure until he'd finished trying, one more time, to put the pieces together.

Norton had changed. The activities of the matrix were growing more unpredictable, and the sight of Norton's heavy, glowing features unsettled him. The man was slowly changing into something primal, something bestial that raised hackles on the back of his neck.

Who had raided him and stolen the bodies of Berg and Calley? Norton denied it, but could he be trusted?

Kraus? The German was capable of it, but the action didn't strike him as characteristic: given full knowledge of the situation, Arthur would simply have slipped a pocket nuke into the complex. Not that it would have done any good—because the matrix itself wasn't there.

More of Norton's prescience? Nakamura had argued for locating the actual chicken brain in the same complex as the tanks, but Norton had refused. For security reasons, he said. And, indeed, those very few technicians who had real knowledge of the location had disappeared mysteriously. Nakamura suspected that he might be the only living human who knew the location, and that made him nervous, too.

Finally, at the beginning—who had suggested using Berg and Calley as a weapon against Norton? He recalled Oranson's face as he'd laid out the plan. So logical at the time. But his security chief had betrayed him to Arthur Kraus. Perhaps, also, to someone else?

He decided that when Hanagan delivered Oranson's unconscious body to him, he would have many questions. What were their names?

Yes. Who killed Collinsworth, Aldocci, Marie?

The thin, gray man set his machines to work on the complicated processes that would allow it to happen. His face was stiff and carved with strain. It was so hard, this, but so incredibly necessary.

The room buzzed with the sounds of his effort. More than at any other time, he was conscious of manipulating the actual matrix itself. All these machines were dreams; his own personality and knowledge ordered the flesh in the end.

He rubbed his eyes and settled back in the chair. For a moment his attention almost wavered, but then he saw the door across from him slowly begin to open.

When he saw the small figure there, he stood. "Ah," he said.

The child grinned, and turned a gaze of crystal and blood on him. "Yes," the boy said.

The sound of it made the gray man's ears hurt.

## 25

"**T**OSHI, COME HERE. I want to talk to you," Berg said.

The deceptively corpulent Oriental nodded. "You mind if I get a refill first?" he asked, raising his empty glass.

"Sure, go ahead. There's plenty of booze. Keep a clear head, though. I need to pick your brain."

Toshi snorted. "Me, keep a clear head? Berg, how many times have I poured coffee into your hangovers? You ever have to do that for me?"

"Yeah, that's a point, isn't it? Sorry I brought it up. Bring the fucking bottle if you want." Berg angled his head toward a hall leading away from the main room. "Meet me in the bedroom, okay?"

"Is that an invitation?" Toshi asked.

"You're not my type," Berg told him. He turned, walked down the hall, and closed the bedroom door behind him. It was blessedly silent in the room. Berg lit a Bolivian Extra, glanced around tiredly, then padded over to the small bar next to the window wall. He poured straight Glenfiddich into a short tumbler, raised it to his lips, and sipped. The smoky fire of the scotch burned away some of the fog. Cigarettes, booze, and drugs: he wondered if bad habits had a cumulative effect on the matrix. He considered that he didn't have a body, at least in any understandable sense of the word. Did the chicken brain, the flesh of the actual matrix, suffer from hangovers? It was an interesting question. Perhaps Norton, the veteran consumer of Russian beverages, would know the answer.

When Toshi slipped quietly into the room, he stopped and stared at Berg. "Uh," he said, "is there any reason why you're sitting on the bed laughing? Aside from softening neural tissue, of course."

Berg chuckled one more time, then turned. "Sorry, Tosh," he said. "I just figured out I don't have to worry about my health as much. I may never have a hangover again."

Toshi glanced at him suspiciously. "Only way you won't have a hangover is if they quit making scotch," he said.

That made Berg start laughing all over again. When he'd finally run down, he waved his empty glass at the Oriental. "Here. Give me a refill. I really think I ought to test this revelation."

Toshi took the glass. "How come I always get to do the chores? I look like the fucking maid or something?" He walked over to the bar and stared at the open bottle of Glenfiddich dubiously. "How much?" he asked.

"Fill'er up," Berg said.

"And you want me to watch the booze?" Toshi asked. "Shit."

Berg took his fresh drink and wandered over to the glass wall. "Toshi," he said, "I think I want to start a war."

Toshi raised his own glass. "I'm always in favor of such things," he said. "I'm a direct kind of guy."

Berg grinned. "Well, we'll see. What I want to do is take over the Double En Tower and wrap up Bill Norton. What do you think?"

"What do I think?" Toshi returned to the bar, put down his glass, picked up the bottle and put it to his lips. His Adam's apple chugged up and down. "I think you're crazy," he said. "This your second bottle of the evening?"

Berg tasted his drink again. "Nope," he said, "I'm dead serious."

"Dead is right," Toshi replied.

"Yeah, well, maybe so, but—if we were gonna do it, how would you go about getting the job done?"

Outside, the lights of Chicago—that toddlin' town, Berg thought suddenly—did their shimmering dance and, for a moment, he experienced an absolutely terrifying sense of dislocation. Would he ever know what was real again?

"I think," Toshi said behind him, "that we'd need a special kind of help. Who would be in on this gig?"

"You," Berg said. "Me, Collinsworth, Aldocci, Marie. Anybody else you think we'd need."

"Cost a lot," Toshi said.

"No problem. No problem at all," Berg replied.

Here and there, roving bands of the labyrinth's denizens had chopped gaping holes in the top of the dike, and moonlight off the lake cast eerie blue shadows over the rotted autos which clogged the tangled paths of the world under the avenues.

"I don't know if you've noticed, but we're not exactly alone down here," Toshi said quietly.

Berg had, in fact, seen faint, flickering movements—the sudden naked skitter of claws, of teeth—at the very edge of his vision. "Ignore it," he replied. "We're expected."

"I don't like wolves," Toshi replied. "They slobber."

"I'm not asking you to keep one for a pet," Berg said. "You said we need special help, right? This should be special enough for you."

"Why don't you get fucking Lassie while you're at it?" Toshi grumbled.

At last they came to the meeting ground. Only a few glowlamps were lit. They stopped and waited. Monotonously, water dripped onto something hollow and metallic, the sound like the beating of a rusted heart. The air smelled thickly of the slime which grew on the dikes' lake side, a heavy, green odor that reminded Berg of an aquarium his mother had once kept by the window in her bedroom. It had grown so solid with algae that the two goldfish inside could only be seen when they came right up to the glass for a goggle-eyed glimpse of the strange world outside. He licked his upper lip nervously and tasted salt. Toshi waited stolidly beside him, but Berg was conscious of the other man's inner tension, a clockwork of flesh and silicon wound tight.

He thought of cuckoo clocks.

The wolves came all at once, many of them. One moment the meeting square was empty, and then the shaggy, feral forms were there, watching. Toshi regarded the circle calmly. "They look friendly to you?" he asked.

Berg shrugged. "I said we were expected," he replied.

"For dinner?" Toshi asked.

"The Lady," Berg said suddenly, his voice strong and clear.

At his words, there seemed to be a certain change in the threatening attitude of the pack. "I came to see the Lady," he said again.

"There," Toshi said.

Then Berg saw it. Behind the pack, growing brighter, came the moving lights, things like the gauzy burnishings of fireflies half remembered from his youth. She moved in the center of them as a queen, slow and stately, the passage of a white ship in the night. The pack's gathered ranks parted for her, and she faced them, her eyes—congealed blood—questing.

"Lady," Berg said softly.

"Berg," she replied.

He stepped forward, waving Toshi to silence. "I need your help," he said. The words seemed part of some ancient ritual to him.

"If you're planning to take out Norton's unconscious, you most certainly do," she replied.

Berg stared at her, his eyes growing slowly wide.

*　　*　　*

They stood just outside the dim light spilling across the meeting ground. Her eyes glowed redly, searching his face. Toshi remained a few meters away, grinning and winking at the immobile shapes of the waiting pack.

"Yes, Berg," the Lady said, "you can use my little ones in your attack."

"Pardon me, Lady," Berg said, "but it almost seems as if you have knowledge of your own. I mean—"

"You mean I don't act like a projection of your own memory of me?" she said. "It's simple: I'm not."

"I don't understand," he said. "How is that possible?"

She slowly shook her hand. "You remember I once told you? You didn't think much of it. You called it bullshit. There are things you don't understand, Berg, but it doesn't matter. I see you still have Toshi with you. I was right, then."

"Yes," he said. "You said he'd be able to protect me."

She let it pass. "How many of my little ones will you need?"

"The whole pack, maybe," he said.

Her great red gaze grew dark. "Yes," she said at last. It seemed to cause her some kind of pain. "You will need them all."

"Lady, do you know what's going on in the outside world? The real world?"

"You, of all people, should know you can't make that distinction, Berg. Not any more."

Again he felt the distant taste of that awful dislocation. If he got out of here, would he ever be able to trust reality again?

"Do you?" he repeated.

Her breath was a soft, sad sigh. "It wouldn't help you, Berg. We do what we have to do. You, me, everybody else."

"Cheap philosophy, and, more to the point, meaningless," Berg said. "You can't tell me anything more?"

"No."

He stepped back, concentrating. "Perhaps I could encourage you."

She watched him calmly. "No, Berg. Not here. Not even you. Take my little ones, take what you need. Do what you have to do." She moved her head slightly, as if listening to sounds beyond the range of Berg's hearing. "I'm not a . . . part of this world." Strangely, the last words held a whispered undertone of regret.

He raised his eyes. His head was beginning to ache. He inhaled once, sharply. "Calley?" he said softly, the plea a naked blade beneath his words.

Her silence was final. He lowered his head and turned away from her.

"Berg," she said.

"What?"

"She's all right. No, nothing more. But one thing."

"What's that?" he said.

"My blessing, Berg. For what it's worth."

Already he was walking away from her, back toward the light. "Yeah," he whispered. "For what it's worth."

He'd never felt so tired in his life.


He needed to talk to her, and so she was waiting for him, sitting on the Weber sofa in his condo, a scene from happier days. He had the feeling that this electronic contemplation of his own navel was dangerous, but the alternative was even worse.

"Hi, Gloria," he said.

"Berg," she replied, stretching. She looked as if she'd just awakened, her jagged hair even more awry than usual, her eyes slowly sharpening to alertness.

"How about a drink?" he said.


He'd called a place he knew on the South Side, and now a mountain of barbecued ribs, hot links, and chicken rested in greasy styrofoam containers on the scarred top of the Lauren coffee table.

"Good?" he asked, watching her eat. Her appetite

had always amazed him. He tended to exist on booze, coffee, and cigarettes, and found her insatiable lust for food almost frightening. Some dim chunk of fear, tossed up from the iron complexities of his own subconscious, he supposed. Maybe I'm afraid she'll eat *me*, he thought. One more rib on the plate of love.

"Great," she replied absently, her concentration on a drumstick coated with dark red sauce. Like blood, he thought. He picked up a damp napkin and wiped his fingers.

"Want another drink?" he asked.

She shook her head, her mouth full. She waved him away with the remnants of a drumstick. He got up and refilled his own glass. So much he wanted to say, but what was the point? She was only a construct of his mind. A construct of a construct, he thought, and sensed the fearful whirl of unreality churning just beneath his awareness.

When he turned, she had changed.

He couldn't quite figure it out. She was still chewing on the drumstick, but she looked different. Then he had it. Older now. Faint lines at the corners of her eyes. A sort of wary tension in the way her body faced him, as if he'd been the source of some kind of pain for her.

The tricks of his yearning. It was Gloria, but now she called herself Calley, and she was a divorced woman. He paused, awestruck by the dissimilarity, suddenly discovered. The process of their parting, the long slow trip down, had obscured what had happened.

It had damaged her, he realized. Now, freed by time and strangeness from the agony of that period, he could see it on her face, in her very bones, and he wanted to cry out loud. For both of them.

"Calley," he said.

"Don't worry, Berg," she replied, dropping the stripped bone onto a mound of them, "I'll do your fucking programs for you. It's probably nuts, trying to crack Double En like that, but what the hell—old times' sake will do it every time."

He walked back, feeling unsteady and faint, and sat down on the sofa beside her. "Is that all? Old times' sake?"

"What the fuck you want me to say? Shit, Berg, we're ancient history. This is a business deal. You want to burn the Double En tower for some reason. Well, you're paying enough for it, and if you don't want to answer questions, that's your business. Although it's stone psycho, buddy. I think your death wish has finally got the best of you."

"Death wish?"

"Sure, Jack," she said, then paused, her face growing intent. "No, wait a minute. You're serious, aren't you?"

His shoulders moved slightly.

"Well," she said slowly, "I dunno, but I always thought you had one. You know, the way you keep yourself bottled up so tight, it's like you're afraid if you let go you'd die. If anybody ever got *in* there, it'd be so terrible you wouldn't be able to hold on anymore. But it's still there, always working away, and someday it'll get you, and that will be the end of it."

She stopped suddenly, as if surprised at the unexpected flood of her own words. She looked down at her hands. "Sorry," she said. "But that's what it seemed like to me."

"I think you've been waiting a long time to say that," he said at last. His voice seemed to be coming from a place that was not his throat, the words thin and reedy. "And I don't know that you might not be right."

She stared at him, blinking once. "Hey, buddy," she said. "It's not that bad. We did all right, for a while. Maybe you're not supposed to get more than that."

"But you tried, didn't you, Calley? You took your best shot, and I turned it into some kind of perverted game, and I won, didn't I?"

"Berg, are you okay?"

"No, I'm not okay. I figured something out just now, and I'm definitely not okay."

She reached out to him, touched his lips lightly with her fingers. He saw the concern in her eyes, and suddenly realized that it had always been there, and only now did he recognize it for what it was.

"Berg," she said softly. "Are you crying?"

He made a low, grunting sound, and it seemed to him that something black and heavy was lodged in his chest, trapped there, and it was pulling him down. "No!" he shouted. She drew back, startled. He leaned forward and put his hands on her shoulders.

"I love you!" he said. "That's all."

"Well, I love you, too, Berg. Always have. Always will, God help me."

He stood up, took her hands, and pulled her gently to her feet. "I'm not very bright, am I?" he said.

"You've always had promise," she told him. "Blow your nose."

He tugged at her hands. "Come on," he said. "The bedroom's this way."

As he led her toward the hall, he was almost able to forget that this one didn't count, and he forced himself not to wonder if he'd ever get the chance to do it when there was a score.

"I remember where the bedroom is," she said calmly.

Later that night he awakened in the dark and felt her there beside him. Gently he touched her face.

Come on, Berg, you're only human, he told himself.

He paused.

Am I? he thought wildly. *Am I?*

While Toshi worked, Berg ran the whole thing over in his mind one more time. Analogs, the second Norton had told him—and that was the key, the heart of the plan. Now, in the chill gray light of the Chicago afternoon, deep in a sub-basement of the Double En tower, the whole idea seemed shakier than when he'd first conceived it.

"That just about does it," Toshi said. He winked at

the two security guards who were bound with strips of super-velcro, propped against the housing of a big transformer. "Half a pound of plastic," Toshi said. "Works wonders if you use it right."

One of the guards was a fat man with a red face. His eyes bulged over the gag at that. Toshi grinned at him. "You want me to drag these guys outside, or just leave them and see what happens?"

"Outside," Berg said. The last of the wolfpack was just skittering through the door. Their weird, shape-shifting coats hurt his eyes. Being in a room full of them was like being haunted by thick, sweating, furry ghosts.

Analogs. He'd finally understood that he had to change the reality inside the matrix. The way he read it, there was only one way to do that: he and Norton had to share an identical reality. So he would send his shadow armies against Norton. None of it was real, of course—but the winner would be the one who exerted the most control over the matrix itself. Another chess game, he thought tiredly, but to the death, this time.

"You sure that will work?" he asked Toshi.

The Oriental bobbed his head. "Sho' will, massa, sho' nuff will. No heat, no air conditioning, and only Norton's private elevator moving in the whole joint. Piece of cake."

"Wrong ethnic accent," Berg said sourly.

"What about the computer stuff?" Toshi asked.

"Calley's taking care of it. The virus moles should be in the system by now." He took a deep breath. "You think this is gonna work?" The heavy weight of the AV15 dragged at his right arm.

"Who thinks?" Toshi said. "Let's do it."

They went through the door and out into a long, concrete corridor. Toshi shut the door. A few meters down the hall, Toshi stopped, his head cocked. "They're upstairs," he said.

"Blow it," Berg said.

Toshi reached into his jacket pocket. Berg heard a

faint click, and then the hallway shuddered. The lights went out, flickered, came back in a dull orange glow.

In the distance, someone screamed.

Berg, Toshi, and a single wolf skidded to a halt outside the closed steel doors of Norton's office. It had been doomed from the start, Berg realized. The wolf was panting, his thick, pink tongue hanging out, his eyes red from exhaustion. His right hand was off at the wrist, the stump hastily bandaged and leaking blood. Berg knew the two bright blue derms on the wolf's bulging forearm were all that kept him going.

Somewhere behind them the low wail of a siren stuttered, then choked off.

"Maybe some of our guys are still functioning," Toshi said.

"You think so?" Berg asked hopefully.

"Not really," Toshi replied.

Berg turned and faced the doors. "Well, what the hell. Let's see if the boss is at home."

Toshi nodded, then knelt and began carefully to wedge a long strip of plastic explosive between the two doors. "Don't bother knocking," he said.

"Hurry up," Berg said. The wolf spun, raising his laser. An orange beam flashed once. The wolf howled, a long, mournful sound, and Berg stepped around his falling body and hosed down the corridor with his machine pistol.

"Blow that fucker!" he yelled.

Toshi rolled the other way. The explosion picked Berg up and tossed him half a dozen meters. He heard shouts in the distance, the sound of running feet. He scrambled up and hurled himself through the shattered ruin of the armored doors, landed on his shoulder, rolled, and came to his feet with the AV15 pointed at the gigantic apparition towering over the desk on the far side of the vast room.

"Christ," Toshi said from his left.

Norton was at least three meters tall. His thick gray

hair, streaked with patches of molten silver, hung to his waist. Two white fangs protruded from his thick lips. His shoulders curved massively down into a barrel chest and arms like tree trunks.

Norton stepped around the desk, his great fists raised, and Toshi threw himself forward.

"No!" Berg shouted, but the Oriental was already there, a blur of movement, and the giant screamed suddenly. He stumbled back, and Toshi did something tricky with his hands. Norton shrieked in pain again, but this time managed to grab Toshi with one hand.

Light bloomed. Norton roared a third time, his eyes bulging at the shredded ruin that had been his fingers, and Toshi laughed.

"Pick on somebody your own size, motherfucker," he yelled.

Berg raised his machine pistol, but held his fire. "Get away from him, Toshi!" he shouted. "Get back!"

Toshi turned for just an instant, but it was enough. Norton's good fist came around, and the sound of it striking Toshi's ribs was thick with the cracking of bone and muscle.

"No—" Berg yelled, but it was already too late. Toshi staggered for a moment, stunned, and Norton picked him up and pulled him to his great chest.

Toshi struggled there, his eyes slitted with effort, but Norton squeezed inexorably with both gigantic arms, blood spurting from one hand, covering them both.

*"Aiieee . . . !"*

Berg heard Toshi's spine crack. Norton opened his arms and the Oriental collapsed with a curious, liquid motion.

Norton raised the bloody stump. "Now, little man," he said softly, and moved forward.

The gun fell from Berg's fingers. He didn't notice. From deep inside him something was rising. He no longer understood anything about the matrix, about reality, about his own status in any of it. All he knew was—

"This is the fucking end of it," he howled, and yanked on that dark well deep inside himself, pulled it up—

Took hold of the very flesh of the matrix and squeezed—

Norton froze.

Berg stared at the giant, huge arms outstretched, towering over him, a grisly statue—

A thin, gray man stepped out of the wall and walked into the silence.

"The chip, Berg," he said. "Use the chip *now*."

## 26

**T**HE MAIN ROOM of the suite on the sixty-fifth floor of the Chicago Marriott was done in Eurochan Eclectic, a gaudy profusion of drapes and painted screens, shimmering primaries—red, blue, yellow—and explosions of tapered light-stems, great flickering bouquets of them set in painted steel urns.

"Did you pick the face?" she asked.

The tall, unnaturally slender young man regarded his features in a polished brass mirror. "Uh-huh," he said. "Why? What's the matter? You miss the old Ozzie?"

She shrugged.

"You know," he continued, "I kinda like it. Maybe I shoulda done it a long time ago." He turned to face her. "Hey, Calley, would you call it . . . uh, handsome?"

"Huh. Handsome," Toshi snorted, from where he was sunk deep into a pillow chair upholstered in scarlet silk.

"I don't know," Calley said, touching her cheek with one finger. Ozzie stared at her, his expression suddenly anxious.

"I mean, it's okay, isn't it?" he said slowly.

"Maybe I liked it better before. . . ."

"No, you said—"

Toshi's gleeful hooting from the corner cut him off. "Kid, you're goofed for real. Don't worry about it, it looks great."

Calley broke into a sudden grin. "Oz, if nothing else

comes out of this, at least I got you to get rid of that godawful kisser of yours."

The lanky young man stared back and forth between them, then broke into his own wide grin. "It's okay, huh?"

They nodded. "Real handsome," Calley said.

"And nobody has it on file yet," Toshi said. "Like they do ours," he added glumly.

Calley flopped down in another chair that looked like a meld between a stainless steel elephant and a pillow factory. "It's gonna be a problem, is that what you're saying?"

Toshi nodded. "You think Nakamura doesn't have us posted in every snitch palace in the city?" he said. "All he knows right now is you're gone, and I was in on the grab. But I bet that's good enough for him to lay down big-time cash to find out where we are. And speaking of which, why are we here? Like the man once said, babe, of all the cities in all the world, you had to pick Chicago. I mean, it's your hometown and everything, but couldn't you take care of biz someplace else?"

She shook her head. "Nope. This city's got something that isn't available anywhere else."

"What's that?" Ozzie asked.

"My computers," she replied.

Ozzie called down for coffee and croissants. While they waited for the food to arrive, Calley paced the big room nervously. "I know," she said, "it's crazy, but I have to get into my machines. There's stuff there I need."

Toshi shifted in the soft confines of his chair. "You know they gotta have that place of yours tagged, Calley. First thing. They may not know where you are now, but they'll keep an eye on your office for sure."

She nodded. "That's why I brought you along, Yamamoto. You're supposed to be good at that kind of thing, so ante up. Get me in there for ten minutes, and get me back out in one piece. Should be right up your alley."

"You got any idea what you're proposing, woman?" he asked. "Double En doesn't hire idiots. Your place is locked up tighter than my maiden aunt's knickers. You can't get Berg back if you're dead, right?"

She sucked her teeth in irritation. "Let me do the thinking around here, okay? If I can't get into my office, I won't be able to pull Berg out of the matrix, either. The two are, you might say, tightly connected."

Toshi's eyes narrowed. "How come you didn't mention that before?"

" 'Cause I was on the Moon," she replied. "For a paranoid Oriental, you're awful trusting, you know? Just 'cause somebody busts you out of a Double En jail, you want to give them the farm?"

He shook his head. "What are you talking about?"

"Well, everybody seems to be buying the Lunies as some kind of Christ figures, just out to do the world a good turn. Save us all from the evil meatmatrix. But while you were up there, did you see any great love for Earth, for us in general?"

"Not so you'd notice," Ozzie admitted. "Remember how Wier acted at lunch that day? But why, then? Why go to all the trouble? LunaCorp is big, but messing around with Double En is not safe, no matter who you are. So what's the motive?"

"I don't know," Calley replied. "I've got sort of an idea, but I need to get into my machines. Until then, I'm just guessing." She turned and glared at Toshi. "So, chubs, can you get me in there? All I need's ten minutes. You think you can get me that?"

Toshi reached into his robe and produced a pair of aviator glasses. He put them on, then turned a blank, silver stare on Calley. She saw herself reflected there as thin, haggard twins, and glanced away.

"Only the Shadow knows," he said in a deep, mournful voice.

"He do, huh?" she replied. "Well, when you find out, you let me fucking know, okay?"

\*     \*     \*

"I been thinking," Ozzie said. He wiped flaky crumbs of croissant from his chin with a linen napkin the size of a small tablecloth.

"About what?" Calley asked. She looked up from her empty coffee cup. There were rings the color of earthworms beneath her eyes. The skin on her face had taken on a stretched, translucent quality, as if her facial bones had been shrinkwrapped.

"Calley, is it absolutely necessary that you get into your office?"

"I already told you—"

"Yeah, but why? Is it something I can do? You gotta figure, maybe they haven't put me into the puzzle yet. And if they have, what they've got, like Toshi just pointed out, is a face that's very out of date. So . . . why can't I go? I'll take Toshi along to guard the body, but you're the one who has the red alarm out. You said all you needed was ten minutes. Ten minutes for what? If it's computers, I'm as good as you are."

"Wanna bet?" she said.

"Calley, I am betting. Offering to, at least. What is it?"

She stared at him for a few seconds more, then shook her head. "Nope," she said. "Wouldn't work."

"What wouldn't?"

"All I need to do is unlock the defenses on my data base. I could maybe crack the programming, but there's manual stuff, too. And it takes my thumbprint and retinal pattern. That's what I've got to do, and I'm the only one who can do it."

"Oh," Ozzie said. He picked up another croissant. "Well, it was a thought," he said.

"Not a bad one, either," Toshi muttered.

"What?" Calley said.

"Calley, don't get me wrong, you're a wonderful, smart woman, but you do have your limits."

"What the fuck are you mumbling about?"

"You know all about programs," Toshi told her. He grinned as he spoke, a long, slow flick of his teeth.

"But I do more than squash people, did you ever consider that? Your bullshit thumb locks and retinal codes will take me about five minutes to get through, not ten, especially if you tell me all about them before I go in." He sat back, his smile hanging like a challenge between them.

"You're not shitting me?" Calley said slowly.

"What you think Berg paid me for?" Toshi said. "Did you think he did all the design work on that condo fortress of his?"

She blinked. "You did that?"

"The hard parts," he said. He looked down at his perfectly manicured fingernails. "Not bad, either, if I do say so myself."

She glanced at Ozzie, then back at the Japanese. Finally she nodded once. "Okay, you little ball of ego, you're it."

"Do I get to send you a bill?" he asked.

She slumped all of a sudden, a weird, limp motion that caused Ozzie to stir a bit.

"Anything you want," she said. "Just do it."

Toshi stood up. "Right," he said, stretching. "Why don't you sack out? You look beat."

"I am," she replied. She grinned wanly. "You wanna know what else?"

"What's that?"

"I didn't really want to go there."

He came over and patted her on the shoulder. "I know," he said. "You can't be superbitch all the time."

"You think we're safe here?" Ozzie asked.

"Maybe," she shrugged. "This suite is Lunie territory. There are treaties. Double En shouldn't be able to bust in here without setting off a godawful incident. And I bet there are a few Lunie hardcases spotted around, just for drill. You think old Wier would let us wander around on our own?"

"Probably not," Ozzie said. He was slurping his fifth cup of coffee. His wiry frame was almost vibrating. "Jeezus, sometimes I wonder how I got into this thing."

Slowly, she pulled herself up out of her seat. Ozzie heard her knees crack, pop, pop. "God, I'm tired," she said. "I'm gonna crash for a while. Wake me up if anything happens, okay? And for sure when Toshi gets back."

"He said it might be a while," Ozzie reminded her.

"Well, whenever," she replied, moving slowly toward the door to one of the bedrooms.

"You want company?" he asked.

"Nope," she said. She raised her arms over her head and yawned. "Maybe tomorrow. I need my energy. You want that new face broken in right, don't you?"

Ozzie blushed. She laughed, and closed the bedroom door behind her.


After three hours he had spotted two of them. It hadn't been hard; he just looked where he would put watchers, and there they were. The two shadowed forms were good, however. If he hadn't known where they should be, he wouldn't have found them. They were doing it by the book. No cigarettes, unauthorized dozing, or conspicuous loitering. Nevertheless, he had the feeling they were bored. Even stone pros tended to lose their edge after days of watching an empty nest.

Toshi sympathized with them a little, so he was gentle when he came up behind the one halfway down the block from Calley's office-apartment and laid a flexible plastic tube filled with brass pellets just under his right ear.

The watcher crumpled without a sound, and Toshi dragged him back into the alley he'd been watching from. The second man was a little tougher.

He sat in a little Hyundai two-seater with the lights out and the doors locked. If things were first-class here, and Toshi figured they were, the tinted glass on the tiny car was armored and reinforced with monomole.

No reason to take chances. Toshi glanced at the still form of the first watcher, then placed the bag he was carrying on the ground next to the unconscious man. He knelt, opened the zipper, and took out a long, dark overcoat. He put it on, took a small oval pouch from the bag, and then a pair of glasses. The guy in the car probably had his face memorized, but in the dark, one man in a bulky overcoat looked much like another. The glasses might add the moment of uncertainty that would be all he needed.

"Sleep tight," he muttered to the silent body on the ground, and stepped out on the sidewalk.

The watcher in the car saw the short, thick shape staggering down the sidewalk toward him. He sighed. Another late night drunk. Best to be sure, though. He opened a briefcase on the seat next to him and removed a small camera, which he aimed at the approaching figure. Unless this guy tried for the woman's apartment, the tech boys could sort it out in the morning.

Carefully he replaced the camera and shut the case before the wildly zig-zagging figure came abreast of the car. He turned his face away, and—

"What the fuck?" he muttered.

The drunk had somehow gotten himself entangled with the small vehicle. Now he was rolling around on the hood, shouting incoherently. The watcher caught a quick glimpse of glasses, of burly shoulders, and then, almost in his face, the man's mouth opened and a gout of thick, chunky liquid sprayed all over his windshield.

"Motherfucker!" the watcher grunted. He stared in disbelief at the disgusting mess which was slowly oozing down the glass, obscuring his view.

The car rocked slightly as something heavy slammed off the fender, and then there was nothing. Silence. The watcher glanced around, checked the rear window. No drunk.

"Shit!" he muttered. No doubt the sonofabitch was passed out right next to his door. He sighed, adjusted the nylon shoulder rig which held his Colt Automag, and reached for the door handle.

The night air was clear and sweet. Something about that sounded the faintest of alarm bells in his mind, but he put his foot down anyway. As he felt the tiniest prick in his ankle, and almost immediately after the black wave began to fill his vision, he realized what had bothered him.

"It doesn't stink—" he managed, before the roaring in his ears picked him up and carried him away.

"Damn right," Toshi said. After he had propped the man upright in the seat, he grinned. He dropped the nearly empty bladder on the man's lap.

"A souvenir," Toshi said, and shut the door.


She awakened to the foggy light of morning, conscious of another presence in her bed. She looked over and smiled. Ozzie's long body was curled next to her, his knobby knees almost to his concave chest, his hands pressed together and nestled under his head. The aqueous light made soft, fuzzy shadows on his face. She watched for a moment, made out a tiny flickering of his eyelashes, wondered what odd Ozzie dream the REMs signified.

It was a pretty good face. The Lunie meditechs had done an excellent job of restructuring. Now, Ozzie looked about nineteen, with a straight, thin nose, high, sharp cheekbones, and a strong chin. Even his eyes, she remembered, had lost their watery, oyster-like shine, and now glowed a clear, light brown color. Amber waves, she thought, and chuckled softly.

She'd never associated poetic images with Ozzie. But then, many things had changed. And as that thought drifted through her dawn awareness, she was suddenly gripped by an almost unbearable longing for Berg.

She remembered the few moments and the few words. Now his body rested in a tank, fed and massaged by automatons, awaiting the return of its master. As did she. She was absolutely certain that somebody—Wier maybe, perhaps somebody else—was fully aware of the hold that tank had on her. Her lips tightened. Which was fine. It just made what she was about to do easier. Not that scruples had ever slowed her down all that much.

"Fuck with me, assholes. . . ." she muttered softly.

Ozzie stirred. His mouth opened slightly, and he made a short, moaning sound.

"It's okay, baby," she found herself saying. "It's only a dream."

The sun was burning the start of a fine day through the tattered remnants of lake mist when Toshi returned, carrying pizza.

"Goddam," Calley said happily. "You eat Italian for breakfast, too?"

"Doesn't everybody?" Toshi replied, placing the big hot-wrapper on the foot of the bed and unzipping it. "Pepperoni, onion, anchovy, two kinds of cheese. You like?"

"I love," she said. "Hey, Ozzie, wake your ass up." She reached over and slapped the appropriate part of his anatomy.

"Ow!" His bleary-eyed head poked slowly from beneath the covers, blinking.

"Breakfast, kid," Toshi said. "You like pizza?"

Ozzie stared at the huge pie. "You bring any beer?"

Toshi grinned and raised a shrinkwrapped twelve-pack. "Old Style okay?"

"Let's eat," Ozzie replied.

"Beer for breakfast?" Calley said. "I think I'm appalled."

Toshi twisted a pair of plastic cans loose. "You want one?"

She reached for a slice of pizza. "Maybe later," she said. "After coffee."

They made a weird kind of picnic out of it. Later she asked Toshi, "Everything went okay?"

He nodded as he wadded up the carton. "Piece of cake," he said. "Told you."

"Anybody there? Anybody see you?"

"Two," Toshi replied. "One of them saw me, but I think I disgusted him. His camera doesn't work any more, either."

"Mm. They'll be on guard now," she said nervously. "I don't know what they'll do with my machines. I better work fast."

"You were planning, maybe, an extended stay?" Toshi asked.

She crawled out of the bed and headed for the shower. Both Toshi and Ozzie followed her progress with interest.

"Is she warm at night?" Toshi asked Ozzie.

"Fuck you," Calley said, and slammed the bathroom door.

"Mm. Touchy," the Oriental observed. "Maybe she didn't like the anchovies."

The afternoon was half gone when Calley pushed her chair away from the house remote and brushed a strand of hair out of her eyes.

"That's it," she said. "I'm in."

The two men were watching the Bears play the London Griffons in their traditional blood match.

"Kill that Limey sonofabitch," Toshi said mildly. "You're in what?"

"Jenny," she said. "My machine. It's gonna be all right."

"Gosh," Toshi said. "I'd hate to think I'd wasted a trip."

"You're sure you can cobble that chip together?" she asked anxiously.

Ozzie nodded. "No problem. You gave me the specs; the rest is drill. Don't worry."

They were dressed for travel. They stood in a small clump next to the door of the suite. Calley put several packed disks carefully into her pocket.

"Is he gonna be all right?" she asked Toshi.

"Who? Ozzie? I don't know why not. As far as we can tell, nobody's ever seen him, and there's no reason to connect him to you, except maybe as a screw buddy. He can always lie. He went to the Moon to get his pretty face done."

She inhaled sharply, then let it out. "Come here, you," she said to Ozzie.

He bent down. She leaned up and kissed him once, quickly. "Take care of yourself," she said.

"You know," she added as he straightened up, "your old face didn't show when you blushed."

Toshi laughed. "You wait here for a sec, while I check the hallway."

She nodded, and the stocky Oriental grinned and let himself out the door.

They hit him halfway down the hall.

## 27

ORANSON STARED AT the wall of small, square white tiles in front of him. The room wasn't large. It didn't need to be. The focus of the room was the chair in which he sat. He was surrounded by machines that at the same time seemed both arcane and threatening. He recognized a retinal analyzer. Overhead, a ring of high-intensity lights blasted every bit of shadow from the sharp-edged corners of the cubicle.

It could have been a dentist's office. But Oranson, a modest student of history, recognized the kinship and antecedents of the place; the robed examiners of the Inquisition would have felt at home here, surrounded by the holy stink of pain.

He listened to Nakamura and the doctor talking about him in low, worried tones, somewhere behind the chair which gently but firmly restrained him from all movement. Oddly enough, he felt no fear. They wouldn't hurt him. Agony was no longer necessary to the ancient rituals of receiving confession. He only worried that they might kill him by accident.

"He's had the standard protections?" Doctor Lewis asked quietly.

"Actually, more than that," Nakamura replied. "He's the head of security, after all."

"You understand the risk, then?" the doctor said. He glanced at the back of Oranson's head, noted professionally the repressed tension in the angle of the man's neck. "The tailored bacteria, in the presence of most of our truth drugs, will create fatal enzymes."

"What about simple torture?" Nakamura asked.

"You said you were in a hurry," the doctor replied.

"I am," Nakamura replied.

"Either way will take time," the doctor told him. "Analyzing information gathered by either method is a tricky business. Certainty is an uncertain matter. We can't undo his protections overnight, and as far as physical means, you tell me he is trained to resist."

Nakamura turned and stared at the former security man. "I think he'll cooperate," he said. "He's a pragmatic sonofabitch, after all."

The doctor lowered his voice even further. "But if there has been tampering, as you fear, he may not know it on a conscious level."

Nakamura made a short, hissing sound. "Doctor, you try my patience. Can you do it, or not?"

"I can do it." The doctor shrugged. "Nothing resists a really determined investigation. Not forever."

"I don't have forever," Nakamura said. "How long?"

"Three, four days," the doctor said. "Maybe more."

"See that it isn't," Nakamura said.

" 'Isn't'?"

"More." Nakamura turned and left the room.

"Tampering?" Oranson thought. He felt suspended in a warm, drowsy haze. What the fuck is he talking about?"

The doctor came around in front of him and stood there for a moment, thoughtfully tapping his teeth with a stainless steel pen. The bright lights reflected off the shiny metal.

"Well, Fred," the doctor said. "I guess we'd better get started."

Nakamura returned to his small office and seated himself behind the oak desk in front of the scarred Picasso. He would have felt more comfortable in his great nerve center atop the Double En tower, where he could make contact with Norton directly, but the suburban compound was a better choice. Behind its kilometers of chain-link fence and platoons of guards, many things were pursued that weren't exactly research, but required the kind of armed seclusion provided here.

He reached into one of the side drawers of his desk and took out a pad of ruled paper. He placed the pad precisely in front of him, stared at the blank page, and began to marshal his thoughts.

He lived in a world of instant information processing, where thoughts were simply anonymous bits of data to be moved, stored, indexed, or erased—but some primal part of him still longed for the slow, luxurious pace of the written word. He hefted the weight of the gold ballpoint in his hand, smiled, and began to write.

The questions first. The right questions were always the key. Answers were often easy and cheap. It was the questions that defined the problem.

How much did Arthur Kraus know, and what would he do about it? What was going on with Norton inside the matrix? Why was his appearance so changed? Who had stolen the bodies? Where were the bodies now? Why were they stolen? Who had killed the three mercenaries Berg had originally hired? How was an obscure cult of body-changers—"wolves," he wrote, and underlined it—involved? How long had Oranson been compromised, and by who?

He paused. It seemed that the questions were endless, but even as he wrote a shadowy pattern began to take shape. It was a pattern of what he didn't know, but order seemed to lurk just beneath the shifting surface of what was, at first glance, chaos.

Behind the questions lay motivations. And motivations, he knew, were subject to history, to information, to probabilities. Greed, fear, hate, anger, lust—the whole eternal box that had plagued mankind, it seemed, forever.

He stared at the words. From what he knew, he

could construct scenarios, could assign motivations. But something was missing.

If he could just discover *what*, it seemed that the whole intricate tangle would collapse into something simple, something totally amenable to reason.

He pushed the pad away and leaned back.

If only he had more time.

Two days later, Nakamura strode into Doctor Lewis's office. It reminded him of his college days at Indiana University. The walls were lined with shelves of books with brightly colored spines. The desk, a thick slab of plex on a spindly chrome framework, dominated the center of the room, in front of windows shaded with thick, brown drapes. The top of the desk was almost completely covered with stacks of hardcopy, several holos showing family scenes, a computer remote, telecom equipment, more books, and several racks of data chips. The room smelled of pipe smoke.

Two low, modern leather chairs faced the desk. Without hesitation, Nakamura went behind the desk and sat there, leaving the chairs for the other two men in the room.

"Well?" he said.

Doctor Lewis shifted in his chair, plainly uncomfortable at this reversal of his normal position of authority. Nakamura could picture him behind that cluttered desk, a cloud of blue smoke wreathing his head, sighting down the stem of his pipe at some hapless subordinate while he cheerfully dismembered the poor sonofabitch for a minor infraction. The thought reminded him of a particularly obnoxious Lit professor he'd been forced to endure at the university.

Academics, he thought tiredly. They're born understanding domination.

Frederick Oranson stared at his boss. His eyes were perfect brown blanks, devoid of interest. Nakamura wondered for a moment how much of a brain was left behind that vacant gaze. That the doctor could have reduced Oranson to this expressionless lump in less than two days was somehow frightening, more so because there didn't appear to be a mark on the security man. No visible marks, Nakamura thought, and placed his hands flat on the desktop.

"You've read the report?" the doctor asked.

"Yes," Nakamura replied. "It is . . . enigmatic."

Doctor Lewis sniffed. "Perfectly straightforward," he said.

"As a report, I agree," Nakamura said. "But in the context of a larger picture . . . there are questions."

"Well, ask them. He'll answer," he said, and glanced at Oranson with all the interest of a butcher regarding a well-carved, but finished, piece of meat.

"What did you do to him?" Nakamura asked.

"We stimulated counter-enzyme production," Doctor Lewis replied. "At the moment there is a balance. A cancellation of effect. The secondary enzymes are fatal as well, of course. But that's of no interest. The equilibrium will maintain for a short time. Afterwards . . ." He shrugged. "Anyway, that was the hard part. Standard interacting drug programs did the rest."

"Yes," Nakamura replied. He wondered what Oranson would feel as the warring enzymes in his brain gradually fought their chemical battles of attrition. Pyrrhic victories of the hippocampus? A Marathon at the vagus nerve?

"Fred," Nakamura said.

"What?" Oranson replied. Even his voice was different. Slower, deeper, a little bit slurred—and totally without inflection.

"There's a certain loss of affect," Doctor Lewis noted mildly, "but he's perfectly lucid."

Suddenly Nakamura wanted very much to finish, to leave the overstuffed, oppressive little office and its not very human occupants.

"Tell me again why you advised hiring Calley and Berg," he said.

"Their names came up on the problem analysis board," Oranson said. "When you first brought me into the Norton situation. One of the options was to kill him. And one of the scenarios called for a direct attack on the personality in the matrix. The Berg and Calley team was given the highest probability of success."

"Yes," Nakamura said. "Were you using the machines in your department?"

"Yes," Oranson replied.

"Which are also the monitoring machines for the tank room?"

"Yes," Oranson said.

Nakamura considered this for a moment. "Was it possible that Norton had somehow compromised your equipment?"

The security man's eyes were blank as silver coins. "William Norton has compromised the entire Double En data base," he said. "That is why I decided to work for him. You are the president of the corporation, but Norton controls it—absolutely."

Nakamura's slender fingers moved slightly, but all he said was, "Then why did you betray him to Kraus?"

"I didn't," Oranson said. "He told me to."

Nakamura glanced at the doctor. "Who knows about this?"

"Just myself," the doctor replied. "As you instructed, I used nothing in the way of data processing. It would have gone faster, otherwise. By the way, you see in the report that this is all deep retrieval? Oranson had no conscious knowledge that Norton was manipulating him. Norton used subliminal messages broadcast directly on Oranson's screens. Simple, but effective."

"Ah," Nakamura replied. Suddenly he nodded at Doctor Lewis. "I may need him again. How long . . . ?"

The doctor moved one shoulder. "Days . . ." he said. "Maybe a few weeks."

"Enough," Nakamura replied. He stood up, came around the desk, and headed for the door. "Oh," he said. "Good job, Doctor."

Lewis smiled, his pink lips parting to reveal red gums. Nakamura looked away.

In the hall outside the office, he paused and spoke

quietly. "Just the doctor," he said. "See that nothing happens to Oranson."

The short, bear-bodied man with the jagged thatch of white hair and the scarred face nodded. "Yes," he said, and opened the office door.

Nakamura waited until the door closed and the faint, ugly sounds began. Then he grinned, turned, and went on down the hall.

Nakamura returned to downtown Chicago in a Nissan-Benz vehicle that looked like a limo, but was of a design prepared for less that a dozen men in the entire world, men of a position and paranoia to require the armor and offense which the disguised tank provided. He rode in a convoy, surrounded by mercenaries whose loyalty their scar-faced commander guaranteed absolutely. As long as they were paid, of course.

Even so, the Japanese executive breathed a little easier when he went past the unusually heavy security forces stationed in the lobby of the Double En tower.

He paused inside the doors of his office and made a short, clicking sound of dismay. Where once had flowed a stream behind changeless waves of gravel, now crouched the low, bulky, functionally ugly shape of a Cray 50-50, the most powerful machine ever built until the advent of the Double En matrix.

It wasn't a matrix, and never would be, but it was in no way connected with the Double En data base. Nakamura hoped that Norton wouldn't be able to crack it before it served its function. The news remotes, hastily stacked beside his desk, further disfigured the elegantly simple atmosphere of the room, but Nakamura had already resigned himself to the loss. Only the first of many, perhaps, but priorities were critical. He could always rebuild. If he survived.

He went to his desk, sat, and began to punch in the codes. He wondered—no, hoped—that his call would disturb Arthur Kraus's sleep.

Three hours later, he knew that the German technology magnate was undisturbed—probably not even asleep. Nakamura's imperative messages had been curtly refused. Now reports coming in from his roving Euro-intelligence groups were taking on an alarming pattern: large-scale mercenary transfers in progress, and data centers buttoned up tight. Nakamura recognized that forbidding web. It was one he'd woven himself on occasion.

Kraus wasn't waiting for negotiations. Oranson's treachery had been far-reaching. Kraus didn't yet have the full picture: the security chief hadn't revealed Norton's existence, saving that as a final bargaining chip . . . but Kraus was evidently aware that Double En was readying a preemptive strike.

The reply would be simple: Preempt Double En's strike.

Nakamura sighed and shut down the Cray. It was too late for the delicate interplay of negotiation. Kraus's Consortium would be gathering all its massive forces into one crushing attack on the Double En empire everywhere in the world.

He turned to the other bank of remotes and began the—he had come to regard it almost as a demonic summoning—complicated process of reaching his former partner.

"I hope the asshole isn't totally zoned," he muttered to himself as he keyed the touchpad.

The hand lay palm down, fingers curled elegantly over the edge of the desk. A thin red stream trailed down the back of the hand and dripped slowly from the fingertips to a small, dark puddle on the carpet below.

Oranson stared at the ridges of veins on the back of the hand, his face expressionless.

"Come on, Fred," the man with the white hair said. He'd done something fast, twisting and awful to Dr. Lewis's head, and Oranson had watched the doctor's eyes as awareness leaked out of them. He didn't look at the white-haired man.

"Are you going to kill me now, Hanagan?" Oranson asked slowly. "I wish you would. It would be better than . . . the other way."

"The Jap wants you in one piece, Oranson," Hanagan replied. "He pays the bills, so that's the way he's gonna get you. I said come on."

Hanagan jerked Oranson roughly to his feet. "Come on, guy, be a man," he said. Then he laughed.

Unprotesting, limp and vacant, Oranson allowed himself to be led from the office. It was important that nobody realize. The doctor might have figured it out, but he was dead. Two days hadn't been enough. He'd told them much, but not all.

Only silence could be his revenge now. He remembered the face on the screen, the childish secret face. He dimly perceived that great forces were on the move and that somehow, they were focused on Nakamura Shigeinari.

So die, motherfucker, he thought. And kept himself from smiling.

Ruby eyes.


Nakamura rubbed his forehead wearily. "Who are you?" he asked.

The gray, drawn face on the screen grinned at him. "You should visit the cancer ward more often, Shag," the man said.

Nakamura stared at the face. "Halloween, Bill? I liked you better the other way. At least you didn't look like a corpse."

Norton laughed. "A little redundant, wouldn't you say? Anyway, you're the one with my, ah . . . *mortal* remains. Which, by the way, you can turn off now. If you hadn't figured it out already."

"Yes." Nakamura nodded slowly. "I don't suppose you've needed *that* for some time now, have you?"

"Not really," Norton replied. "Did you call to tell me so?"

"Why did you compromise Oranson?" Nakamura asked. He found it hard to organize the words. Norton's features reminded him of masks of demons, visages that had frightened him as a child when he'd visited the old stone temples of Japan.

It would have been better had he never left those mountains, those temples.

"Greater imperatives," Norton said.

"Yes," Nakamura replied. "Is there room in them for the survival of the company?"

"Possibly," Norton told him. "By the way, thanks for sending me Berg. Calley isn't here, however."

"You have their bodies, of course?"

"Sort of," Norton said. "More accurate to say I have access."

"Who are you?" Nakamura repeated.

"I'm the one who should have been here all along," Norton replied. "But it didn't work out that way. Sad. I didn't want it to turn out like this."

*"Damn it!"* Nakamura suddenly raised his fist and slammed it on the desktop. The sound rattled in the air between them. Nakamura glared at the screen, breathing hard.

"I'm going to save your fucking company," Norton said softly. "And your ass, too. If you're willing to listen. You think you can do that?"

"Why should I?"

"You've got no choice," Norton told him.

Slowly Nakamura nodded. He moved closer to the screen. He began to listen.

His neck ached as he handed the man with the white hair a sheet of hardcopy. The scar on the man's face moved slightly, a worm of ruined flesh crawling, as he read the name at the top of the sheet.

"Arthur Kraus," Hanagan said.

"The rest of the information is there," Nakamura told him.

Hanagan nodded. "When?" he asked.

"Now," Nakamura replied. "Tonight. Tomorrow. Immediately."

"All right," Hanagan said.

"Do it yourself," Nakamura said.

Hanagan nodded again. He stared at Nakamura's drawn face for an instant, then turned and left the room. His feet made no sound even when he crossed a patch of gravel, remnant of the eternal garden.

Nakamura sighed. His eyes felt dipped in acid. His head throbbed. He put both hands on the back of his neck and squeezed, heard cartilage pop.

So tired. He turned. The Cray had been a mistake. Now, staring at its ugly, boxlike shape, he wished he had the stream back. The sound of water flowing. The changeless, ever silent sand.

He shook his head. Then he walked back to his desk and began sending out the killer teams.

# 28

THE MOMENT STRETCHED. Berg felt himself frozen in its fluid stasis, an ice cube caught in amber. Melting.

"The chip," hissed the gray man.

The moment broke and fell on the floor. He was faintly aware of the matrix writhing in the grip of his will.

"The chip?" he said slowly. "Yes, I suppose you want that," he said. Norton—petrified, gigantic—hung over him like a rockslide.

The gray man drifted closer, a spectral fog of tension. "Everything comes to this, Berg. This instant. Use the chip. Bring us together. It's your only way out."

Berg refused to look at him. "Is it?" he asked, and let the dark web of information, lodged for so long next to something blacker and harder in the precise heart of him, let *that* go free.

Slowly, from the pores of his skin, the exotic dew began to form. Light without shape, flowing. In his outstretched hand. The midnight ball, so bright it hurt to see it, shot through with traceries of silver pain.

Sound of bells. Wings.

"Here," he said, and spread his palms. "Your gift."

*Coming together. . . .*

Things changed.

The sound came from outside, and then he realized

he *was* outside, and the unbearable noise was somehow ringing from his own chest, from a hole there that would never be filled.

From him swept endless neon lines, emerald roads that, momentarily, had found a center. Nearby—far away?—the spectacle slowly unfolded, the turgid heart began, finally, to beat.

The matrix hung before him, suspended in its agony. It had become a great fist of blue fire, turning upon itself, holding the ranked data cores like shards of sapphire in its gelid, scorching fingers.

Berg, transfixed with his wonder, silent, felt movement—a vast rushing of forces upon his center, delicately balanced and unutterably strong—channeled through him, invisible and pervasive.

The matrix screamed.

All the matrices vibrated slowly, like brass bells struck once.

Blinding light.

"What?" Berg said.

The office was small, separated by a low glass partition from the wide expanse of the main laboratory. It was a working office, cluttered with hardcopy, remotes and monitors of several sizes arranged in random constructions. In the center, a gray steel desk was almost buried under papers, books, telecom equipment, a large, brown glass ashtray filled with half-burnt pipe tobacco, and an unopened bottle of Stolychnaya vodka. Next to the bottle stood two wide-mouthed chemical beakers filled with ice.

"You want a drink?" Norton asked.

Berg stared at him. His shape had shifted again, and Berg somehow felt that this was a final—perhaps the original—version of the man. Where one personality had been huge and full of an obscene vitality, and the other small and dry, the corroded edge of a blade, Norton was now an amalgam, an alloy of the two. Berg noticed that the feeling of menace was gone, as if this

Norton was at last satisfied—relaxed, confident, *comfortable*.

His power must be immense, Berg warned himself.

"Sure," Berg said. "A big drink."

"I've only got one bottle," Norton said as he filled both beakers with the clear fluid.

"I bet you can get more," Berg said.

"All I want," Norton agreed, and pushed one beaker toward Berg.

Berg sipped, pursed his lips, then took a larger sip. The vodka went down his throat like burning honey.

"And can you get anything you want?" Berg asked.

Norton regarded him over the lip of his own beaker. The ice made small, clear cracking sounds. "Pretty much," he replied. His gray eyes were unclouded, but there was a brooding cast to his strong features. "That was the point, wasn't it?"

"For you, maybe," Berg said. "What about me?"

"What about you?"

"I mean, is it all over now? You got what you wanted, right?"

"How about you, Berg?" Norton asked. "You got everything you need?" He shrugged. "Maybe not. How about a few answers? Would you like that? I bet you would."

"You probably win a lot of bets, huh?" Berg asked.

"All the big ones," Norton said. "I just won the biggest, so I guess I owe you."

"That's right," Berg said. "You do. And you're gonna pay off, 'cause I know something else."

"What's that?"

"It's not over yet. Right?"

Norton's gray eyebrows rose slightly. "That's right," he replied. "It's not over yet."

Berg crossed his right leg over his left and watched his foot begin to jiggle. "It occurred to me that this is the first matrix. But nobody ever built one before—an organic computer. It must have some strange properties, something maybe no one else anticipated. Is that possible?"

"It's possible," Norton said. "And it's possible that the creator of the matrix would discover those abilities first."

"Everything about this begins to make sense once I put in one missing piece," Norton said. "At first I kept trying to untangle it like a detective, you know? Cause and effect, motive, the scientific method. All that shit. And I didn't get anywhere. It was like a chess game where half the moves were missing."

Norton put one finger into the brown glass ashtray and gently stirred the little mound of burnt tobacco. He raised his finger and smelled it. "You weren't supposed to figure things out," he said. "Nobody was."

"I can see that now," Berg told him. "You had too much at stake. One thing I'm curious about: did you know what was gonna happen? Did you know what your body would become locked away in that tank?"

"I should," Norton said. He sipped his drink. "Since I gave myself the cancer. Nakamura thought he did it, and I let that stand. Smoke. But it was me all along."

Berg blinked. "You *what*?"

The other man tilted his head back, his eyes slightly unfocused. Perhaps he stared at something only he could see "Properties, Berg. You want to talk about properties? Well, there's the properties of Henrietta Lacks's cells, for one."

"I don't—what about her cells?"

"Henriette Lacks died in Baltimore in 1951, of cancer of the cervix," Norton said slowly. "Not much to say; a common enough death for that time. They hadn't discovered the carcinoma techniques we have today. But there was something very strange about the cells of the tumor that killed her. When researchers placed them in a culture medium, they grew. In fact, they did better than that. The cells doubled every twenty-four hours."

"You talked about that once," Berg said. "Is that so odd?"

"Back then it was," Norton said. "See, nobody had been able to grow human cells successfully. This was the first time, and, like a lot of such things, they hit the bull's eye first time out of the box. Not only did the cell cultures thrive, they were unbelievably hardy. Survived damn near anything. For a while they were a scientific wonder. Till, years later, the techs figured out it was too much of a good thing. Henrietta's cells—they named them HeLa cells—had contaminated cell cultures worldwide. And still went right on growing. Immortal cells. It took a lot of fancy stepping to get that contamination under control."

"You said—" Berg stared at his foot. It had stopped jiggling. "You said you used her cells when you built the matrix."

"I did something better than that, Berg," Norton told him. "I wasn't after a matrix, I was gunning for bigger game. I told you I didn't have cancer. I just used that as smoke—a coverup for what came later. I was after immortality, Berg, and I found it!"

"Right," Berg said. "That matrix."

"No, you idiot, that came after. What I did was isolate the factors in HeLa cells that kept them multiplying and surviving. Those cells had a different spring, Berg. You understand? They didn't run down—the genetic clock was set for eternity!"

"I think you've lost me," Berg said. "You found the secret of athanasia?"

Norton nodded. Then he sighed heavily. "At first I thought I had. Maybe I still do. But I made a little mistake, and that led to everything else: my condition, the matrix, all of it."

"Nobody's perfect," Berg said.

Norton laughed, a harsh, biting sound. "Right," he said. "Everybody thinks the matrices are augmented chicken brains."

"Why, aren't they?"

"Nope." Norton shook his head. "Remember, I didn't set out to build a matrix. I wanted to live forever. I think there was a lot of hubris involved.

Certainly a lot of punishment. Anyway, I wasn't about to turn over the techniques to anybody else. Not until I had them, at least. Things like that, they have a way of getting classified, and their discoverers locked away in luxurious hidey-holes out in the desert for the rest of their lives. Which often aren't all that long. You know what I mean?"

Berg pushed his empty glass forward. "Russia makes a lot of vodka," he said. "Got something to do with their balance of payments, I think."

Norton grinned and tipped the bottle. Berg listened to the soft boop-boop of the liquid filling his beaker. No ice this time, he noted.

"Anyway, I started testing some of the techniques. You know what?" Norton's voice was tinged with disgust. "I found out enough to know that they would work. And I gave myself cancer."

"Oops," Berg said.

"You're not very solicitous about this, are you?"

"Fuck that," Berg said. He felt his lips flatten over his teeth, and wondered what the smile looked like to Norton. "You goofed, okay. But now I'm stuck inside this—you say it isn't chicken brain—anyway, I'm here, several people are dead, my ex-wife is God knows where, and you want me to hold your hand. Are you stone nuts, or what?"

"Maybe I'd just better finish the story," Norton said. "I didn't bring you into this because of your compassionate personality." He rubbed the side of his nose. "So I infected myself, as I said, and all of a sudden my options became much more limited. It was pretty obvious I wasn't going to have the luxury of pursuing the scientific method on myself. I needed a quick fix. So I turned the same techniques, with more stringent precautions, on the creation of the matrix. That did work."

"You said it wasn't chicken brain. So what is it?"

Again, that bitter, barking laugh. It was almost a cough. "My brain, Berg, my own fucking brain. What'd

you think? I just wanted a place where I could survive.
What better choice was there?"

Berg blinked.

"That's right," Norton said. "And, of course, there
were ramifications to that, too. Always fucking ramifications. Open one box, find a smaller one inside. Ad
nauseum. Life sucks, and then you die."

"Except maybe not," Berg said. "There's always
that."

"Uh-huh," Norton replied. "The transfer fucked
things up. That's where you came in."

"I got that part," Berg said. "I'm like some kind of
key. But I don't understand it. Why am I so special?"

"It's all programming, Berg," Norton told him.
"Something about the way you're wired. You could
take Calley's stuff and combine it with yours and hold
it all together. You still haven't figured it out? It's
simple, Berg: you don't sit down at your touchpad and
punch in instructions for a matrix. Not at first. You
use whole personalities: it's the only thing that will
work. And when you want to reprogram, you have to
do the same thing. All you are to me, Berg, is software on a grand scale."

Berg had ignored the last part, his attention snagged
on one word. "So you do know about Calley!" he
exploded. "You cocksucker, what happened to her?"
He stood straight up, his drink splashing, forgotten, to
the floor. "Where is she?"

Norton stared at him. "Sit down, Berg," he said
wearily. "You can't do anything to me here—I'm in
control. Not even your trick of manipulating the matrix itself—all you'll touch will be the little part of it
supporting your own personality." He raised his hands,
palm out, a weary gesture. "But she's okay. She's all
right. She's back in her own body, as a matter of
fact."

"*How do you know that?*" Berg was surprised at the
shrieking whine in his voice. He paused, then sat
down suddenly.

"I know," Norton said. "Don't worry, I know."

"That's what I figured out," Berg said at last. "You—somebody—knew. All along. There was this big, un-explainable hole in everything, and nobody to fit in it. I took too many precautions. Too many people were involved. Even Nakamura couldn't have been aware of everything. Collinsworth, Aldocci, Marie. That was you, too. Right from the very beginning. You had them snuffed. How come, Norton? That was the part that didn't make sense. Why kill them? Just because I hired them?"

"Give me your glass," Norton said.

"What?"

"Give me your glass. You want another drink, don't you?"

Berg glanced at the empty beaker rolling on the floor by his left foot. "Yes," he said. "I guess I do." He bent over, picked it up, and slid it across the desk. Norton refilled it carefully.

"Berg," Norton said, "all I needed was you. And Calley. Her programming functioned as a—well, call it something like a hypodermic needle. My projections told me my unconscious would oppose your entry into the matrix . . . of course. So it took Calley to get you in. Once you made it, she was no longer necessary. Which is why she isn't here. But what I didn't need was your bully boys. Of course, if I'd arranged for you to know the real details of the job beforehand, would you have taken it?"

Berg remembered his first glimpse of the tank, of the black, coiling mass of cancer cells, of the ghost of a face hidden in them. He shuddered. "No," he said.

Norton shrugged. "So I lied. You bought the lie and brought in those three. It was simpler to remove them. So I did."

"Nakamura hired me," Berg said. "But he didn't know. I was with him. I believe what I saw. If he'd known what was really going on—"

"Yes. But when you control all the matrices, it means you can access any data bank in the system."

Berg nodded slowly. "That's what I sensed, then.

That pervasive, shadowy influence. It was you. Whenever he went to a machine—any machine—you were there. All his projections, his analyses, they were all gimmicked to make them come out the way you wanted, right?"

"I'm afraid so," Norton replied.

"How did you do it?" Berg asked. "You were subordinate to your unconscious until I came along."

"I had help," Norton said.

"Calley's okay?" Berg said finally.

"Uh-huh."

Berg paused. "One last question. How come you blew up my condo?"

Norton shrugged. "Simple strategy, Berg. I didn't want to give you time to think about all of it. I knew that would hurt as bad as anything, keep you moving, keep you thinking about revenge. Instead of what was really going on."

"But it's not over yet," Berg mumbled suddenly. "What else is there? You're together, one integrated personality. What else is left? You've accomplished what you set out to do. Why can't I just go home?"

"Two things, Berg. All the matrices are part of my brain. And I've never changed from my original goals. I want to live forever. *Live* forever. You think about what that means. No, it's not over. Not yet."

Berg stared at him. At his smoke-colored eyes. And realized that whatever Norton had once been, he was no longer even remotely human.

He drew all the drapes with a word, then washed the taste of the vodka from his mouth with a large tumbler of straight scotch. The big living room of his condo was dim and shadowed, a haunted place. He knew what burned outside his windows, cold and viscous and without mercy. The scotch took him in its warm velvet grip and soothed the wave of unreasoning panic that threatened to send him screaming though the plate glass, to descend forever in the oceans of swirling data.

He wondered if he could still call the ghosts, but the memory of Toshi's liquid fall was etched on a painful place behind his retina, and he didn't want to try. It was Norton's matrix now, anyway. He poured another scotch, and noticed that even after a full day of almost continuous drinking he felt dreary and sober.

Norton was behind it all. Manipulating Nakamura. Using the Lady as a messenger girl. Kidnapping him and Calley. Snuffing Aldocci, Collinsworth, and Marie. Bombing his condo.

Norton everywhere. And somehow it was still wrong. A hole remained unfilled. He recalled Norton's words.

"I had help," Norton had said.

Help? What kind of help?

He sat there in the shadows, and realized that the puzzle still didn't come together. Norton was too powerful. And he was Berg's only ticket home.

Something else, then. Why am I here in the first place? he asked himself. I put things together. I am the key, but I have already turned the lock. Or have I?

What other lock is left? he wondered.

"I want to *live* forever. . . ."

The fear took him then, picked him up and marched him across the room, crashed him into the bathroom where, without pausing, he knelt before the toilet and puked until his skinny ribs were like bands of flame around his chest.

"I am the key!" he shouted wildly. His chest heaved with the effort of the words. After a time he was able to pull himself upright. His stomach was a pit filled with acid. But deep inside pulsed a tiny knot of knowledge, of certainty.

He staggered back to the living room and collapsed on the sofa. "Calley," he whispered.

But nothing in that night held an answer to his desire, because he knew what was coming, and vengeance was the only answer left.


"Will he figure it out in time?" Norton asked.

The reply was the kind of sound that strained metal makes when it finally rips. A bandsaw cutting acres of bone. The scream of small animals. Not a human sound at all.

"Yes," Norton said. "But will everything else be ready?"

Again, a shattering to make men put their hands over their ears and lock their doors.

Norton sat behind the small desk, sipping his vodka, as sleek and self-assured as a great feline prince. "Is Collinsworth ready?" he asked.

The child's eyes bled great slow rivers. He seemed to be struggling to maintain his shape, and Norton perceived the tiny edges, like fluttered wings, which betrayed awesome forces just offstage from reality.

"Soon," Norton said. "It will be over soon."

Life and death and birth, flesh and sand and dreams. Norton saw the dance, and understood it. "Soon," he repeated.

Eyes of smoke, eyes of ruby.

Hunger.

## 29

**C**ALLEY SAW THE elevator door slide open and four men step out. At first glance they were businessmen, dark-suit types in big shoes and short hair, but then she saw their eyes.

Toshi was already facing them and moving forward when she saw the guns.

"Get back!" Toshi yelled.

She jerked her body into the doorway. Behind her, Ozzie was pushing at her, mumbling, "What is it? What's going on?"

She jammed an elbow into his skinny ribs. "Trouble," she said. "Stay inside."

"Trouble? What about Toshi?" He pushed against her again, and she braced herself in the doorway.

"It's what he's supposed to be good at," she said. "Let's hope he is." Her voice was grim.

She carefully slid her head past the doorjamb, exposing herself as little as possible. Now Toshi had somehow gotten between the four men and the elevator. As she watched, he did what appeared to be an intricate dance step, almost a pirouette, and out of the whirling movement came one flashing hand. A gout of blood exploded on the forehead of the nearest man. He dropped like a bag of wet cement.

"Get that mother!" another man shouted. He was older, and seemed to be in charge of the squad. Toshi moved forward, splitting the attack of the two younger men, getting between them. The leader hovered on the fringe of the struggle, trying to get a clear shot at the Oriental.

One of the men held his left fist in a strange position, thumb forward, as if there were a knife there, but Calley couldn't see anything. Then she realized: monomole switchblade. The blade, an invisible thread of monomole stiffened by static electricity, would slice through bone as easily as butter.

"Look out—" she started to yell, but Toshi, grinning and winking, reached out, and she thought she saw a bit of flashing metal somewhere in the middle of the melee.

The man with the switchblade stared in disbelief at his wrist. Blood fountained where his hand had been. He went white and toppled over as Toshi kicked his partner in the balls. The man doubled up and the Oriental brought both elbows down on the man's shoulders. Calley heard a sound that reminded her of kitchens: the moist, sharp crack of a carrot snapping.

The fourth man, the leader, was already running down the hall. Coolly, Toshi shot him in the back. His dark suit grew a sudden pattern of darker spots as he slid down the hall on his stomach.

Toshi stopped for an instant, listened, then turned back to the door. "Come *on*," he hissed. "There'll be backup, bet your ass. We got to get *out* of here!"

Shakily, she stepped out into the hall. "What about Ozzie?" she asked. Her voice shivered, and this surprised her.

"Bring him with us," Toshi said.

A second elevator door opened, and wolves appeared.

"Oh, fuck," Calley moaned.

Toshi whirled to face the new invaders, but the first wolf in the hall held up both paws.

"Friends," he said, his voice damp and guttural.

Toshi remained in his strange, tippy-toed position, his pistol dangling loosely from his left hand. "Yeah? What kind of friends?" he asked.

The lead wolf jerked his half-human, half-lupine muzzle at the bloody humans on the floor. "The' wah thee othahs," he growled. "Nah mah," he added, and glanced at his claws. Toshi saw blood there.

"Can you get us out of here?" Toshi asked quickly. The wolf nodded.

"Good. Let's do it, then," he said.

Ozzie stepped out into the hall and the wolf saw him. "Tha one," the wolf said. "Comes wi' uth. The Lay say sah."

Calley joined the small group, stepping carefully over the leaking corpses underfoot. "The Lady?" she asked. "What's she want with Ozzie?"

The wolf shrugged. "He be safe."

Toshi glanced at Calley. "Hurry it up," he said. "That was a killer team. There'll be more."

She nodded. "How about it, Oz?" she asked. "You trust these furry fuckers?"

The lanky youth grinned. "Why not?" he asked. "They've done okay so far, right?"

"Not much of a reason," Toshi grunted.

"You got something better going?" Calley asked.

"Fuck it," Ozzie said. "Let's get going."

Just before he stepped into the elevator, Toshi bent over and fired his pistol into the skull of the man whose neck he'd crushed. "Still alive," he said tersely as he joined them. "Not any more."

The door slid shut.

"You think Ozzie's gonna be okay?" Calley asked.

"Who knows?" Toshi replied. "You think any of us are?" He shrugged. "We aren't in the best position, you understand. Luna doesn't have all that many escapes hatches."

Calley stared at the small bundle of tapes on the table between them. The room seemed oppressive. She remembered the way blood had bloomed on the forehead of the man Toshi had barely seemed to touch.

"We gotta play it to the end," she said. "You see any other way?"

Toshi shook his head. "We got Nakamura looking to snuff us," he said. "It's better here."

"Don't forget Berg," she said.

"I haven't. You gonna get him out?"

She nodded. "If I can."

Wier knocked gently on the open door of her apartment.

"Hi," she said. "Come on in."

Wier approached the table almost diffidently. "Mind if I join you?" he asked.

She pushed back a third chair. The Lunie scientist smiled and sat down. "What's up?" he asked.

"Why don't you tell us?" she replied. "It seems you know a lot more than we do. Like, where did that rescue force of wolves come from so conveniently?"

"From us, of course. You didn't think we would depend just on diplomatic immunity down there, did you?"

"Who the fuck knows?" she replied, her voice burred with exhaustion. "Listen, Wier, I've got a few questions, if you don't mind."

"Fire away." He grinned. "Maybe I've even got some answers."

She stared at him for a moment. "Sure. Well, why don't you tell me what you're really after?"

"I don't understand. We've explained that all along. Take out the Double En matrix. It's dangerous to us. It's a threat to everybody."

She sighed. "Can you cut the bullshit for a second, Wier? You think you can do that? I can buy the part about it being dangerous to you. That's a reason I can understand. Self interest. But saving everybody else? And why bother with me? Or Berg? There's no reason to try to get Berg out of there if all you want is to trash the Double En matrix. I get extremely suspicious when big corporations tell me all about their altruistic urges. Some of this programming you've had me do—it doesn't make sense."

Wier spread his hands. "It doesn't? How so?"

She tapped one of the tapes in irritation. "This stuff," she said. "A lot of it is straight attack systems. That makes sense, I guess. But the rest of it, these suction programs. . . . What's in the Double En matrix you want so bad? My attack sequences will get you in. But I got to wonder—is there anything you want out besides Berg?"

"Of course there is," Wier said. He smiled suddenly. "We want the techniques."

She blinked. "What are you talking about? What techniques?"

"The same stuff you want, I guess," Wier said. "That's why Ozzie's down on Terra right? Their matrix is the first, and it's the only one with a human personality in it. So how did they do it? How did Norton work the transfer? We can't hold a personality together for more than a few hours—too complicated. Information drain scatters the data after that. So we punch in and we pull out. What we analyze in those few microseconds will move our own research forward two, maybe three years. You know what that means."

"It means you dominate. With what you've already got, that information will put you so far ahead, Terra will never catch up. That's the whole idea, isn't it?" Her voice rose slightly.

"Now I do see it," she said. "This isn't some normal kind of corporate infighting at all. It's a revolution Free Luna, right? You guys get a big enough club, you never have to worry about dirtside corporations again. Or governments, either. No if you can take their data cores apart like so much tissue paper."

"You said it, Calley," Wier said, staring at his fingertips. "We aren't altruists. Never have been. And never can afford to be, not if we want to survive. It's no secret that a lot of Earthies would like things to go back the way they were, before we bought ourselves out and went private."

"Yeah," she said slowly. Already she was growing tired of the conversation. Wier was not going to tell her anything he didn't have to, anything she couldn't figure out for herself. Nor did she expect him to. But there was one more thing. . . .

"Tell me." she said. "It doesn't bother you that I've

got Ozzie down there all set to pick up the same stuff
you're after?"

He shrugged. "You got a matrix, Calley?"

"No."

"Then what good is it going to do you? Sure, you'll
get your data—but it's useless. And any other stuff
you pick up, stuff you can use, well—welcome to it.
You can't hurt us with it, and maybe you get rich. Call
it a bonus."

"A bonus," she repeated. "And, of course, if I get
to be too much of a pain in the ass, there's always
wolves. Or something like them, right?"

Wier only grinned.

"Right," she said, and stood up. "Okay, I guess we
understand each other." She glanced at the tapes.
"That shit won't take long to load," she said. "So
when do you wanna do it?"

Wier pushed his chair back and stretched. "Tonight,
Calley. We do it tonight."


It was hotshot equipment, the best she'd ever seen.
She swiveled in her padded seat, taking in the rest of
the big, brightly lit room. The air smelled like all
Lunie air, dry and cool. There was a hush that reminded her of a cathedral she'd once visited in Spain,
where robed acolytes moved like reverent ghosts among
the sacraments.

Her console had a faintly unfinished look to it, as if
components had been covered with cosmetic plastic to
hide the hasty nature of their manufacture. She sighed,
took one end of the fiber-optic cable in her right hand,
and gently touched it to the socket beneath her ear.

Her programs were loaded. She'd attended to that
earlier. Now all she had to do was sit and wait, while
the great Lunie matrix chewed and digested the
data—no, more likely while the small army of techs
reviewed one more time their duties during the attack.
The matrix was always faster than its human creators.

To her left stood the tank, an enigmatic coffin bereft of its tenant. What, she wondered, did they want with Berg?

She still didn't believe Wier's explanations. There was no logical reason to rescue her ex-husband, beyond the fiction that might be used to keep her happy. Then, slowly, she thought she understood. She was the cutting edge of the attack: they were using her programs, and until the Lunie juggernaut had battered down the defenses of the Double En matrix, she was necessary. Since that matrix would be defended by Berg, the job was a bitch, and would require every ounce of her concentration and comitment. They must know that, and hence the elaborate charade—if charade it was. Perhaps, once the attack was successfully mounted, it was as easy to rescue Berg as to ignore him.

And they still didn't understand Ozzie's real purpose on Terra. She wondered for a moment if he was okay, but there was no way to find out till later. Did Wier know? He seemed to be a man who understood self-interest, and she'd gone to great pains all along to convince him of her own motivations.

Her eyes itched.

"Just a few minutes now," she said.

Toshi swung in his seat to face her. "I feel about as useful as left-handed toilet paper," he said.

"You're useful," she said, and glanced once again at the tank and the three techs who were fussing over it.

Toshi's dark eyes were shadowed. He only nodded, then turned away, sunk in his own thoughts.

Wier came up then, his ever-present grin flashing reassuringly. "You'd better get linked up now," he told Calley. "We'll be getting the show on the road in about five minutes."

She nodded, staring at the cable jack. "Okay," she told him.

He turned, then paused and turned back. "Good luck," he said.

"Right," she said, not looking at him. "Thanks."

He seemed to want to say something more, but

thought better of it. Without any further words, he turned and walked back toward the command consoles.

The room was slowly growing electric with tension. It was contagious; she could feel her own shoulder blades tightening up, and she rolled her head and flexed her back muscles. Finally she looked over at Toshi, but the little Oriental was lost in his own private visions.

"Okay," she said to herself. "Here we go." With one short, fluid motion she plugged the jack into—

—*click*—

—and was there.

She'd almost forgotten what it was like, and the raw glory of it smacked her in the face like a sucker punch. The metamatrix: all around her, spread out below in shimmering organic order, glowing and flickering like the biggest Christmas tree anybody could imagine.

It was utterly silent, the controlled bustle of the Lunie computer room completely gone. The graphite dark surrounded her, cushioned her against the unforgiving blaze of light. Off in the distance the Double En matrix burned malevolently, white light shot with emerald sparks. Somehow, to her, the matrix appeared to be spinning slowly, and from it emanated an expectancy that unsettled her.

The goddamn thing is waiting for me, she thought.

She shook off the unwelcome thought and concentrated on her own programming. Distantly she was aware of her fingers entering the endless ranks of data, and she wondered if anybody had figured out the tiny gimmicks in her routines. She'd been very careful. Even matrix analysis should not have identified anything out of the ordinary.

Somewhere in the back of her skull an invisible clock ticked down. Now she began to feel it, the slow rising of an awesome wall of power, as the Lunie matrix began to kick in behind her attack programs like water backing up behind a dam.

Then she saw them, the faint, flickering wings of shadow forming around her, and on the edges of those wings, whirring knives. The myriad interference programs, endlessly duplicated by the matrix itself, a trillion tiny mouths. Biters and gnawers, teeth to cut the flesh of the Double En matrix, open it up for the heavyweight assault programs coming in behind.

This wouldn't be a subtle attack, she thought. No sneaking here, just naked power, as fast and as much as she could handle.

For one instant, she saw a picture of herself. Small moth fluttering, caught in the flame. Smoke. She pushed the picture away.

Now the wings were taking on solidity, vast, revolving panes of glistening darkness, shiny on the flat black of matspace itself. Ponderously they moved to enclose her, their edges flashing like hardened oil slicks.

Thirty, she thought. Twenty-nine, twenty-eight. . . .

Toshi got up from his chair and moved over to stand by the tank. One of the techs glanced at him.

"What's up, guy?" Toshi asked.

The man grinned. "Pretty soon now," he said.

"Seems weird," Toshi said. "The guy in the tank, I mean. I can't figure it, you know? Is he dead, or what?"

The tech regarded him with the mild condescension all experts hold for those not lucky enough to pursue their own peculiar grails. "Nothing to it," the tech said. "We'll have him back together quicker than shit."

The tech glanced over at Calley, motionless before her console, the optical cable trailing from her head like a gossamer chain. "You a friend of his?" he asked.

"You might say that," Toshi told him.

"Well, don't worry. We'll pull him out okay. His girlfriend, though. . . ."

"Yeah? What about her?"

"She's got the tough job."

"Why's that?" Toshi asked.

"You got any idea how much power she's tossing around there?"

Toshi shrugged. "A lot, I guess."

"Shit. She makes one mistake, her brains look like scrambled eggs. Burned scrambled eggs."

Toshi swiveled around, taking in the entire room. The air of barely controlled stress had risen until the entire area seemed to vibrate slowly. He inhaled. "We'll know pretty soon, then, won't we?"

The tech nodded. "One way or the other," he said.

Now something rumbled up beneath her like a frozen volcano, ancient stone succumbing to unimaginable stresses. The Lunie matrix was bringing everything online, and she began to sense something else.

There was a center to that massed energy, something bright and clear and hard. She tried to track it down, but after a moment the sensation disappeared, leaving only a faint uneasiness in its wake.

Three, she thought. And two. . . .

The gigantic wings locked together with an almost audible snap, their leading parts revolving faster and faster, like a drill. And now the volcano stretched beneath her, cracks widening, as molten light poured through. Slowly, the vast assemblage lumbered forward, directly toward the waiting Double En matrix.

Calley, caught like an angel on the head of Heaven's pin, screamed ecstatically as she fell out into the vastness of the metamatrix, her face to the enemy stronghold.

"I'm coming, Berg! Hold on, I'm coming!"

## 30

**B**ERG HAD LOST track of time. He felt it suddenly when he pushed himself away from his remote, as the muscles at the base of his spine creaked and popped, sending jagged lances of pain up his neck.

"God damn it," he muttered. He reached up and began to knead his shoulders as he twisted back and forth, trying to loosen things up a bit.

It was dark in the room. His face glowed phosphorescent in the backlight from the monitor screen. The green glow made the bags under his eyes into black, heavy bruises. He put his hands down and stared at the screen until the rows and rows of instructions began to blur into tiny, meaningless patterns.

"It should work," he said.

"It better," Norton said from behind him.

Berg jumped. "Damn it," he said, "you ever hear of knocking first?"

"You forgot 'asshole,' " Norton said mildly.

"It seemed superfluous," Berg told him. Norton chuckled.

"You going to sit here in the dark?" he asked.

"Why not?" Berg replied. "Does it make a difference?"

"Nasty," Norton said. "You are a nasty man, Berg. Maybe I told you that already, though." Berg watched him move off into the dark. He heard a click, and the lights flashed brightly. Berg squinted.

"Well?" he said.

"Well, what?"

"Did you just drop by to irritate me, or you want something? I got lots of vodka."

"So do I," Norton told him. He leaned against the back of the sofa, facing away from Berg. His shoulders moved slightly. "It's time," he said.

"Time? What's that mean, 'time'?"

"Don't be too much of a jerk, Berg. What little patience I had to start with is just about gone."

"Too bad," Berg said. "I'm in a wonderful mood."

"Nice to hear that. You finished tinkering with your programs?"

Berg keyed the touchpad: the final instructions flashed once and disappeared. "Yeah," he said. "Is that what you mean about time?"

Norton turned around and stared at him, his eyes flat and gray. "You want to get out of here, don't you?

"Uh-huh," Berg said. He swallowed.

"Then now's your chance," Norton told him. "Right now."

"Wait a minute. I don't—"

"Just key up those fucking routines, Berg. It's all coming to a head. I had hoped to arrange things a little better, but this will have to do."

Berg exhaled slowly. He felt a thousand years old. He let his fingers play idly across the touchpad, watched the strange, flickering patterns fall across the monitor. "A drink first? One for the road?"

Norton shrugged. "Why not?" he said. "Why the fuck not?"

Nakamura watched the endless strips of hardcopy flowing from the outlets behind his desk: bad news. He didn't even bother reading them. He knew what they said.

Kraus and the consortium were on the move. Already some of his key executives had been taken out. Hanagan was undertaking reprisals, but it was too soon to tell. Kraus himself had dropped completely out of sight. For a moment he wished that Oranson was still able to lead the troops. No matter how good Hanagan was, he was still new on the job. He would never be able to get the efficiency from Double En's security people that their former chief had extracted.

He stared at the calm gray face on his monitor. "This is what you wanted, isn't it? It's all up to you now. Your choice to make—whether I live or die. Well, make it, damn you. You said you can burn their matrices. It's the only way. I can't take them all on by myself without an edge. Fry their cores, and I won't leave anything but ashes. Without that—"

The gray man nodded. "Quit worrying, Shag. I said I would, and I will. The timing has to be right, though."

Nakamura pushed the heels of his hands into his eyes. "You have anything to do with that team I sent over to the Marriott? Somebody spotted that little Oriental there. Nobody came back."

Norton blinked. "Not me," he said. "I've got other fish to fry."

"Like me, maybe?"

"No, Shag. You just keep on keeping on, and everything will work out fine. You've got your people in the field?"

"Of course I do. Everybody. I'm moving against the consortium physically, financially, and politically. But it won't be enough. You can project that, can't you?"

Norton nodded. "Yeah. You can't win this without me. They'll take some hurt, but you'll take a bad case of dead."

"So?"

"So, what?"

"So when are you going to burn them, you asshole?"

"Pretty soon, Shag," Norton said. His voice was soothing. "Don't worry. I won't let you down."

"Motherfucker!" Nakamura screamed in impotent rage; the monitor suddenly went black. He sat alone in his office and listened to the printers spit out news of his ongoing demise.

Finally he keyed up his telecom and said, "You have the location monitored?"

The scarred man, his chopped white hair a brutal flag flying from his skull, said, "You give the word, boom. Whatever's there won't be anymore."

"Stay in touch," Nakamura said softly.

He didn't believe in hari-kari . . . not, at least, without company.

You don't really need that, you know," Norton said.

Berg turned and glanced at him from the giant console where he sat, strung from strands of optical fiber. "It's all analogs," Berg said. "So this analog makes me feel comfortable. You got any idea how much power I'm pushing?"

Norton's teeth flashed once. "Since it's me you're pushing, yeah, I've got an idea." He walked over to the wide glass wall, open onto the neon night. "How come this view?" he said. "I thought you like Chicago."

Berg turned back to the console. "If I'm going out there, I figured I might as well look at it. The metamatrix is reality, too."

"Yeah," Norton said slowly. "One reality, at least." He sounded gloomy.

"It doesn't matter," he said at last. "Whatever reality is, it is. Chicago, the matrices, the metamatrix. . . ." His voice trailed off. He sighed gently. Then he jerked his head up briskly, suddenly full of determination. "Come on, Berg. Let's get it done."

Berg nodded. "You're right," he said. "I'm tired of all this, too."

"You won't die," Norton said, as if Berg had asked a question. "I don't think."

"Yes," Berg replied. "Maybe not." Slowly, as if he were playing a musical instrument, he began to punch up the great pattern of his routines. Norton watched him, in the freckled diamond light cast by the shadows of the matrices.

*     *     *

Now Berg was alone, riding like a great bird above the surface of the matrix, the iron rhythm of his programs slowly marshaling around him. He felt cloaked in dark numbers, wrapped in them, muffled by their weight. In the vast distance glowed the Lunie matrix, and it was as if he'd known all along:

*There!*

Some mysterious thing was forming there, and he felt the answering resonance.

I am the key, he thought again, and felt Norton—lost somewhere behind him in the glowing heart of the Double En matrix—shiver in response.

And still the routines took their tenuous shapes around him, a giant flower slowly opening. Across the metamatrix the hunter replied, a blind, insectile seeking. Machine pollination, the ultimate violation of the flesh.

Did Norton know fear? Somehow he knew that he did, and that this moment was his alone, that, in truth, everything had been channeled to this final instant.

And he laughed. *"Fuck you!"* he screamed, and fed the power of the matrix to his great blossom.

They met in a great joining of light and sound. The metamatrix whipped and fractured about Berg as he rode the final copulation down to climax, and in the white-hot core of that unendurable joining, he felt her once again.

"Calley?"

"I'm here, Berg."

Around them the matrices ripped and shuddered, and Berg wondered what was happening to the world of information on real-time computers. Were bewildered techs pulling out bizarre fantasies and shaking their heads? What kind of hardcopy trail was this unimagined event forming?

"Calley, what is it?"

"What they wanted," she replied. He felt her close to him, invisible but comforting, and in the greater joining around them he pulled her to him, a smaller melding in a vaster whole.

"Ah, God . . ." he breathed.

"No," she replied. "Us. We two. Finally."

And knew what she meant, twisted against it for a moment—*Don't fight me, Berg, not now—I can't—just relax—I will die—no, be a part—I—you—we—*

*We!*

The metamatrix began to twist and flow and they were one within it, while around them titans screamed and blazed and melted—

To a star.

Bright core.

Burning.


"We'll die now, won't we?" he asked sadly. He had tasted her heart and given his, and felt only an unutterable sadness, a wordless sense of loss. "What a fucking waste."

Her reply flowed through him. Calm and cool, full of love and forgiveness. "No. Not now."

In the distance a new star burned, equidistant between the shrunken husks of the two matrices, now gray and colorless in the awful light of their creation.

He felt the fabric of his personality begin to unravel. "I love you," he said.

"I've always loved you," she replied.

"YOU ARE FREE, BERG."

The voice filled the metamatrix like blood frozen in a cup, and the star began to spin. From it came silver rays that cast shadows on every part of the data cells, illuminating them.

Berg nodded slowly. Free, yes. His personality was no longer supported by the matrix, so he was free. Free to dissolve. He felt a momentary sadness, mixed with bitter triumph. With an effort, he held himself together for a few final ticks of time.

"Bury the body, Gloria," he said. "Do that much."

"Don't be an asshole," she replied, and her voice

was brisk and sure. He wondered at that as the darkness pressed in around him, until only the star remained, focus and destroyer.

So he never saw the strange construction rise from the base of the metamatrix, a construction of geometric hexagonal forms linked in patterns of indexed beauty, never felt its power as it caught, lifted, carried him away, there beneath the lurid light of the pitiless and unforgiving star.

Nakamura stared at the monitor, his face a bleak yellow mask, his eyes slits of onyx and blood. "Have you got him yet?" he asked.

The white-haired man was changed. His scar was livid on a face smudged with black streaks. He shook his head. "I sent in three teams. Nobody came back."

"Then go yourself," Nakamura hissed. "You're supposed to be the best." He turned away from the screen, then turned back. "No, wait. That's no good. Kraus will be after me, too. I can't stay here." He glanced around his office, repulsed by the dim, shadowy forms of the cannabalized processing equipment, the fractured beauty of the ruins of his garden. "Come back here," he said finally. "I need you here."

The white-haired man nodded, smiling.

Toshi dropped the last technician with a blow as direct as the strike of a snake. Calley slipped around him and ran up to the tank. The lab was chaos. Alarms throbbed, lights flashed, men and women ran from station to station, shouting at each other.

In the center of the riot, Wier waved his arms, trying to restore order. "The matrix is down temporarily!" he called. "Only for a moment. We'll be on line with Arius in seconds!" His angular face was red and strained, his eyes wide.

"Arius?" Calley asked as she fumbled with the catches on the lid of Berg's tank.

Toshi shrugged. "The mystery honcho?" he asked. "Beats me. You need help with that?"

She stepped away from the tank and pointed at the latch which had defied her efforts. Toshi came forward and brought his hands together on the metal. She heard a sound that flesh should not have made, and looked away. When she looked back, Toshi was prying up the lid.

She ignored childhood nightmares, forced herself not to think of coffins, of vampires. Toshi forced the lid fully open, and she stared at Berg's thin, white features.

"He's dead," she said flatly.

"Hardly," Toshi replied, his fingers fluttering on Berg's neck like tiny wings. Berg lay unmoving, the silver cap of input jacks crowning his skull.

"He's alive," Toshi said. "Something's pumping, at least."

She pushed him away and bent over the sleeping man's body, placing her long hands on his face as if their warmth alone would return the—soul?—to its natural home.

The great overhead lights began to strobe, their pattern lengthening until full seconds of darkness were interspersed with frenzied light. Nobody seemed to notice the strange tableau, the short Oriental standing protectively next to the woman who cradled the sleeping man in her hands.

Things stretched. . . .

"My God," Calley breathed.

"What?"

"His eyelids—they moved."

"That's just—"

Berg opened his eyes and smiled.

She stared at him.

"Welcome back," she said.

Toshi moved beside her, and she heard bone and cartilage snap. Another tech, curious enough to ignore the general bedlam, had decided to investigate. She saw him join the others on the floor.

"We should probably think about leaving," Toshi said.

"Yes," she replied. She pushed the insectlike chair toward the tank. It had been designed to articulate motion for paraplegics. Together they lifted Berg from his tank and fitted him into the chair.

"This should be fun," Toshi muttered.

The lights went out completely, and Berg began to laugh.

Hanagan watched the smaller Japanese, his eyes heavy and hooded. Perhaps, Nakamura thought, he is wondering if I can still afford to pay him. He smiled at the thought. The hired killer had so little comprehension of the secrets of great wealth, of the power that money, even in extremity, could always buy.

"Don't worry," Nakamura said. "Your Swiss accounts are being fed."

Hanagan nodded.

"Don't misunderstand," Nakamura continued. "Double En is in ruins, yes. Kraus's teams hunt me now, and for a time I will have to run, to hide. So be it. But I am not powerless."

The white-haired mercenary moved slightly, his eyes questioning.

Nakamura sighed. For one moment he paused, his button eyes taking in the outlines of his office, the pitiful remnants of the power that once had been his. Now, all that remained was money, secret accounts, hidden caches—but it would be enough. Money to buy secrecy, and flight, and protection, even as it paid for the services of the deadly thug in front of him.

So much, and yet so little, compared to what had been. He stared at the blank monitor screens.

"I tried to reach him again, there at the end, but he was gone," Nakamura said, knowing that Hanagan had no idea what he was talking about. "And true to his nature, he betrayed me one final time." His voice was low, musing. "Did the company mean so little to him? Or was it just another piece in the puzzle?"

Nakamura stood suddenly, his shoulders straight, his face at last calm and peaceful.

"At least there will be revenge," he said. "I will never know, but maybe he will lose, after all." He faced Hanagan and said sharply, "How far?"

"What?" Hanagan asked.

"The place you wired to destroy. Can we do it from here?"

"No," Hanagan said. "But not far. Do you want to go there?"

A slow grin spread over Nakamura's golden features. "I want to push the button, you fucking asshole."

Overhead, the afternoon sun pounded out a blinding symphony, and Nakamura shielded his eyes against it. Of course, he thought, I must be denied even a final vengeance.

The scene replayed itself swiftly, bitter little frames of memory, and he pondered again the limits of even great wealth. You buy the best, and even that may not be good enough.

They had come from the crowd as he and Hanagan stepped across the sidewalk toward the waiting limo. Normally he would have boarded the vehicle deep within the Double En basements, but the shadows there worried him. In those garages were corners and turnings that could hide a hundred of Kraus's killer teams.

So he chanced the street, and lost his chance.

The tall, lanky one was waiting. He seemed faintly familiar as he stepped forward, a light coat covering his right arm and hand, and Hanagan had moved instantly, not knowing the face but recognizing the intent.

The lanky man was impeccably dressed. His long, horsey face moved slightly as he stepped back smoothly from Hanagan's attack, and he smiled.

"Stupid," he said, and moved one more time, turning the white-haired killer just enough for Marie to neatly bury eight inches of monomole wire in Hanagan's kidney.

Nakamura recognized them then, as they pushed him into his own limo. "You're dead," he said.

The man nodded. His voice was slow, lazy, aristocratic. "If you believe the evidence of your own computers," he agreed. "And that has been completely accurate all along, hasn't it? Pity all three bodies were pretty much destroyed. It certainly made identification difficult."

"You are Collinsworth," Nakamura said.

"At your service," he replied. "You know of Marie, I believe?"

Nakamura nodded. Outside the streets of Chicago floated past, a comforting, familiar world that tugged at Nakamura even as he resigned himself to its final loss. "How much is Kraus paying you?" he asked. "I can double it, of course. Or much more."

Collinsworth's lips parted, revealing slightly yellowed, even teeth. "Oh, we don't work for the kraut, old man. But we *do* require a few thing of you."

It was a dark room; Berg slept for two days. Finally she touched his lips with her fingertips until his eyelids fluttered open.

His weakness had finally passed. He stared at her, and wondered how to ask the question. Then he understood that the simple way was easiest, and he said, "Do you remember it all?"

She nodded. "Everything. Right up to the time Ozzie snatched us out of there and rammed us back down the throat of what was left of the Lunie matrix."

"It was an artificial intelligence, an AI," he said softly. He seemed upset.

"Arius," she said. "I know. We should have figured it out before. All those strange cores stuck to it like barnacles."

Berg stirred slightly. "I was the key," he said. "That's what Norton really wanted. Me and my programs—I joined him to himself, and then I joined him to the AI. That's why it was so hard, why they needed you to blast through the natural barriers between man and machine." He paused. "Between flesh and sand," he added, almost to himself.

"What?" she asked. She stroked his chest gently.

"Something Norton said," he told her. "Not important." He seemed to drift a bit, then returned suddenly. "What happened? Nakamura will be after us. . . ."

She shook her head. "Double En collapsed," she said. "It was all over the Net—big raid by a European consortium. And there was some kind of convulsion in the world data storage systems—a lot of information garbled, lost. The Euros took some hurt, too." She grinned at that.

He stared at his fingers, as if seeing them for the first time. He moved them, watched the movement as if it were alien to him. "I poisoned them," he said finally.

She blinked. "You what?"

He turned his head. "My programs—I wrote the keys inside the matrix, and I loaded them with lethal feedback routines. When Norton joined the AI, whatever was created had a bellyfull of shit. I don't know what will happen."

Now she stared at his fingers. So delicate. . . . "It doesn't matter," she said at last. "I got more than you out of there. Ozzie took enough stuff from the collapse of the two matrices to make us all rich forever. And I don't think whatever was created in there is all that interested in us. Never was, really, in any humans."

"You're wrong," Berg told her. "They both were interested in exactly that. I remember what Norton told me. He wanted to live forever, he said, and stressed the word 'live.' A body. He wanted an immortal body, and I think that's what the AI promised him: true immortality. If that fusion survives my killer programs—and I didn't plan on the AI—then you can bet that we're not done with it."

She took her hand in his. "We were joined in there, too," she reminded him.

"I am the key," he said. "Of course we were. And are. And will be, as long as we live."

She put her head down on his chest and closed her eyes. "None of it seems real," she whispered. "Only this."

Slowly he wrapped his arms around her, and pulled her warmth closer, trying to dispel the icy core that threatened to overwhelm him.

"What's reality?" he asked.

# Epilog

THE TINY BEACH was shadowed and empty, a short strip of white sand surviving in the protection of the great dike, its ragged edge lapped continually by the cold waters of the lake. Overhead glittered stars that chipped sudden bits of light from the sand, and from the lacy tips of the curling wavelets.

She stared out on the silent scene from her vantage point deep within the darkness of the dike, and then moved slowly forward, carrying her burden. As she always had.

Her eyes were red in the starlight, great and seeking, and found only cold, and the night.

She remembered the days of her agony, when her swollen body had been almost too huge to move, times when the cables and cords had held her pinioned like an insect to the spidery nets of technology.

She moved through the gap in the dike and stepped down onto the sand. Her breath made soft, silvery clouds in the darkness. She felt the silicon crunch beneath her feet, and shivered slightly as she moved to the very edge of the water. Of the sand.

Her wolves followed, and the others. Without looking at any of them she said, "It goes well?"

Collinsworth's slow drawl replied, "We've purchased both matrices, Lady. Neither the Lunies nor Double En have any use for them. The Lunies, of course, feel betrayed. And Double En doesn't feel anything. Nakamura will say whatever it takes to let him have his vengeance on Kraus. Meanwhile, the company is 'being reorganized,' as the Net likes to say."

She remembered the agonies of giving birth, and the further agony of giving birth again, as a star was channeled through her into . . . something new.

"My acolytes," she murmured, staring out at the great glistening inland ocean. The tiny thing in her arms moved, and she hugged it closer.

There was great safety in religion, and great power to protect, as well. Especially if the god was a living god. She looked down at the swaddled, infantile form and carefully stroked its lumpy, alien skull.

Human, yes—and other, as well. She wondered why it didn't cry. It *was* alive. There was brain function. It could move—did move—between the human structure and the matrices as easily as another might step between apartments. My mansion has many rooms, she thought.

But it was silent.

She sensed the struggle and knew that eventually it would be won—in time. It had all the time in the world.

She sighed, and listened to her wolves, her advisers, around her. So hard to be the Lady. The Mother. And the Daughter, the High Priestess of the New Religion.

She wondered what they would call it, what sleek words they would use to camouflage the reality of it, that something new moved in the worlds of man.

Carefully she raised the tiny body, held it for a moment suspended between the stars and the water. It struggled faintly and then was still.

"Remember," she said softly. And gathered it back to her warmth, and turned away.

She gathered her wolves about her and began the short journey back to darkness and dreams. Bearing, one more time, the flesh across the sand.

# About the Author

W. T. Quick was born in Muncie, Indiana, and now lives in San Francisco. He was educated at The Hill School and Indiana University. He is fond of single malt scotch and writing about the near-infinite possibilities of technology. He is not fond of Senator William Proxmire or cats. He has been publishing science fiction since 1979 and intends to continue.

All Futura Books are available at your bookshop or
newsagent, or can be ordered from the following address:
Futura Books, Cash Sales Department,
P.O. Box 11, Falmouth, Cornwall TR10 9EN.

Please send cheque or postal order (no currency), and
allow 60p for postage and packing for the first book
plus 25p for the second book and 15p for each additional
book ordered up to a maximum charge of £1.90 in U.K.

B.F.P.O. customers please allow 60p for
the first book, 25p for the second book plus 15p per
copy for the next 7 books, thereafter 9p per book

Overseas customers, including Eire, please allow £1.25
for postage and packing for the first book, 75p for the
second book and 28p for each subsequent title ordered.

# interzone

## SCIENCE FICTION AND FANTASY